City of Brotherly Love

City of Brotherly Love

Stories by

Ned Bachus

Fleur-de-Lis Press 2012

Printed in the United States of America
First Edition

Library of Congress Cataloging-in-Publication Data
Bachus, Ned
City of Brotherly Love
I. Title
Library of Congress Control Number: 2012931725

ISBN: 978-0-9773861-7-8

This is a work of fiction. Names, characters, locations, and incidents are a creation of the author's and are fictitious. Any resemblance to actual persons, places, or occurrences is coincidental.

Some of the stories in this collection were originally published, in sometimes slightly different form, as follows: "Demonstration" in *The Louisville Review*, "A Baker" in *Calliope*, "The Wig" in *Antietam Review*, "Home" in *Carve*, "Some People Just Stick Out" in the anthology *Meridian Bound*, and "The Interpreter" in *The Evansville Review*.

Jacket and type design: Jonathan Weinert
Author photo: Michael Bailey
Cover photo: Ned Bachus

Fleur-de-Lis Press of *The Louisville Review*
Spalding University
851 S. Fourth St.
Louisville, KY 40203
502.873.4398

louisvillereview@spalding.edu
www.louisvillereview.org

For

Kathleen Bachus

and

Jim Brady

City of Brotherly Love

Demonstration

THE TRAIN LURCHES to a stop at Suburban Station. People who get on here and at Thirtieth Street will have to stand until the packed car starts to lose people. I am still panting from having raced half of Philadelphia through the concourse and down the escalator at Market Street East. I consider pulling the Rosatti case file from my briefcase, but instead I close my eyes. There are twelve more stops, "station stops" as the conductors call them, until we get to the end of the line and my Toyota. Fourteen stops. Ordinarily, I don't mind the ride. It beats sitting in stalled traffic on the expressway or the river drives. Beth hated the train ride home. Probably still does. She once called it the Fourteen Stations of the Cross, and I laughed out loud. We spent the entire ride home trying to remember the Stations of the Cross from childhood and then coming up with equivalent commuter indignities. I remember her whispering in my ear, "Station Number Nine: The conductor falls for the third time."

Two years ago she left. For six months I tried to figure out why. She was in love; she apologized for the inconvenience. Now, I have our almost seven-year-old daughter during the week, and Beth is the weekend parent. She's got an investment broker named Clint from Monday through Friday, and I've got Eugenia. Beth and this Clint tool around town with Eugenia on weekends while I do next week's work. That Beth no longer loves me is no more or less explicable than that she loved me in the first place. For Beth, love has not died; it's just moved on. A mystery of faith has become a mystery of faithlessness. I understand the laws of love about as well as I understood James Joyce or particle physics in college. But I get to see my daughter's little face greet the dawn five mornings a week, six times this week because of the performance tonight. These mornings and evenings I claim as the spoils of battle, a battle fought with the only weapons which I, like my literary namesake, Joyce's Stephen Dedalus, have allowed myself: silence, exile, and cunning.

When I hear the conductor announce our arrival at Thirtieth Street Station, I realize I've dozed off for a minute. I shake my head from side to side a few times and stretch my legs. Outside, people scurry across the platform. I decide to review the day's activities. The videotaping of Mr. Rosatti in the hospital took up most of the time. The old man won't be around by the time the case is settled. Even if we win, someone else will reap the benefits. I see myself crossing the hospital lobby, after the taping, telling Rob from the firm and the audio-visual guy that I can't stop for a drink. They bustle through the sliding doors, and I'm left standing in front of the McDonald's that the hospital has allowed to set up shop next to the pediatrics section. Disgusting. Then I remember that little Allysia Pettigrew, daughter of our next-door neighbors when we lived in Mount Airy, is in the hospital with sickle cell problems. I get her room number at the front desk and go looking for her room. After spending half of the day in one wing of the hospital, I barge around like I know the place. I think I'm on the right floor when I stumble into a corner lounge that somebody's whole extended family has taken over: kids, teenagers, adults. A man, in his thirties like me, stops speaking Spanish and looks right at me, as if he had been waiting for somebody in a suit to show up. I pivot away and head up the nearest corridor, happy to get away from that waiting room. Nothing good is going to be told to that group. In the hallway, none of the room numbers are close to what I'm looking for, but I keep going anyway. I hear loud voices coming from a room ahead on the right. I stop in the doorway. It's a normal-sized patient room, but it is filled with agitated people who swarm around a little bed. White lab jackets, green scrubs. Meters, gauges, tubes, lights. I can't see past the backs of the doctors and nurses, but somehow I know that this child belongs to the people in that lounge. I see swinging doors, an elevator, a nurses' station. I see Eugenia. We are at some beach town down the shore, but now I have a second child, a little boy. The three of us are in a ground floor motel room. A storm rages outside, and we've just learned that there might be flooding. Then we're walking down the street toward the ocean, and people start screaming and running toward us, and we see a wall of water coming down the street, and we turn around and run with all the others trying to get away, and the surging water grows louder with each step, and we make it to our car in the lower parking area of the motel and find the rear of every car is sitting on the front of the one behind, and our car is pressed against the back wall of the garage, the last car in the line.

The man in the window seat elbows me out of my dream and squeezes past me to get off at one of the Mount Airy stations. I realize I've sweated through my white shirt. I wonder if I moaned or called out when I was waking from my dream, so I glance around to see if any of the passengers are looking at me, but they're still absorbed in their newspapers or are staring ahead. The car is half empty now. I have the whole seat to myself for the rest of the ride.

Eugenia frowns when she sees me from the doorway of the after-school center. She's already got on her coat, hat, and mitens and is holding her backpack. She says something to Mrs. Jeffries and is out the door.

"We're going to be late, Daddy," she cries and runs past me to the car. She's already in the passenger side door and buckling her seat belt by the time I get my door open.

"You must be hungry?" I say.

"We had a snack, Daddy. I can wait til later."

"Okay." I start the car and back out of the parking place.

"You remembered my outfit. Didn't you?"

"Yes, honey."

"And my violin?"

"Oh, I knew I forgot something," I say.

"Daddy!"

"No sweat," I say. "Everything's in the trunk. We're all set."

I hope a day spent in the cold trunk won't make the violin impossible to tune. I floor the gas pedal, and we pull into the rush hour traffic on Reynolds, squeezing between a pickup truck and a Buick. The guy in the Buick lays on his horn. The light's a full yellow when I come to Grover, but I make it through, leaving the Buick back at the intersection.

"So, school was good?" I ask.

"Pretty good."

"How was lunch? Did you eat all of it today?"

"Most of it."

"You've got to tell me if there's something you don't want to eat. I don't want to put stuff in your lunch box you won't touch."

She mumbles her agreement. Her words are like hugs. I will take any she is doling out.

"How'd the spelling bee go?"

"Spelling test."

"Right," I say. "How'd you make out?"

"One wrong."

"That's real good."

"The spelling bee's next week. That's what I stink at. I always lose on the second word, or the third. Marjorie Gruber and Janeen never make a mistake." She pauses and watches the cars through her window for a while. "Marjorie called me a jerk," she says.

"She did?"

"She said I was hogging Janeen, that I'm selfish."

"That makes you selfish?"

"Janeen and I never have any problems playing. It's just when Marjorie joins in. And I can play alone with Marjorie, too."

I make a right onto Bethlehem Pike, the last turn before we get to the school entrance.

"She said I was stealing Janeen."

"It's complicated. Isn't it?" I say. I calculate that there are three more traffic lights between us and the school and look at the clock on the dashboard. Unless I hit three red lights, we'll make it on time.

"I never told her that she was hogging Janeen."

"Well, that's good."

"At recess when we tried to use the swings, Robert and the two Jeromes pushed us."

"Pushed who?"

"Marjorie and Janeen and me. They called us some stupid names. They said we were too girlie to play touch football. That's when they pushed us."

"What do you mean they pushed you?"

"They acted like they were going to be nice, giving us pushes on the swings. But then they were rough. They said they'd push the swing all the way over the top. Janeen kicked Robert when he tried to push her higher."

"Guess that showed him."

"He just laughed. He likes her. I think she likes him, too, but she says she hates him. They pushed me higher and higher until the bell rang. The boys in our school are so stupid."

"Well, none of them are performing in a recital tonight," I say.

"Demonstration," she corrects me.

"None of those bozos are doing anything as great as you are tonight." After I pull into the driveway, I have to drive to the back section of the lot to find a parking space.

"You should be proud," I say as we get out of the car. "Only a few kids get a chance to play tonight. Not like the Spring Concert." I pop open the trunk and retrieve the clothes and violin. *A chance for kids who are doing well to show off*, I think. I'd been surprised when Olivia, Eugenia's teacher, had called two weeks before to ask if she could be part of the demonstration. Eugenia was the tallest in her practice group, if not the oldest, but other kids in the group knew almost all the songs in Book One; Eugenia was still working on "Lightly Row."

"I am proud, Daddy."

"Good," I say. I slam down the trunk door. "Very Good."

Eugenia takes her performance outfit into the ladies' room of the school annex. I listen to the other children tuning up their instruments in the adjacent room. When she swings the bathroom door open and steps into the hallway wearing her black skirt and white blouse, I inspect her.

"Did anyone help you in there?" I ask.

"No. I used the mirror."

"You look great," I say.

"Here," she says, giving me the bag into which she's put her other clothes. I hand her the violin case, and she turns and walks toward the room where she has her weekly lesson and where the other children are tuning and playing bits of melodies. She takes a seat in the second row of violinists. Fourteen other kids are dressed in the same white tops and dark slacks or skirts. I recognize a boy and a girl from Eugenia's group and kids who were featured at the last concert, kids who were well into Book Two back then. A thin, graying woman stands by the grand piano, towering over the ranks of student violinists. After she explains the order of play, she reminds them to stand and play only on the tunes they know. They begin the rehearsal with a complicated tune then move on to somewhat less intricate pieces, involving more kids with each tune. The kids who know the tunes stand and play, while the others sit and wait for the ones that they can play. Now all but Eugenia and two others are standing and playing.

"All right, now," announces the gray-haired lady, "'Go Tell Aunt Rhody.'" Only Eugenia remains sitting. "Ready," the woman says.

"Begin." I watch the back of my daughter's head. She's looking up at all the bows sawing away above her. Just when it sounds like they are done, they move into a second part of the piece. It sounds so full with all these instruments. If they make any mistakes, I can't hear them. Then they stop, tuck their little violins under their arms, and bow from the waist. The parents and Eugenia applaud.

"Next, 'Song of the Wind.'" While Eugenia has started practicing this one, I know that she is not ready to try it in front of people. "Everybody for 'Song of the Wind.' Ready. Begin."

Eugenia sits alone. I clench my jaw. I cross my arms over my chest and breathe out through my mouth. Why did Olivia choose her for this? Why didn't she choose other students of the same level?

Finally, they get to "Lightly Row," and Eugenia stands. I notice that my glasses have fogged up a little bit, so I reach for my handkerchief and start to clean them. The tune ends before I'm done, so I stick one of the temples between my teeth and clap over the handkerchief, as the glasses dangle from my mouth.

They all play "Twinkle, Twinkle, Little Star," the first tune each of them learned. Then it is over and the teacher tells them to report to the auditorium fifteen minutes before the performance. I grab Eugenia's coat and violin case, walk over, and tap her on the shoulder.

"You guys sounded great." I take the bow and violin from her and put them in the case. "Do you want to go out by the swings? It's crowded in here." She nods. We button our coats and leave the chattering violinists and parents.

She runs up the path to an old maple tree. She stands by the tall bare tree and looks down at children playing on the swings in the playground.

"That was super," I say. "The audience is going to get a great show."

She nods, still looking at the other kids.

I pat her blonde hair. "Are you all right, Sweetie?"

She looks up at the big tree then back at me. "I feel funny with all them."

"You probably wish you knew every song in the book, huh?"

"I only know two of the songs. Nobody else only knows two songs."

I crouch down and look up at her round face. "You did fine on your songs. Fine. You just go out there and do what you do. That's all."

"Do they want me here because I'm like a beginner?"

"No, honey," I say. I look down the hill at the group of kids on the swings. They're shouting and laughing. "I think they want you here," I say, still watching the other kids, "because of what you already can do and what you will do."

"Mm," she says. "Like a good beginner."

"I think they can tell you're going to be pretty good at music."

A fat blonde boy on the end swing screams out someone's name. I turn back to Eugenia. She stares intently at the kids on the swings. When the fat boy leaps off his swing and runs to the sliding board, she bolts down the hill and takes possession of the empty swing.

The audience is composed of parents of the kids who are in the performance and parents of prospective students. A good show means new students, fresh tuition money. The school administrators pace around, calling parents by name, smiling every time they make eye contact with anyone. They know the hall is nearly filled. Spotting a single seat at the end of the second row, I slip past families who need two, three, four seats together and plunk myself down while the other people work their way toward the open spaces in the rear rows. A grand piano dominates the floor below the stage that is high and small.

Eugenia finds me. "You've got a great seat, Daddy."

"Where's your violin?" I ask.

"Back with the other kids. I saw you and I wanted to say hi before we start."

I spot Olivia Dunning across the aisle chatting with a couple about my age.

Eugenia plops herself on my lap and says, "I'll sit here, so I can see what you're going to see."

Parents clog the aisle, and I peer around Eugenia's head to catch a glimpse of her teacher.

Eugenia twists her head around and looks up at me. "You've got a good view of me, and I've got an even better view of you from up there," she says.

Olivia hugs the woman she's been talking with and starts for the back of the hall. "Olivia," I call. "Olivia!"

"Oh, hi, Mr. Kraft," she says, stepping over to us. "Hello, Eugenia. You look lovely."

Eugenia beams.

"I'm glad we caught you before the festivities begin," I say.

"Well, good luck, Eugenia," Olivia says, edging away.

"You're not leaving, are you?" I say, keeping my eyes on hers.

"Why, no," she says. She forces a smile. "No. I'll be backstage once they begin."

"Good," I say. "I wouldn't want you to miss Eugenia's numbers.

Both of them."

"Of course not," Olivia says. She averts her eyes for a moment then brings them back to mine.

"You know which ones she's doing. Don't you?"

She starts to say something then hesitates.

"The last two," I say.

"'Lightly Row' and 'Twinkle,'" Eugenia says.

"Great crowd," I say, still looking Olivia in the eyes. "Big crowd."

"Eugenia," she says, bending down and touching my daughter's cheek. "You'll do just fine." She straightens up and turns back to me. "Mr. Kraft, I need to get ready, so if you'll excuse me." Flashing a smile, she spins around. I watch her march to the back of the hall.

"I better go, too," Eugenia says.

I kiss her cheek. "Break a leg, Sweetie."

"Break a leg?"

"It means good luck," I say. "Remember. I can't play a note on that fiddle without sounding like a dying cat. You can. So, go have some fun."

She pops out of my lap and puts her hand up to slap me five. "Should I tell the other kids to break their legs, too?"

"Maybe you should just wish them good luck," I say.

She walks off to join the other kids backstage. I turn around and survey the packed hall. Olivia is nowhere in sight. I consider trying to find her again, but decide it would be in everyone's best interests if I don't.

Then the lights dim and the audience chatter subsides. Applause erupts as the kids come out and form three lines of five. Eugenia is in the second row, at the far end. Next to me, a grandfatherly looking man holds a two-year-old girl on his lap. A four- and a five-year-old sit on the far side of the grandfather and after them a woman who I figure to be the mother of one of the musicians. The head administrator taps the microphone next to the piano and clears his throat. Clarence Willoughby. I remember him to be the husband of the gray-haired woman who led the rehearsal. As he gives a short history of the school and discusses the procedure for enrollment, I check my pockets for chewing gum. Nothing. No candy, either. With this many kids in the room, I guess there must be hundreds of sticks of gum within these four walls, but none that I can get to. I run my tongue behind my teeth as I half listen to Willoughby's speech and scan the audience.

I spot Ellen Loober sitting near the back of the hall, the only other single parent I know in this crowd. Our eyes meet, and she waves. I smile at her then turn back to the stage. I can still picture her face when I close my eyes. She was Beth's old jogging partner. I remember seeing her once when her daughter had finished a lesson with Olivia, and Eugenia and I were going into the room for the next session. We hugged, and I smelled her perfume, a scent Beth had once sprayed on her wrist in a downtown department store and turned up her nose at. I touched Ellen's hair, soft black curls, as we came together. She kissed the air, and the perfume just lifted me. I thought, *this is the first woman's smell I have taken in since Beth left.*

I wonder if scent had anything to do with Beth discovering Clint. I remember tucking the thought of Ellen Loober's soft hair and dizzying perfume into that part of the brain or heart where we keep such treasures secure until we feel safe to bring them out like old photographs for the occasional private glimpse. After Beth went away, but before the settlement, when I looked around the house at things that were only mine, not hers, I knew fear. The only way I might end up with Eugenia was if I made myself into some kind of near saint. I would fight back by not fighting back. When Eugenia picked a star in the sky for Mommy and one for Daddy and then asked if we should pick one for Clint, I told her to pick a nice, shiny one for him, because all of God's creatures deserved one. I did not tell her that I wished that the star she picked for him would fall into the sun. I was the perfect gentleman, the best possible loser, and I got a better custody deal than anybody at my firm dreamed possible.

The concert starts with a piano piece by a seven-year-old boy. I look over at Eugenia sitting on stage. She looks so settled, comfortable. The program alternates between the group violin pieces and kids playing other instruments. Eugenia watches them, with her head up. She's got my posture, if nothing else. More of the violinists rise to play. Eugenia looks fine. She probably is fine. I look out the window to my right. Streetlights are shaking a little in the January wind. I think about Mr. Rosatti in his hospital bed downtown, how he managed to crack jokes on his deathbed. I think about little Allysia whom I had never gotten to see. And that kid with the big family. I hope Eugenia is thinking about nothing.

Behind me I hear people shuffling around. A man crouches in the center aisle trying to get a good shot with his video camera. Scanning the crowd I realize that there are nearly as many video units as there are families. Beth ended up with ours, a lost battle I can live with.

Mr. Willoughby introduces "Song of the Wind." I hope Eugenia doesn't stand and try to play it or, even worse, pretend to play it. She remains seated. I figure that with the lights Eugenia cannot see me, but I smile broadly and hope that maybe for one moment she might catch my eye. The violinists move into the second part of the tune. The little boy standing in front of Eugenia stops playing. He shrugs his shoulders and sits on the floor.

When the tune is over, Eugenia and the front row boy rise to play "Lightly Row." I cannot hear her above the fourteen other violins, but I watch her bowing and her fingering. She is playing it right. And then they are done, and they sit for a final piano offering.

An eight-year-old girl sits at the grand piano, pauses then launches into that Mozart sonata that everyone recognizes. The parents with video machines make way for a cameraman from Channel Ten news. He sets up in front of the piano, turns on his big lights, and starts filming. The girl holds up her left hand to shield her eyes from the glare and shoots a look at the cameraman. He cuts the lights and camera. I want to hug the little girl.

When she finishes, it is time for the finale, the medley of "Twinkle" variations, sort of a national anthem for Suzuki violinists. All fifteen of them stand up and roar away. The cameraman carries his equipment to the foot of the stage, turns on his lights, and pans across the players. He works his way down the front of the stage and takes a shot of the audience. I notice Eugenia shift slightly so the cameraman can see her.

When it is over and the applause has died down, Mr. Willoughby tells the audience to watch for clips on the eleven o'clock news. Eugenia runs over to me. "You did it," I say. "God, you were wonderful." I hope I do not sound too surprised.

"Daddy, that was great. I love performing. I want to perform every day."

*

On the way home, we stop at McDonald's for hamburgers and French fries and then at Earl's Ice Cream for sundaes. My little violinist talks and talks, and I enjoy the moment, watching her ride the adrenaline. I think we both wish the ride home could last longer than it does. I park in front of the house, and after I close the car door behind Eugenia, I hear another car door slam.

"Stephen," my former wife calls from across the street.

"Mommy!" Eugenia squeals. She runs to the edge of the curb and flings her arms out wide. "It was so great. I got to perform in front of a huge crowd."

Beth reaches our side of the street and kneels down to hug Eugenia. Clint looms up behind her, his camel's hair coat glowing under the streetlamp's light.

"Hi, Stephen," he says.

I nod to him. The fact that they're here, now, has me feeling queasy. I walk to the trunk of the car, open it, and pull out Eugenia's schoolbag and clothes.

"Stephen," Beth says again, standing with her arm around Eugenia. "I've been trying to catch up with you all afternoon."

I step onto the curb and look at Eugenia, resting her head against her mother's side. "What's up?" I say. I know I'm about to hear something I don't want to hear.

"Look, Stephen," Beth says. "I guess you didn't get any of my messages. I know this is a special evening. It's just that Clint got tickets for the new Disney movie tomorrow."

"Oh," says Eugenia, swiveling her head up at her mother and grinning. Then she looks over at me and lowers her eyes.

"It's for the first show," Beth says. "But it's in New York."

"And?" I say.

Clint clears his throat. "We'd have to leave pretty early, Stephen."

For a moment, no one speaks. I notice that everyone's breath makes a cloud in the cold night air at exactly the same time.

Finally, Beth says, "Clint just got the tickets this morning. We thought we could go ice-skating at Rockefeller Plaza afterwards. And have dinner with Clint's sister and her family."

Again, silence. I already know I've lost. I realize, all at once, that part of me is relishing their discomfort.

"Of course, Stephen," Beth starts up again, "you don't have to go along with this. It's just that it came up on such short notice. I tried to contact you." She glances at Clint. "Eugenia's usually with us on Fridays, anyway."

Eugenia separates herself from her mother but stays right next to her. "I don't have to go to New York, Daddy," she says.

"It's up to you, Stephen," Beth says.

"We thought it would be easier for Eugenia," Clint says. "If she woke up in our place, that is."

The three of them stand there in a row with the light from the streetlamp shining down on them making their hair glow.

"Come here," I say, reaching out my hand to Eugenia.

She looks up at her mother and then steps over in front of me. I crouch down and put my hand on her shoulder.

"It will be a special thing," I say. "Just like tonight was a special thing."

Eugenia looks down at the pavement. Just then a gust of wind pushes her against me, and she shivers. I hug her tightly.

"It's okay," I whisper in her ear. Then, louder, I say, "Come in and change. We'll pick out what you need for your trip tomorrow. All right?"

She pulls back just enough for her face to be right in front of mine. She looks sadder than I've ever seen her before.

"It's okay," I whisper again. "Come on."

She takes my hand; I rise, and we walk off toward the house.

"Thanks, Stephen," Beth calls after us.

"We'll wait out here," Clint adds.

I turn and look at them. They're holding hands and smiling as they stand there under the streetlamp. I shake my head then turn back and follow Eugenia to the front door.

After the three of them leave, I rinse out Eugenia's lunch box and straighten up the living room. I open my briefcase and put the Rosatti files and videotape on my desk. I find a note I wrote to myself to start doing the taxes tomorrow. I know a pile of laundry waits for me down in the basement. It can wait. I go to the refrigerator and pull out a beer. It's eleven-ten. The Sixers are playing in L.A.; I can catch the first quarter before going to bed. I take my beer into the living room and turn on the television. The Sixers are down five. I put my feet up on the coffee table just as the Sixers call a time-out. I watch a beer commercial about frogs that like beer. The clock on the VCR reads eleven twenty-five. "Damn," I grunt. I grab the remote control on the couch and press 1-0. The newsman says something about hearing from the next generation of musicians after a commercial. I scramble to the shelf across the room where we keep the cassettes. There are no new ones, so I snatch up one with two Muppet movies on it. Back at the VCR, I put it in the machine and hit the Play button. Fozzie Bear is in a diner in New York City. I hit Fast Forward. Channel Ten comes back on while the tape speeds forward. The smiling newsman is talking about Eugenia's school while they show the entrance to the auditorium. "No time," I yell. I hit Record and then realize that I have fast-forwarded to the end of the tape. On the TV, I see the little girl from Eugenia's practice group. They are all playing "Twinkle."

"Muppets!" I yell at the TV. "Muppets."

I crouch in front of the television screen. From a close up of the little girl the camera makes a slow pan across the stage. I see Eugenia, looking straight into the camera's eye as she plays. The music keeps going, and the camera cuts to the audience. There are people sitting all over the floor at the foot of the stage and then rows and rows of people in chairs. The shot makes the demonstration look as impressive as a concert at the Academy of Music. I pick out the grandfather with the little girl, but I almost do not recognize the serious looking man next to the grandfather. On the screen, I look like I am planning, calculating. There is cunning in my eyes. The shot cuts back to the boy who sat down on "Song of the Wind." He is fiddling away with his mouth open and his tongue hanging halfway out. The credits run over a last pan across the violinists. I see Eugenia again for a moment between the boys in the front row. Then it is over. An announcer introduces the talk show that comes on next.

I turn off the video unit and the television. I sit back on the couch with the beer in my hand, feet on the coffee table, and I stare at the blank screen. I close my eyes and try to play the demonstration back in my mind. When I see the stage full of violinists, I think I can see Eugenia. Then I see the grandfather and then me. I see those calculating eyes again. I open and close my eyes, thinking it might help me to find her face, but it does no good. I cannot see the face that I want to see.

Some People Just Stick Out

It's WEDNESDAY AFTER the morning rush. Mary—my fellow first shift waitress—and me and Earl the cook are talking about characters. Mary says she's done with her first two cigarettes and half *The Daily News* and is ready to be human. I've got tips to count and no business, so I plant myself on the stool next to her. We always take the stools at the left end of the counter where the cash register keeps anybody but a midget or a kid from eating.

Earl tells Mary to wait while he checks on the home fries he's left on the grill. Mary's daughter Pat comes in and joins us. She's dropped her youngest off at the sitter's and has time for coffee before going to her job at the bank. Earl the C returns from the kitchen smelling like a giant onion. He always smells of onion, and now, as he gets fatter and balder, he even looks like one. The C stands for cook and also for the way the poor bugger stands.

Thirty years over a grill and anybody'll stand like that. Never gets flustered back there. Nobody says it, but we all know he's the big reason we get so much business.

A good place like this gets everybody. You know you got a good diner when the help from other restaurants stop in on their way to work. So we get them all. The pizza guys from down the hill. Even the people who work at nice places like the Keg and Cleaver. Bankers and lawyers. Even the minister next door. There's always a real mixed crowd, but some people just stick out.

We have a good laugh over old lady McBride. Old lady McBride who can't be more than ten years older than Mary or me. Mary's got this way of acting just like the person she's talking about in a story, so me and Earl the C are laughing as soon as Mary starts in. Old lady McBride used to try to steal a little something every time she came in. Mary likes to think she can spot any funny business going on a mile away. She let the old lady go on with her sugar and creamers and silverware for a while, and then one day she wrote her up on her check for a bottle of ketchup. Mrs. McBride never said anything, just paid the bill. Hasn't stolen anything since. Hasn't left a tip, either.

Mary laughs so hard telling the story she has to hold her hand on her uniform to keep her belly from breaking through. There's maybe six people in the diner at the time. They can't help hearing her tell it. Everybody just roars at Mary's story. Except for the one guy in the booth. The professor we call him. He sort of smiles and nods his skinny old head, then goes back to shuffling pages of *The New York Times.* My doctor's the only person I know, besides the professor, who reads *The New York Times.* Costs twice what the price says because they have to truck it in from New York. Doc Willis tells me he gets *The Sunday Times* and spends all week reading it. And here's a smart man, a doctor, paying good money for out of town news and old news at that.

So, the professor reads on. He's got to be about my age. I can tell by his face, although his hair keeps him from looking like most men my age. Black. His is black. It is thin in parts, and he flattens out the black strands across the back of his head where it's almost gone, like somebody stretched a few strings of spaghetti, jet black spaghetti, over an old softball. His coffee cup's about half-empty, so I grab the pot and head over to his booth.

"You're probably going to charge me rent here someday, huh?" he asks as I pour.

"Only before ten o'clock," I say. "But you never show up during the rush." It's true, he manages to get here after the breakfast rush and usually leaves before the lunch crowd fills the place and the line goes out the doorway. Then he likes to come back in the afternoons, too. He's one of those with a bottomless coffee cup. But he's no problem.

"You don't think I'd break the rules?" he says. He points to the sign next to the clock that asks single customers to sit at the counter during the breakfast rush.

"No sir. Is there anything else I can get you?"

"I'm fine," he says. He stirs his coffee, taps the spoon on the top of the cup, then points the spoon at me. "What do you think about these diner characters, Ruth?"

"What do you mean?" I ask.

"Well, I couldn't help but overhear. What do you think about the characters who come in here? Do you have a favorite, or a favorite story?"

I don't know what to say. Here's this man who hasn't said two words to me outside of "More coffee" or "Check, please" in the maybe two years he's been coming here for breakfast. "Mary's the one with the stories, sir. I think that one about Mrs. McBride's my favorite."

"You're not Mary," he says. "That's for sure."

I flush redder than I have for years. I don't know whether I should tell him off or what.

"Please," he says, "don't misunderstand. There's a wonderful quality here, and you're a part of it."

Now, I've been in the restaurant business since I was a girl, and I know a line of bull when I hear it, but this guy I can't figure out. It sounds like bull to me, but I can't figure what kind of bull. Or even if it really is bull.

I start burning inside. The kind of feeling where the burn gets the better of you, and the words don't come out. He starts in again. "This place has color. Colorful people. You were just talking about that, right?"

I set the coffee pot on his classified section. "Yeah," I say slowly.

"Well, Mary and Earl are part of that, aren't they?"

I nod.

"And you are too."

"We ain't freaks, Mister."

"Of course not."

He looks up at me, and for the first time in our little conversation I wonder if anyone else can hear us. I look around. Earl is heading into the kitchen. One of the customers is showing Mary something in *The Inquirer.* I realize that it just seems like we're on stage in front of them all, that they really aren't listening.

"There's an atmosphere, an ambience here," he says. "I know you're going to think this is crazy, but there's something French about it."

Well, you're right about one thing there, Mister, I think to myself. I'm ready to march off to the kitchen, but he goes on.

"Well, obviously I don't mean the cuisine. I guess it's the people. There's a wonderful directness, a simplicity. A strength, really. Believe it or not, it makes me think of places in the south of France."

I try to picture Earl in a beret. I shake my head.

"I can see that you misunderstand me. You're a special person, Ruth. And this is a great place. That's all. Forget the French business. You don't understand. You're special. Thank you for being you."

"Well, they want me to be me in the kitchen right now," I say and grab my coffee pot and spin around. Ambience. French. Some people fart higher than their asses, as Mary would say.

Next day all my booths are filled when the professor comes in, and he sits on Mary's side. I'm glad I don't have to serve him. Let him dazzle Mary with his bull. Pat comes in just as her mom's side of the counter gets filled. Al, the mailman, leaves my side, and Pat takes his seat.

"Hi, Sweetie," I say.

"How's it going, Aunt Ruth?"

"Good," I say. I give her black coffee and two sugars. She's called me her aunt since she learned how to talk. If I'd been able to have a baby, the kid would have been about her age. I place a donut on a small plate in front of her. "Forget the diet," I say.

I notice the professor down the way paging through his paper. He's sitting at the end of the counter where you can see the cemetery. I wonder if he's ever noticed it, but of course he'd have to. The diner sits at the front corner of Leverington Cemetery, next to the Baptist church. My Walt used to tell Earl that for a big chrome mausoleum, the diner had some pretty good food. With the open spaces and the sky, the cemetery's not the worst thing in the world to look out on after the morning rush. I look forward to break time when I can curl up with a cigarette and enjoy the view. I think how I'm glad Walt's in Holy Sepulchre out on Cheltenham Avenue, how I like going over there after Mass on Sundays, how different it would be if he were right here behind the kitchen or out past the big window on Mary's side.

On Friday, the professor comes in a little later, and the place is almost empty. Mary goes on break the second he sits down at the corner booth. I feel funny about going over to him, being as how our little conversation went the other day. Then I start feeling funny about feeling funny. I bring him a cup of coffee and three creamers.

"Good morning," I say and put the coffee down in front of him.

He kind of smiles and begins nodding his head. "You remembered how many creams I like. You people always know how each person takes his or her coffee."

"Everybody drinks coffee here," I say. I look at him, and he's got that smile that makes one side of the face rise up. I sort of blink a smile back at him. "No big deal."

Now he smiles on both sides of his face. "Curious," he says.

"So what would you like today?"

He orders a bacon Eye Opener with a grilled corn muffin. I write the check up and bring it back to the kitchen. Earl backs away from the pancakes and sausages grilling in front of him and wipes his forehead with the bottom of his apron. *"Bonjour,"* I say and clip the order above the grill. Earl blows out a long blast of air that becomes a tired-sounding whistle.

I go back out to the counter to stack some fresh plates. The professor's lost in his newspaper. After that first real conversation last Wednesday, I asked Mary and Earl what they made of the guy. They both thought maybe he ought to start getting a salary like one of us. Mary said, "The guy can nurse a piece of pie all right. He spends more time on an order of pie than the baker does making the damn thing." Earl liked him all right as long as he didn't tell him what spices he ought to try on the eggplant parm. He said he could be an all right guy, but like with most people, there's probably something up his sleeve. Mary said, "I don't know about his sleeve, but he's got something up his keester. Like a mop handle, which I don't suppose he's too used to using." It's true, the guy sits straight up, and even his chin seems to be held up by something. A lot of our roofers eat with their heads about four inches above their plates. This guy's head keeps stretching for the ceiling. Even when he eats while reading his precious *New York Times,* he never slumps down, just tilts his whole frame forward a bit. As I watch him sipping coffee over his newspaper, I can picture Mary's mop doing its work. I swallow my laugh and grab his order.

I hear him talking before I get to his table. The words fly by like he's speaking in some other language, even though I'm sure it's English. In fact, I look around to see if maybe he's talking to somebody else. All the while he's holding up his half empty coffee cup and looking off at the ceiling, like he's seeing right through it. I slide his eggs in front of him.

"'Sometime too hot the eye of heaven shines, and often is his gold complexion dimmed. And every fair from fair sometime declines, by chance or nature's changing course untrimmed.'"

I look around the diner. The booths next to his are empty. He's still at it. No one at the counter seems to notice.

"'So long as men can breathe, or eyes can see,'" he says. "'So long lives this, and this gives life to thee.'"

He sets his cup down in the saucer and looks at me.

"Shakespeare," he says.

"B-5," I say, "with a corn muffin substitution."

He admires his food for a moment and then turns back to me. "That was one of the Bard's sonnets, a little something I learned as a schoolboy. Timeless words, aren't they?"

"Very nice," I say. "Can I get you some more coffee?"

He's got his face in his *New York Times* when I return with the coffee pot. I give him a refill and get back to the customers at the counter. We make eye contact when I'm behind the counter, and he gestures to let me know he wants more coffee and the check. A half hour later he walks past me. He shows me his hands as he passes. "*New York Times* ink," he says. He wiggles the tips of his fingers. They look like he's been tinkering with a car engine. He disappears into the bathroom. Next thing I know he's gone. At his table I find his bill and enough money to cover it, plus a tip. People don't usually leave pennies in tips, so I grab a pen and calculate what fifteen percent of his bill would come to. It's exactly what he left.

Saturdays always feel funny. Different faces from the weekdays, no predictable rush. There's always lots of kids, usually with one parent. People getting haircuts across the street stop in before or after their haircut. This Saturday drags more than most. I don't expect to see the professor. He probably gets that hair of his cut at some fancy place down in Manayunk. I imagine him out and about on a Saturday, passing his time in a little bookstore or a museum.

When I get done, I check the schedule. Next Saturday's my day off. And then the place is closed for Easter Sunday, so I'll have the whole holiday weekend to myself.

I take the A bus as far as the shopping center and figure it'll do me good to walk the two blocks home from the Acme there. Kids are crawling all over the McDonald's at the corner. There's a crowd at the sporting goods store. Maybe they're all getting baseball gloves for Easter. The library's the only place on the strip that's not jumping. I have to look twice in the window to see if it's open. At the Acme I get a quart of milk, some eggs, a loaf of bread, and a little apple pie that's on special. I thank the checkout girl for putting the pie in a separate bag.

On the way home I stop in the library. I ask if I can leave my two bags at the counter. The pale little man behind the counter tells me that it won't be necessary, that I can tote my things with me wherever I go.

I glance at the magazine section over by the window, the section of the library I am familiar with. I am relieved that I don't see anyone there that I know. I step past the children's section and see a librarian sitting against the back wall next to a computer terminal. She's alone. I move across the room. There's a man standing in front of a wall of books and a woman across the way who's down on one knee by another bookcase. The people here are as quiet as Mary and the rest of us at the diner are loud. The phone rings as I arrive at the young woman's desk. She takes the call. I set my bags on the carpet. I stand before her, tapping my fingers against my sides. I mouth the titles of the books on the shelf behind her. She's speaking, not whispering, on the telephone, but her voice is so low that I can barely hear her. I wonder if I could ever speak that quietly.

"What can I do for you?" she asks me.

"Oh," I say. "How are you today?"

"I'm fine. Thank you. I'm just fine." Her voice is warm. She sounds like she's from down South.

"Did you want something, Ma'am?"

"I'm looking for something by Shakespeare," I say. "I didn't know what section that would be."

She rises from her swivel chair and glides by me. She gestures for me to follow and I do, keeping within a few steps of her. Pat, Mary's daughter, describes herself as medium everything, and that's how the librarian looks. Medium height and weight. Light brown hair. Medium length. She's about Pat's age. Out of college, old enough to be married, established, maybe with a child or two. I wonder what brought her all the way from Alabama or Mississippi. She might have come to study at one of the colleges in the city. Or maybe she married someone from up here, although I see no ring.

"Eight twenty-two," she says. "He's the only person who gets his own number."

"Well," I say.

She touches one book and points to the end of the section. "This whole area is Shakespeare. Anything in particular you're looking for?"

I wonder if what the Professor recited is from a particular

play. "This might be impossible," I say. "I heard this spoken by someone. I think it was a sonnet, but I have no idea what book it's from."

"I can find you a collection of his sonnets," she drawls.

"I don't know if it's from *Hamlet* or whatever," I say.

She pulls out a volume and places it in my hand. *Love Poems and Sonnets of William Shakespeare*. I feel my face redden. She explains that a sonnet is a special form of poem and that I wasn't crazy to suggest a play because he actually slipped some into his plays. "But I bet," she says, "that if it was called a sonnet it's probably in here."

"So long as men can breathe," I say, "or eyes can see."

She smiles and clamps her hand around my shoulder. "So long lives this, and this gives life to thee," she says.

I nod.

"Oh, please," she says waving her hand at me. "I only know that because it's one I happened to study in college. That's the final couplet, the last two lines in the poem. They always rhyme."

I nod again.

She takes the book and flips through it. "Shall I compare thee to a summer's day?" she says. She glances up at me. "That's the first line. Shakespeare's sonnets are all numbered. But people know them by their first lines, too." She finds the page she's looking for and runs her finger partway down the page. She clears her throat. "Thou art more lovely and more temperate." She offers the book to me. "Here we are," she says, "Sonnet Eighteen."

The book is opened to a page with Sonnet Seventeen on the top half and Sonnet Eighteen below. There are two more sonnets on the page to the left. I scan the words of Sonnet Eighteen. I recognize some of the phrases.

"Beautiful, isn't it?" she says.

"Yes," I say.

"And how did you run across this particular one?" she asks.

"At work," I say. "Someone recited it."

"Just where do *you* work?" she says. "I'd like to work there."

I laugh. "I'm a waitress in a diner. Somebody said this. Said all this."

"My," the librarian says.

I feel my face turning red again.

"You know what you might like?" she says. "Would you be interested in something about sonnets themselves? That might make reading this, or reading others in this book, more interesting. I'd be glad to find you something like that."

"Sure," I say.

"Are you going to stay for a while?"

"Yes, I guess I'll find a table and read for a bit."

"I'll find you," she says.

I pick a spot at her end of the room but not too close to her desk. I figure fifteen minutes won't kill the milk. The book is filled with these sonnets, tons of them, and they all look alike. I see that they seem to rhyme in the same place, and they have that little pair of lines that's set off at the end. I read the professor's sonnet over and over. I shake my head at the *thou arts* and the *haths*, but after a while I feel like I almost get it. It's a love poem. I see that. I'm sitting here and not only am I reading freaking Shakespeare, but I'm reading love poems by the guy, a whole book of them. The librarian brings me a book opened to the part about Shakespeare's sonnets, and I page through it. It explains the stuff I was guessing at. I'm pleased that I was sort of on the right track.

I go over to her desk and ask if I can take the books out of the library.

"The book of poems is a circulating book," she says. "I'm afraid the other one is considered a reference book. That one has to stay."

"I see."

"How about if I show you where it lives here?" she says. She flashes a smile.

"Then I'll be able to use it here," I say.

She writes the call number of the book on a slip of paper and hands it to me, leads me to another part of the room, and then puts the book back on its shelf. I thank her and lug my groceries and *Love Poems and Sonnets of William Shakespeare* over to the checkout area.

At home I make an omelet for myself and then settle in Walt's easy chair with the book. I read the professor's poem and then skip around in the book doing my best to make sense of the stuff. At nine o'clock I turn on the TV with the remote. There's nothing interesting on, so I turn the sound off but keep the picture on. Mostly, I read sonnets. At eleven, I realize I'm nodding off, so I drag myself and the book to the bedroom. I find the holy card I got when Lester Magee passed away and tuck that in at the page with the professor's poem.

The next day is Palm Sunday, and I go to the nine o'clock Mass as usual, but instead of taking the buses over to the cemetery, I decide to go for a walk. I tell myself the weeds won't take over in a week. I drop off my church bulletin and the palms they gave out at Mass and then walk up the avenue for a good twenty minutes before turning around. A little voice inside tells me that the air is just as fresh over at Holy Sepulchre Cemetery, but I remind myself that Walt would be happy just knowing that I offered up my communion for him. I get home and do the house cleaning that I usually get to on Saturday. I eat some leftovers and a piece of the pie, do the dishes, and then bring *The Sunday Inquirer* to bed with me. When I'm done with the paper, I make a cross out of the lengths of palm leaves I brought home from church. I do it automatically, as I've done since I was a girl. I think how I could probably show somebody how to braid the pieces of palm into a little cross, but I couldn't explain it, couldn't put it into words if my life depended on it. I can't decide in which room I should hang the cross, so I set it on my bed stand and then turn off the light.

The professor comes in the diner on Monday but sits on Mary's side. I see him from my end of the counter and give him a quick wave when I catch his eye. He's there for over an hour, and when my side is almost empty, I'm tempted to walk over to his booth. Surely, he knows that I always work the north end of the diner.

Tuesday, he's back to a booth on my side. He orders the chipped beef. I bring him coffee and then his food. I walk near his table every time I have to deal with another customer. I hear nothing about Shakespeare. No sonnets, nothing. He gestures for his check. From the counter I can see him reaching for his wallet and then standing up. He sees me looking at him and winks at me. I blush, and he gives me a big smile.

After work I stop at the library again. I go directly to the shelf the librarian showed me and pull out the reference book. I take it back to the section where the young woman was last Saturday. A woman closer to my age is sitting in her seat. I inquire about the other librarian and learn that Tuesday is her day off. I re-file the reference book and go home.

In bed I finally get around to reading the church bulletin. They're to have a big to-do on Holy Thursday with foot washing and all. Then it's all the somber business on Good Friday. The place'll be dark until Saturday night. Pat and her husband had dragged me to the Saturday night Mass last Easter. The candles and the choir were nice, but two hours up and down on your knees was a bit much for me. I'll wait for the morning Mass on Easter Sunday. For Holy Week I can read my prayers at home, do my own stations of the cross right here. I know I'm not a very good Catholic, but I like the shorter, simpler Masses where you can actually say your prayers to God. I turn out the bedside light and ask for forgiveness for my old fashioned ways and also pray to God to help keep me from being foolish.

I slip the Shakespeare book into my bag and bring it to the diner even though I know I won't touch it in front of anyone down there. I start thinking about the professor as soon as I get to work. It occurs to me that I don't really know what he does for a living. We call him the professor, but nobody really knows what he does. He doesn't wear a tie, that's for sure. Unless he takes it off and leaves it with his *Inquirer* on his desk or wherever he works. He looks neat enough though. Always a nice sharp looking shirt. Most men his age don't care what they look like. They seem to take pleasure in looking like they don't care. The man does like his sports coats. My Walt wouldn't have thought to wear a jacket without a tie any more than he would have thought to give up bowling on Thursday nights or our two weeks in Ocean City every August. This guy looks like he's got a metal ruler in his jacket ready to pull out and point at some daydreaming student. He could be a professor, all right. Head always in the clouds. Going on about this and that.

He walks in at ten o'clock and sits right at the counter on my side. He orders pancakes and bacon. I wonder how a man can eat all that starch and not gain an ounce. And this one doesn't strike me as a walker or a gym user. I decide it's just his metabolism. I bring syrup and packets of jam, as well as extra butter.

"That Sonnet Eighteen sure is something," I say.

He looks up from his pancakes. "What?" he says.

"The poem you were reciting the other day," I say. "I think it's really something."

"Well, yes," he says.

"I just think it's a great sonnet," I say.

He nods.

"I like One Hundred Sixteen also," I say. "The one about admitting impediments?"

He nods again. He takes a sip of his coffee. "What was it about the poem from the other day that you liked?"

"The feeling," I say. "The feeling and the idea that it would last forever."

"And it has," he says.

"It has?"

He stares off beyond my shoulder. His face looks like he's deep in prayer. "Shakespeare knew what he had," he says.

I feel myself start to blush.

He keeps looking past me. He nods. "That love," he says.

"Such love," I say.

He turns back to me. "To love one's own work so much. To be so sure that one's words were so good, so lasting." He wipes his mouth with his paper napkin. "That's an artist."

I write up his bill at the counter next to him, and instead of scribbling my name on the bottom of the order form, I fill up half the sheet with the R in Ruth. He pays at the cashier and walks back to leave a tip. I clear the change off the counter and slide it into my pocket without counting it.

At break Mary asks me if I got my hair done. I tell her no.

"You look like the Easter Bunny gave you a giant chocolate cream egg," she says. "Semi-sweet chocolate, so you can eat the whole thing at once. Anyway, you look good."

I tell her she's got chocolate on the brain.

"A couple of days more," she says.

I remember that she gave up candy for Lent. I thank her for the compliment. She says Pat's noticed, too. She gives my cheek a pinch like I'm her little sister.

On the way home I go to the library. I head straight to the back room. The young woman is at her desk, paging through something. She looks up and sees me. She smiles. "How's Shakespeare coming?" she says.

"It's coming," I say. "You were very helpful the other day. I wanted to thank you."

She smiles again. "Do you remember where that book is?"

"Oh, yes," I say. "I was in last night. It's a good book. I appreciate you showing me the book and also talking with me about Shakespeare."

"Sure," she says.

"So, how is everything tonight?" I ask. "How are you doing?"

"Fine," she says. "Just fine." She pushes the book she's been reading aside. "And how are the sonnets treating you?"

"I thought the sonnets were all about love," I say.

"Well, they're about love," she says. She leans back in her chair. "They're about love, and some of them are about themes like time and death, about friendship, about the immortality of poetry."

"I guess I thought from the title of the book that they were all about love."

"Different kinds of love," she says.

I roll my eyes. "*Tell* me about it," I say.

She laughs, and then I laugh, too. "One great thing about poetry," she says, "is that there is usually more than one way to read it, to understand it."

"I think I see that," I say. I'm old enough to be this woman's mother, but she puts me in mind of my own mother. "It's tricky," I say, "when people see things differently. I mean, I can read something one way, and another person can have a completely different idea."

She points to the chair next to her desk. I sit down. "There is this person I know from my work," I say. My voice is low, like hers was the other day. "I guess I want him to understand things the way I do."

"Oh," she says.

I can't believe I'm telling anyone, let alone this woman, these thoughts, but it's quiet, and no one's near us. "I don't know why this is," I say. "I think maybe he's more interested in the actual poetry than I am." I look around. A teenager is sleeping at the table I used the other day. The librarian looks relaxed, like she is in no hurry to go anywhere or do anything. "I know very little about him," I say. "I mean, I don't *know,* but I've certainly imagined. I've invented a whole life for the man."

She leans a little closer.

"He's been widowed for years now. Children all moved away. Teaches his classes and is always in the middle of writing some book. I'm imagining all this. You know?"

"Yes," she says.

"When he talks, he sounds like the real deal, as my friend's niece Sally would say. He could be talking about plumbing or restaurant work, never mind Shakespeare, and he'd sound like he knew all about it."

She smiles.

"It's education," I say. "It shows in the professor like the lack of it shows in me, my co-workers, most of the people I know. My Walter, too. God rest his soul. He was always too busy puzzling over some new thing to make much noise about some other thing he'd already learned." I let out a long sigh. "You must think I'm nuts."

"It's all right," she says. "Go on."

"I got no right to bend your poor ear like this," I say.

"You know something?" she says. "For all the books and magazines in here, there's not a heck of a lot of talking going on. Of course, I like the quiet. I wouldn't have gotten into this kind of work if I didn't, but it's good to hear a real person talk about real things sometimes, too."

"I don't usually do this sort of thing. I mean, talking with strangers about strange men. You know?"

"And Shakespeare brought all this on?"

"I guess," I say.

I mention that I really do enjoy the book. She asks me if I have any favorites. I take it out and open it to Sonnet One Hundred Sixteen. I laugh about how I'm getting used to the Roman numerals in the titles. She reads the poem in that quiet voice of hers. I tell her I like the way some of the words run together.

"That's good," she says. "That's good."

We read and talk about Sonnet Seventy-three. I point out that it's almost closing time. She thanks me for making the evening pass quickly for her.

I get home and climb into bed. I set the Shakespeare book on the bed stand. I've done enough reading and talking about poetry for the night. I scold myself for the liberties I took with the librarian. I'd left feeling like I should have paid her something, and she ended up thanking me, for God's sake.

I wake up before the clock radio goes off but feel rested. I watch the local news on the little TV in the kitchen and still have time to catch the early bus. I help set up Mary's side, as well as my own, before Earl the C opens the front door to customers. Mary sends me on break at nine, and I sit at the corner and look out at the cemetery. I'm glad I don't have anyone in this cemetery. At least, as far as I know. I wonder if any of the people out there ever sat here in the diner.

The professor comes in just before ten. I bring him a cup of coffee and a saucer full of creamers. He tells me he needs time to decide what he's in the mood to eat. He smiles at me over the top of his newspaper. I smile back and go off to my other customers.

At twenty after ten I see his finger up in the air. He asks for an order of toast. When the toast is up, I bring it and some jam to his table. His hands are folded on top of his *New York Times*. He's just staring out the window at the traffic. He looks like he just lost his best friend.

*

The afternoon crawls along. Sally can't come in until six, and I tell Earl that I won't mind staying through the beginning of the dinner rush. The after lunch business is slow, and I end up looking at the clock all the time. Busy day, you don't even notice the radio. Not that it's worth noticing most of the time. Right in the middle of filling all the sugar containers I catch what they're playing. I get this feeling before I can even think of the name of the song or the singer. Like I'm whizzing to a stop in one of those high-speed elevators in the big buildings downtown. I think I'm going to lift up right out of my skin. It's not so much the words or the melody. I'm rushed back forty years. I can smell Johnny Wilkins's hair and my parents' big stuffed parlor chairs and my grandmother's vegetable soup from off in the kitchen. A song can bring back all those sights, sounds, and smells. Especially smells. Johnny's smell was soap and talc and a touch of his mother's garlic sometimes. We saw each other one spring. That was it. Walter has his own songs that bring back his smell. I hear those songs; I think about my Walter, back when we met and later. And then one thing leads to another, and it's just not a happy ending.

I tell myself a long shift today won't kill me. I'm not going to the Holy Thursday services anyway. I find Earl's paper when I go on break and wonder what story it was the professor was talking about. I start with the metro section and work my way though all the local crimes, accidents, fires. The national and world news section has stories and opinions on wars and near wars. There's a piece about the Holy Land and problems they're having there. I wonder how all these stories might have hit the professor. The features section has a piece on eating disorders and a story about a woman who used to be homeless and now isn't. I keep looking

"It's a nice day," I say. "Supposed to stay like th days. Herb said so."

"Herb?" he asks.

"Herb on Channel Ten."

"Oh, yes. Of course."

He looks out the window but not at anything in The A bus is making it through a yellow light. There school kids waiting to cross the avenue, but he doesn notice them either. I have to ask is he all right.

"Yes, yes. Just fine." He gives me a brief smile like sor taking his picture and just said, "cheese," then he p hands on his newspaper and looks down at it. I picture Powell from one of those old films. I see him in a smokir in some posh living room. The professor is the first per ever spoken with who could actually wear a smoking ja certainly is a glorious day out there," he says. "And I am to be here. I was just thinking about something I came ac today's *Inquirer*."

He sees me looking at *The New York Times* laid out befor "I left *The Inquirer* at work—not that *National Enquirer* thin *Philadelphia Inquirer*."

"Yeah," I say, "*The Inquirer*."

"Anyway, I pick up *The Times* on my way here."

"Right," I say.

"Ruth, I'll see you tonight at dinner time."

"What?" I say.

"There are some problems at the office. So, I'll be aro tonight."

"Oh," I say, "then I'll see you tonight."

"Right," he says.

for the one piece that's going to steal my smile, make me look out the window, and tell somebody about it. They all could, I guess, but none of them do.

There's no telling what got to the professor. I don't know a thing about him, really. *There's no fool like an old fool,* I think to myself. I'm just a stupid schoolgirl worrying about some boy. I know that's foolish, but I can't stop it. I'm not sure what I want from this man, but for some reason I want to see him walk in the door. I ask myself what kind of feelings this man has for me, and as the words come to me I ache in embarrassment. I haven't felt this kind of foolishness in several decades, and why on earth should I feel it for this character?

By five o'clock it's clear that the professor is not coming back, and I'm taking it with as much grace as I can muster. He will never ask anything more of me than the daily specials. I serve the early dinner crowd cheerfully and whistle the high harmony to "My Blue Heaven," Walter's favorite driving song.

At quarter to six, the professor saunters in with another man, a young guy in his twenties. They sit at one of my booths. I'm surprised to see him with someone. The way he said he was coming sounded like it was just going to be him. I wonder how I would feel if he came in with a woman. I grab two waters and menus and head over to their table. Maybe he's a student or a young teacher.

"Coffee, professor?" The words come out of my mouth before I realize what I'm saying.

"Professor?" says his companion. He gives the professor a funny look.

The professor looks from the young man to me. "No," he says. "I'm not in a teaching position."

His friend says, "Oh, I can understand, Ma'am. When I started working for the state, I thought Richard was a unit supervisor or something, considering he's so experienced, established."

The professor bows slightly, as if he were receiving the young guy's applause.

I nod and pull out my pen and order pad.

"I come here for coffee occasionally, Larry. You know, if I'm doing field visits." The professor opens the big dinner menu. "While we don't have time to do more elaborate fare, I'm sure we can muddle through here. "

"Oh, it's fine," his friend says.

"And we *don't* want to be late for the meeting," the professor says, sounding like he means nothing of the sort. He leans across the table toward his friend. "Someday, you and your wife will both be my guests for some memorable dining. I'll pick the place."

His friend looks back up at me. "Well, what would you recommend for tonight?"

I roll off the daily specials like I'm some kind of game show host. They sit there studying their menus.

"People always like the meat loaf. And the stuffed cabbage. When I want something a little special I usually go for Earl's pot roast. Green beans, maybe a side of macaroni and cheese."

Larry lowers his menu and looks at the professor. "I appreciate you taking me out like this before all the nastiness starts. Really, it would have been a tight squeeze to run home, get a bite, and be back on time. I know it's not one of the places you talk about, but this'll do just fine."

I click off my ballpoint and tuck the pen and my order pad back in my apron pocket. "I'll give you a few minutes, okay?" I rush off to work the other booths in my section. When I head back, I can see they're done with their menus. The professor is talking a mile a minute, the other guy nodding his head.

"They're beautiful people, Larry. Gentle. It's a different pace than with this culture."

I stand next to them and take out my order pad and pen and wait.

"I can see why all the crap from on high gets to you, why you hate it so much in this environment," Larry says. "I'd love to visit some of those haunts of yours. More exotic than what I'm used to."

The professor clasps his hands together with a flourish. "Well," he says. "All in good time." Then he smiles up at me. "Ruthie, Ruthie," he says. "And your diner. Ruth, it may be called Bob's or Whoever's Diner, but it's your baby." He beams at me as if I'd just won a blue ribbon. "Larry, Ruthie here makes this diner."

Ruthie it is now. I wish he'd called me Ruth a while longer before calling me Ruthie. Still, it sounds good in his voice. He lifts his water glass in a toast. "To the house that Ruth built."

The younger guy laughs and lifts his glass up to clink his friend's.

I laugh despite myself. "That's what Walter always used to call our place on Jefferson Street," I say. "The house that Ruth built. He always said that." I smile. They're still laughing. "He was my husband," I say. The professor starts ordering his dinner before I can say anything else. I want to explain, but I have all I can do to keep up with his order and then his friend's. It's just as well, I figure. At least this way I'm not saying anything else that needs explaining.

When I come back with their rolls and butter, they're talking about outdoor cafes in some other country. How people's jobs allow for siestas and everybody sleeps late and eats dinner at ten at night. Really, only one of them is doing the talking. The young guy listens and nods sometimes.

When I bring the soup and salad, the professor reminds me that he had asked to have the salad served after the entree. I can't believe I didn't write that down on the check. I look the order over to make sure I didn't mess up anything else. I hear him explaining his reason for serving the salad later in the meal, and I'm not sure whether it's for my benefit or for his friend who seems as surprised as I am.

"It doesn't seem very American," I say.

He laughs like I just told a great joke. "No, Ruthie, it's not particularly American."

I move to the couple at the adjoining table without excusing myself. The professor is talking about people who know how to live. It's not clear to me who these people are, but I get the feeling that they don't run after customers or punch time clocks. Not a care in the world, I hear him say.

Back in the kitchen, little Louis is banging on the pots and pans over at the sink. I stick another order in front of Tom, the dinner cook. I look over all of mine to make sure I didn't forget anything. Colleen swings through the door, plants an order next to mine, and whooshes her way out front again. The door shuts off the chatter from out at the counter and beyond, but standing here I know every word the professor is saying. I don't have to hear the words or read them. I know them. I know this man like Shakespeare knew his Hamlet. Right now his friend is telling him it's a shame how their supervisor is coming down so hard on the professor. The lack of trust is unbelievable, the professor says. His friend says, if you say you're out in the field, you're in the damn field, and who are they to say otherwise? The professor says, hey, the work gets done, right? Then the professor is telling him about better jobs, better countries, better restaurants. Yes, I know him. I could write a book.

I feel a hand on my shoulder and hear my name. It's Tom. He reminds me of what time it is. "Get out of here, Ruthie. Gina and Mary are long gone."

I nod.

"Enjoy your Saturday off," he says. "Have a nice Easter."

"Yeah," I say. I pull off my apron and walk to the change room. I put my tips in my pocketbook. I can count them at home.

The professor and his friend's seafood specials are up. I go out to the counter and tell Sally to take over. She'll finish them and my other tables. "And the seafood guys," I say, "they get their salads *after* their entrees."

"Whatever," she says.

There's an *Inquirer* sitting on the end of the counter. I pull out the travel section. I find my pen and draw a big circle around the article about the increase in airfare costs. It seems the cost of flying abroad is going through the roof. I dump the other sections of the newspaper into the trash. I fold the travel section in half and tell Sally she can give it to the old man with the seafood order.

I don't even look down at their booth on my way out. I shiver in the cold of the evening at the corner. I have lots to tell Walter when I go to the cemetery Sunday. I can already hear him telling me I'm a bold one. Well, thanks, kiddo. I can see him shaking his head. Ruth, he'd say, there's a time to be bold and a time to just let be. I turn and try to make out the professor's head in the windows. You can't see anybody from out here. I go back in and stand at the inside of the doorway.

"Yo, Sally," I call.

"Yeah," she says from the counter. "Did you forget something?"

"You didn't deliver that newspaper yet, did you?"

"No," she says. "Not yet."

"Well, eighty-six the newspaper," I say. "He doesn't need it. Eighty-six it."

"Sure thing," she says. She takes the paper off the counter and drops it into the trash.

There's an A bus coming right as I go out the door again, so I hustle to the corner just in time to catch it. I let myself sink into a window seat and look out the window as the graves and monuments on the other side of the wrought iron fence go by. I blink at the lights of the businesses on the avenue and think about where I should buy flowers for Easter. I try to think of just how I can ask my librarian friend to go out with me to Holy Sepulchre on Sunday morning. I figure something'll come to me.

September

"THEY'RE DEAD!" Chuck screamed.

The kid who was bagging froze, eyes wide, and the box of mac and cheese he held suspended over the paper bag.

Chuck bolted, leaving his groceries at the register. He slowed only to allow the automatic door to open, then charged outside.

On the dark street, he ran through the powder-clogged air, away from the market, away from Simone and the apartment, away from the smoldering remains of the World Trade Center. At the first corner, he dashed headlong into the street, cars swerving around him, a cab horn blaring at him all the way through the intersection. A couple wheeling a stroller toward him pressed themselves against the facade of an apartment house as he shot past. Blocks ahead, a Chinese restaurant's hanging sign, yellow with red lettering, blinked on and off. When he reached the sign, he cut left. A church loomed in the distance; he swung right before he reached it. The streets were darker here. Panting, he staggered to a stop in front of a small park he had never noticed before in this mostly residential area. A hunched-over man with a newspaper tucked under his arm shuffled along a path on the far side of the park. Chuck stumbled to the middle of the park, plopped onto a bench between two old sycamore trees and waited for his breathing to even out. When it did, he touched his white-hot face. For the first time since he had started running, the sirens and traffic noise registered fully.

He'd fucked up again. Not as bad as when he'd refused to attend his mother's funeral, maybe, but he felt a familiar twinge because he'd fucked up just the same. This time, at least he'd tried to put his best foot forward, but the result was the same.

Since Tuesday, Simone had stopped asking about his missed psychiatrist appointments and the two refills in the unopened CVS bag atop the dresser. She'd cried but had not said a word about leaving him. On Friday night, when he'd finally turned off the TV, he'd said, "In a way, it's better to know what I feel." *Or,* he thought, *to know I feel it, not like some zombie.*

"Chuck!" she'd sobbed, throwing her arms around his neck. She'd hugged him so hard he'd thought he'd pass out.

And tonight, he hadn't wanted to flip out on the bagger at the market. Being able to relate to people for a few days had been oddly comforting, but now, people like the bagger kid were going all out to find silver linings.

"You said 'hero' five times in the last minute," he'd told the bagger. The kid said something else, but Chuck was all head, no ears. "People on TV," Chuck yelled. "With photos of dead people. Since Tuesday. Think they're going to find the dead people."

Whatever the bagger had said next was part of a seething blur. Still panting, Chuck stretched back against the park bench, trying to even out his breathing. Images and ideas swam in his head:

those planes last Tuesday, the old house in Germantown, Sun Ra's Arkestra playing that mad music, the toxic smell in his mother's hospital room. He thought he heard someone yell, "Yo!" the way his father, the South Philly trolley driver, used to. He turned toward the sound.

Across the street, people in grimy uniforms exited a red van outside a bar, their noisy voices not those of an out-on-the-town crowd. They shouted, as if out of habit, slowly, as they practically stumbled toward the entrance to the bar. Their calling to each other irritated him. A man with a leashed dog locked the vehicle and then crossed over to the park. The others had gone inside now, and only the whoosh of street traffic and the ever-present wail of sirens in the distance filled the air.

Even under the dim park lights, the man's clothes looked rumpled and dirty. His harnessed German shepherd, panting quietly, trudged along the grass at the edge of the sidewalk then stopped to sniff a no-littering sign. Chuck knew where they'd come from.

When the man noticed Chuck, he stopped and said something in a low voice to the dog before scanning the rest of the empty park. Chuck did not know where to go next, but he felt the urge to start moving again. The man and the dog started toward him, slowly. They stopped about fifteen feet away, and the man waved.

Chuck nodded. "I was just leaving," he said, rising from the bench.

"I'm not a cop," the guy said. He and the dog came a little closer but stopped again.

The guy's face was haggard. The dog's eyes were filmy, its fur matted, and its features aged. Chuck wondered how old those dogs got before they retired from this work.

"Fire Department?" Chuck said.

"Special Unit," the guy said, nodding toward the van across the street. "We're up from Philly since last night." The dog whined.

"How's the old fella doing?" Chuck said.

"Candy?" he said. He knelt and patted his dog. "She's three."

"She's younger than me," Chuck said. "I mean, in dog years." The guy was not much older than Chuck.

"She didn't find anybody today," the fireman said. "Know what I mean? A couple of false alarms, but nobody came out of there alive today, again." He stood up. "You don't have to do this if you don't want to."

"Do what?"

"I want to get a beer like the rest of my unit and call my wife on my cell," he said. "But I just can't put Candy in the van yet."

Chuck looked at the dog, and the dog's eyes locked on his. *Just tell your human what you want. Tell him you want a bowl of water or maybe a steak. I wish you could.*

"When I put her vest on, she's all work," the guy said. "I don't know what you do, but trust me, you don't work any harder than she does."

Chuck felt that familiar twinge.

"She's not right, not herself," the guy said. "I can't take her back until she finds somebody."

Candy cocked her head to the side, like the RCA Victor dog, her eyes still on Chuck. "What would I have to do?" he said, turning to the guy.

"Hide somewhere in the park, under some leaves, some newspapers, then I'll bring her back."

"I don't know," Chuck said. "What'll it do for her?"

"Wonders," the guy said. "You'll see."

When the fireman turned around and went off with the dog,

Chuck looked closely at the little park. He walked behind the trees, where two lines of shrubs formed an X. The junction of the bushes seemed too obvious, so he kept going. He settled on a wild section near the end of the brushy shrubs. Once behind them, he knelt down, waiting for the guy and the dog to reappear. When they came into sight on the far side of the park, she was wearing her vest and was pulling the guy along. Chuck crawled under the bushes, tucked himself against the lower branches, and curled his knees against his chest. It wasn't enough. She'd see him right off. He broke off a branch from the bush, wincing at the sound it made. Across the park, the dog sniffed the base of a tree. Chuck pulled himself into the fetal position as tightly as he could and held his camouflage over his shoulder. He heard the dog's panting and the padding of her paws. They were over near his bench.

The guy whispered something to her, but Chuck could not make it out. He closed his eyes and waited. He could not hear them, but he knew they were closer. His right foot was in an awkward position. A branch was poking his neck, but if he moved it would make noise. He breathed slowly through his mouth, trying not to move his chest. The dog couldn't be more than twenty yards away. *Come on,* he thought, *work, work.* The branch pressing into his neck felt like it was spring loaded. *A zombie wouldn't feel this,* he thought. *None of it.* The end of the branch pressed deeper with every tiny breath he allowed himself. But he was not going to make a sound. He was not going to fuck this up.

Ray

Two nurses call in sick, and nobody can come in to cover, and all hell breaks loose in L and D. I'm sure I'm going to win the Olympic Gold Medal for bladder control this time. After circulating for back-to-back sections, I finally run to the bathroom, give report to the next shift, and get the hell out of there. At the exit, I stand under the awning and smoke a cigarette. Some appetites won't wait. There's an all-night hoagie shop on the way to the parking garage, but I'll wait until I get home and play another game of Refrigerator Miracle Worker.

It's nearly one in the morning, so I don't expect Ray to be up, but he's sitting at the kitchen table when I walk in.

"Late," he says.

I nod and pull a Budweiser out of the refrigerator.

"Bad?"

I pop the top and pour the beer into my pilsner glass. "Of course," I say. "Maybe if the hippies weren't siphoning off our help, we all could have had a break tonight."

"I thought midwives went out before the Hula-Hoop," he says.

"Retro," I say. "You have no idea." I open the refrigerator again and study the shelves before grabbing the package of American cheese.

"What happened?" he says.

"Nothing happened. It's what *could* have happened. Never mind not peeing for nine hours." He's looking out the window. Floodlights in the middle of the backyard illuminate a row of roses he put in a month after I moved in with him. They mostly obscure the yews at the back of the yard, the tall shrubs that I told him made me feel like I'd be living in the woods, a nice thing for a city girl. Now, one night, it's mums on the right. Another night, it's something I don't even know the name of up front.

"You're wasting a lot of electricity," I say. "It's not good for them."

"I'm going to bed."

"I'm one grilled cheese sandwich away from joining the ranks of the dead," I say, watching him pad across the linoleum.

When I'm ready to sit down and eat, I dim the overhead kitchen lights, switch off the outside lights, and enjoy looking out the window into the blackness. "A regular gabfest," I say to myself.

When I wake up, he's already sitting in front of that monitor screen. "You need to get off that computer and talk to someone," I mutter.

At least, he doesn't drink. Nor does he give me a hard time about my smoking. And people slow down when they drive by all his flowers and shrubs. He doesn't meddle with anything I do inside, and I don't say anything about the arboretum he's developed in the yard.

When I get home from my shift, he comes into the kitchen.

"Next Saturday," he says. "You working night shift?"

I check the calendar. "A twelve," I say. "The extra money will help get an edge on the furniture payments. I go in around dinner time."

"I located some guys from the area. They were in the Nam when I was. It's going to be like a meeting."

"You don't know them?"

"The Internet."

"You think the Internet's safe for that kind of thing? You hear stories. People get into all sorts of trouble on that thing."

"They won't bother the house."

"Strangers," I say. I wish he wanted to go out to dinner or a movie, but I tell myself this is at least a small step.

The shift is quiet, for a change. It stays that way all night. They send me and another girl home before dawn.

The place is like a ghost town when I pull in the driveway. I figure he's packed off all of his little buddies by now and turned in. The floodlights are off. Maybe he was so excited about this meeting thing that he forgot to leave them on. Or maybe he figured the moonlight was enough.

I tiptoe into the kitchen and turn the dimmer on just enough so I don't bump into anything. My eyes adjust bit by bit. Some coffee cups and glasses sit in the dish rack. I open the cabinet door under the sink and shake the trash bag. Empty cans. I turn up the dimmer a bit. The table is empty. The counters are just the way I left them. I walk to the window and strain my eyes.

I open the yard door and stop. The trench starts about fifteen yards out, where the gladiolas were, then stretches all the way to the yews. Two black guys are sprawled out in the bottom of the part of the ditch nearest to me. One of them is snoring. Then there's a white guy whose back is against one dirt wall with his feet up against the other. I scan the row of guys and spot Ray, slumped over, shoulder-to-shoulder with a guy who looks a bit like our mailman. At the far end, I see a short balding man, perched on the berm of the trench. He is alert, as if on guard. He watches me take in the whole scene. His face is blank, but he's got these eyes. He just stares at me.

Back inside, I go up to the bedroom. I am panting even though I feel that I must be quiet. The sky has started to turn from black to that deep blue that tells you the sun is on its way. From the window I see them out there. At the edges of the yard, the grass and flowers look as if nothing's happened. I slip out of my clothes and put on my nightgown. Standing against the wall mirror, I feel as if I'm still panting, even though I've stilled my breathing. Across the room, the sheets on the big bed are pulled down, the way a maid might leave a bed for a hotel guest. It is enormous. I cannot move.

Indian Summer

I NEVER WOULD HAVE caddied that summer before high school if it hadn't been for Paul Bacon. "Even a retard could caddy," Paul assured me one evening, standing by the playground swings. "If you can play that miniature golf course in Andorra, you can caddy." I might not have completely believed what my friend was saying, but I believed that he believed it.

"What about that big golf course across the Wissahickon, near Dalessandro's?" I said.

"Public course guys don't tip for shit," Paul said. "Besides, my dad and his cronies go there."

He'd hatched this scheme before I could think. We settled on a private course out in Spring House, near his grandmother's. We'd thumb a ride out 309. End up with the money he wanted for clothes for the upcoming school year. I'd get my grubby hands on the new Gene Pitney and Roy Orbison records.

"We tell our parents we're going to the woods," he said, answering the question on my mind.

I got to Paul's house around nine o'clock the next morning, sweating from the five block walk between my rowhouse block and the Bacons' large stone single. Paul's mother opened the door and ushered me in.

"My, you're quite the early bird, Thomas," she said. "And still a husky one, at that. Wait in the living room. I'll get him up."

Just as I settled back into the couch, she swept into the room. "This just came," she said, dropping a *National Geographic* in my lap. I sucked in my stomach. She switched on the large window fan across the room and started out.

I glanced at the magazine's cover. "On Safari in Kenya." The wafting air from the fan made my damp shirt suddenly feel chilly. The radio was tuned to a classical station.

"Tchaikovsky," Mrs. Bacon said, stopping on her way out the hallway entrance.

In her long house dress, she looked like Loretta Young, ready to sweep from the living room. I tried to picture my mother or father saying "Tchaikovsky."

"I only know because the announcer said so," she confessed. "Piano Concerto No. 2 in G major." Her eyes seemed to focus on something far beyond the living room. Suddenly, her expression hardened as if someone had just smacked her face. "You're not sitting on my cigarette lighter?" she said, glaring at me.

I fumbled through the cushions. "Sorry, Mrs. Bacon," I said. But when I looked up, she was gone. Paul's mother was odd that way. You never knew which Mrs. Bacon you were going to get.

I opened the *National Geographic* to an article about some guy who'd explored Newfoundland and Labrador. I knew that Labrador was north and that it stuck out into the Atlantic. The local Eskimos took this explorer out in a little boat to look at an iceberg up close. Icebergs were tricky, these people told him. They could flip over on you, drop you and your boat down under them. The guy was surprised that the icebergs had other colors in them, like blue. The article had no photos of this particular iceberg, but I pictured it as a floating island. When the guy got right next to it, something was floating around in a pool up on top: a jellyfish, stranded up there within the iceberg's walls, under the sun, going wherever the iceberg went, with all that ice between it and the ocean. *Jesus,* I thought. *Some ride.*

I heard Paul banging around upstairs, so I put the magazine down on the couch. I had to admit the music was all right. All sorts of instruments swelled, not just the piano. It sounded like movie background music. It wouldn't work in a movie about this explorer guy though, not scary enough. Tchaikovsky's Second Piano Concerto in G Major. I wondered if this was the second piano concerto Tchaikovsky had written or if it was the second one he'd done in G major. I was sure that these were not questions you could ask in high school and expect to live afterwards.

When we left, Paul announced that instead of paying bus fare to get out to the expressway, we would walk. "So even if we don't earn anything, we'll still have bus fare for later, plus some food money," he said, poking me in the gut.

We reached the expressway in under an hour then walked up the shoulder until we came to a shaded underpass, where Paul plopped down out of the sun. I pulled two cigarettes out of my pack and passed one to Paul.

Paul produced a shiny Zippo lighter that I was sure was his mother's, lit his cigarette, and then held out the flame for me.

"Just stick your thumb out like this," Paul said, suddenly the expert on hitchhiking. "And act like you don't care. Nothing to it."

Standing by the road with my thumb out, it seemed to me that drivers were actually speeding up when they saw me. I told myself it was just a matter of time. "You know, Paul," I said. "Life needs background music."

"What?"

"Like in the movies," I said. "Don't you think?"

"You are so mental," he said, shaking his head. "I used to think stupid shit like that. Everybody grows out of it."

After about fifteen minutes, a guy in a business suit stopped his Fairlane for us. He had Mantovani playing faintly on the radio. *Fool,* I thought. *What a waste of a good radio.*

When we got to the clubhouse, dripping wet, a bald man with a purple splotch of discolored skin on his forehead cracked open the door just wide enough to poke his head out. He gave us a look as if one of us had farted, pointed to the caddy shack, and then slammed the door in our faces.

A dozen guys lazed about the caddy shack, an old wooden hut with benches along three walls. Nobody even looked at us as we went to the far end. Two boys were called to caddy, then four others. Three hours later, just Paul and I remained in the little hot house, swatting flies and wondering if we would ever see any other part of that golf course. Finally, the old bald guy stuck his head in and gestured for us to follow him. Two of the caddies who had been in the shack when we'd arrived were standing with a foursome of golfers at the putting green.

"I'm glad to be your caddy today, sir," Paul said to the golfer he was assigned to. "Perfect day for golf."

My voice cracked when I tried to say something to my golfer.

"Don't offer any advice," Paul whispered, as we headed off to the first tee.

On the fourth hole, Paul's golfer and mine ended up in the same sand trap. I saw Paul offering his man a particular iron. I couldn't tell which one. When my golfer approached me, I tilted the open bag toward him and managed a weak smile while I waited for him to choose a club.

We didn't make enough money to get clothes or records, but we had enough for bus fare and hoagies. While I paid for the sandwiches, Paul slipped a *Playboy* under his shirt. Instead of going right to the bus stop, we crossed the street and found an empty bench at the edge of the park. When we had wolfed down the hoagies, Paul flipped open the magazine to the centerfold. "Now, *that's* entertainment," he intoned.

I wondered how I would confess all this. I had only gone once at the start of the summer, and my list of nasty deeds was getting way too long for one visit. "It's going to be weird," I said. "You not going to Catholic school anymore."

"No first period religion ever again."

"And you'll go to college," I said. "Everybody from Central gets in."

"You'll have to listen to some old priest ranting about religion for four years. And some of those priests have masters degrees in cruelty."

I'd heard those stories too. In the eight years we'd gone to Holy Martyrs, the worst thing Father McMullen had ever done was yell at us for feeding chocolate chip cookies from the rectory pantry to his overweight Basset Hound, Beauregard. Monsignor Day took a carload of kids to Willow Grove Park every year. For confession, I usually maneuvered to get either him or that old visiting priest with two hearing aids.

"You'll have to go to C.C.D. classes after school," I said.

"I'm *supposed* to show up," Paul said, grinning.

I was about to ask him what his parents would do if they found out he cut the classes, but I stopped myself. Paul, no doubt, had some perfect answer that he was dying to spring on me.

The next day, Saturday, we told our mothers that we had been building a fort in the woods, and they packed us lunches. We ate the sandwiches at our expressway hitching spot. I'd bought two more packs of Marlboros with the money I'd earned the day before, and I gave one to Paul. I took out a pair of butts, and Paul lit them.

"Isn't that your mom's lighter?" I said.

"I'm gonna swipe my own soon," he said. "Then I'll stick this in the couch."

Our second ride took us practically to the entrance to the caddy shack. The heat had broken; in fact, clouds had moved in, so sitting in the caddy shack wasn't torture. Only a half dozen other guys were in there. I plugged in my earphones and listened to my transistor radio. I pulled the weekly WIBBAGE Top Ninety-Nine song list from my back pocket and sat it on my knee, noting which records I owned. Two Gene Pitney songs were climbing the list that week.

Paul found a pack of matches with a picture of the three Pep Boys on the cover. He made holes at the crotches of Manny, Moe, and Jack and stuck a match through each hole from inside. Then he started pushing the matches back and forth, making it look like the auto supply big shots were jacking off. The faster he pushed them, the louder the shack full of caddies howled.

At twelve-thirty the caddy master took us and two local boys aside.

"You better look sharp," he warned us. "The archbishop doesn't put up with any shenanigans. Now wait over there by the pro shop."

"Shit. Archbishop Strahle," Paul said.

When Paul went inside to use the bathroom, I sat on the pro shop's wooden steps. Please, I prayed, don't stick me with the archbishop of Philadelphia.

"Move it, fat boy," boomed a gruff voice.

I jerked around and looked up at the stern face of the man who had confirmed me six years ago. He held a putter in one hand as he chomped down on the business end of a half-smoked cigar. He blew out a thick cloud of smoke.

"Fore!" he bellowed.

I jumped to my feet before the archbishop could take another draw on his cigar. He stomped down the wooden stairs and headed toward the putting green. I watched the tall man stroll away, slicing his putter through the air like a sword.

Paul slipped out of the pro shop. "Move it, fat boy," he whispered in my ear.

One of the experienced local caddies ended up with the archbishop's bag, thank God. Paul carried for a priest about the same age as the archbishop, and I got a younger priest who introduced himself as Father Jerry. The other guy got the really young priest.

"If you make me laugh," Paul whispered to me at the first tee, "I'll kick your ass from here to Vatican City."

I had chosen Paul for my confirmation name. Thomas Paul Lord. Paul for my friend. And for Saul, who became Saint Paul on the road to Damascus. Of all the Bible stories we had learned, that was one that had stuck in my mind when confirmation time came around. I remembered some others, but I'd liked that one, the magic in it, the strangeness. I liked Paul's luck, which the nuns would have called grace. The nuns had drilled it into us kids that we would never get any direct contact from God; regular people had to find God in other people. Still, I imagined how cool it would be if God knocked me off a horse or my bike, or at least sent the Blessed Mother on a quick visit to Philadelphia to unravel a few of life's mysteries for me. A year ago, Father McMullen had taken me and three other boys on a weekend retreat to a Franciscan seminary high school out around Gettysburg. They were trying to recruit us. But after watching those guys pad around the whole weekend with their mouths clamped shut, only to leap up as if zapped by a cattle prod every time a bell rang, I knew damn well I wasn't going to be the priest in my family. By the beginning of eighth grade, I knew I wasn't going to write off girls for the rest of my life.

The archbishop teed up his ball and swung. He whacked it straight down the fairway; he'd be on the green in two. He tucked his red Ban-Lon neatly into his trousers, then leaned on his driver and waited as the others teed off.

I avoided looking at Paul as his priest made his first drive down the fairway, sure that if he made me laugh, my days would be over. Just then, I noticed a foursome of women over at the putting green, wearing flowered tops and long shorts. One of them bent over to pick a ball out of the hole, and I watched her shorts ride up her leg. I turned away, fast. I really didn't need a hard-on in front of the archbishop of Philadelphia and three of his priests.

Father Jerry arched a high shot toward the first flag. I stowed his club and then lifted the bag to my shoulder. As I followed the others down the fairway, I realized that I was praying to not screw up, to not laugh, to not get a hard-on. I had to use every bit of strength I had to keep a straight face.

On the fifth hole, the archbishop, Paul's priest, and Father Jerry all ended up in the same rough. The archbishop lined up his second shot and then slammed his ball into a chestnut tree from which it bounced straight back and landed almost exactly at his feet. He and the two priests laughed. I glanced at the other caddies. All of them were looking in different directions. I forced myself to stifle a laugh. The archbishop set up his shot again, working what was left of the cigar with his mouth as he waggled his hips. He needed to drive the ball to the left of the chestnut tree and over a cluster of bushes. He drew his club back and then struck the ball squarely. It smacked off the same tree again and this time ricocheted into a jungle of overgrown vines and brush at least thirty yards away from the fairway.

"Son of a bitch," he muttered, looking straight at the tree. His face started to redden. None of the priests laughed this time. When I saw Paul's back shaking, I bit down on the insides of my cheeks. The archbishop spewed out clouds of smoke and then threw his cigar on the ground and stomped on it. The others shot out of the rough. I went with them to the fairway where we waited. The archbishop dropped a new ball and took another swing. A loud crack filled the air as the ball struck the chestnut tree once again and this time sent the archbishop sprawling as it zipped past his head.

"Goddamned son of a bitch!" he screamed. His face was now nearly the color of his shirt. "God damn it, you goddamned son of a goddamned bitch!"

Paul tiptoed around in little circles trying to make his squeaks of laughter sound like coughs. He let out a hiccup. Then another. When he turned away from the archbishop, I could see tears streaming down his face. All of the priests had averted their eyes. I felt sorry for the poor bastard of a caddy who had to stay with the archbishop until he finally gave in and chipped out onto the fairway.

At the seventh hole, thunder started to rumble overhead. The ninth hole was the farthest out from the clubhouse and that, of course, was where we were when the rain and lightning started. The archbishop and one of the other priests wanted to wait out the storm. We gathered together under a maple tree. The sky darkened and the rain pelted down harder and started to penetrate the maple's foliage.

"We could jog back to the clubhouse," the young priest suggested.

"It'll blow over," the archbishop growled.

Almost immediately lightning lit the sky just above the first hole, and less than a second later a clap of thunder boomed behind us. Another flash, even closer than the last one, made me jump.

"I don't believe it's safe," Father Jerry said, "to stand under a tree during a lightning storm."

"Son of a goddamned bitch," the archbishop muttered. Then he started striding back toward the clubhouse. We shouldered our bags and followed behind the fast moving priests and the archbishop.

Except for Father Jerry, the other golfers disappeared into the clubhouse. He stood under the caddy shack doorway and joked with us about the weather.

"Here," he said, doling out five and ten dollar bills. A sly smile came over his face. "Let's just say that fifth hole was worth as much as the whole back nine."

I counted the money in my hand and realized that he had paid us for the full eighteen holes and had given us a nice tip.

"We have a huge car," he said. "If anyone wants a ride back to the city, wait out front." Then he strolled over to the clubhouse.

"Hot damn, Boss," Paul said. "A free ride."

We were drying off with towels inside the shack. The storm had passed and the sky was getting lighter by the minute.

"No way," I said. "I've seen enough of Strahle today." Paul saw some wisdom in my flat-out refusal. We walked toward the expressway, taking turns doing impersonations of the archbishop. Whenever there was a lull, one of us would scream, "Goddamned son of a goddamned bitch," and we'd both explode into gales of laughter again.

We'd made enough money for each of us to buy what we wanted, but we realized that we couldn't do so without explaining to our parents where the money had come from. So we decided to spend some of it on a couple of things and try to pass it off as old gift money. We'd use the rest of it for sodas, snacks, maybe a movie. We also decided to quit caddying. If we had enough money for smokes and sodas, what was the point?

Labor Day weekend came and went, and with it went the heat. The following Thursday, when I became a lowly freshman at Cardinal Dugan High, the weather was so cool that no one even considered opening the windows. The other kids from Holy Martyrs acted like they were friends with the other freshmen, and I wondered how they had mixed in so quickly. I was relieved when the other kids didn't seem to notice me. I wondered how Paul was doing.

On Friday, at the first gym class, they made us change into gym suits even though all we did was sit on the floor of the basketball court and listen to Mr. Long explain what we'd be doing in class during the school year. When the bell rang for English class, I was still fiddling with my lock in the locker room; everybody else was gone. A tall priest with pink splotches on his cheeks and oily black hair marched into the locker room. "Detention!" he hissed. "Report to Room 109 after your last class." By the time I got there, I'd found out from some other Holy Martyrs kids that he was the school disciplinarian, the one they'd told me so much about. I couldn't remember his real name, but everyone called him Bastard Bob. His office was off the administrative area. He opened the office door and pointed inside. "You'll get to know this office very well," he boomed. The secretaries around us looked up and smiled wanly. I felt myself redden. "Come along," he barked. I followed as he stormed out of the administrative area, down an empty hallway toward the science labs. Whistling a familiar sounding tune that I couldn't quite place, he suddenly stopped walking, pulled an enormous key ring out of his cassock pocket and then opened what looked like a storage closet door. He pulled on the overhead light string and closed the door behind us. He stopped whistling. It was stuffy and warm in the room. When he sat down on a large carton of paper towels and pointed toward an identical container across from his, I sat down. "Smoke?" he said, pulling out a pack of Newports.

I shook my head.

"Smart," he said, lighting his cigarette. "Bad for your health."

The light bulb above us was still swinging, dim light and shadow playing across his splotchy face, the boxes, mops, and buckets behind him.

"Looks awful," he said, frowning at me, "a freshman getting detention the first week of school." He leaned back against the wall and gazed out at the wall behind me, as if he were looking out the window of his office. He took a drag from his cigarette, blew out the smoke, and smiled in a way that made me a little queasy. "I suppose we could overlook this little transgression," he said. He warned me that I shouldn't expect any breaks after the first week, however.

"What are you interested in?" he asked abruptly. "You have hobbies?"

"Music," I said. "Sports, I guess." Caddying for the archbishop two weeks ago was just about the last thing I was going to bring up.

"You're a good lad," he said. He smiled that way again. "I won't breathe a word of this to anyone, son."

"Thank you, Father."

"It's important to have someone you can trust."

I nodded.

"You're shy," he said. "Isn't that so? You were the last boy in the locker room because you are so shy."

"I guess," I said, shrugging. I listened hard but could not hear a sound out in the hallway.

He took another drag on his cigarette. "It can be embarrassing," he said, in a dreamy sort of voice. "Taking off all of your clothes in front of so many other boys. Ashamed of how you look to others." He exhaled a slow stream of smoke.

I was scared now, even though I might be misunderstanding everything he was saying. I took a quick look at the closed door, but I couldn't tell if it was locked or not.

"It's okay to be shy," he said, bringing his cigarette to his mouth again. He paused. "Modesty is a virtue, after all!" he said, with a laugh. Then his face darkened again, almost as if he were in pain, and he smoked his cigarette. "But high school brings with it such newness. You're thrust into awkward situations with strangers." He exhaled a cloud of smoke and crushed the cigarette on the floor. Then he picked up the butt, put it in his pocket, and scuffed the spot on the floor with his shoe until only a small black smudge remained. "Never be ashamed of your body," he said. "You'll get comfortable being around other people, other bodies."

I cursed myself for being late. *What was he going to do? If I screamed, would he really go nuts?* I took a deep breath. I thought about the jellyfish on that iceberg, the sun drying up his little pool a bit every day. *Did the heat of the sun melt the iceberg enough to keep him floating?*

He turned and his eyes met mine.

I felt light-headed and hot, like the time I stood up too fast after getting a blood test. I tried to focus on the mop bucket.

"There's nothing to be afraid of," he said.

I felt like I was free falling in an elevator. My body went rigid. People and places whirled past me, making no sense.

"Are you all right?" a man's voice said.

Strange faces loomed above me.

"Where am I?" I heard myself say. A bright light seared my eyes. "What happened?"

"You fainted," a kind voice said. It was Father Rogan, the principal. "You were moving boxes for Father Ladd, and the air in here must have gotten to you."

I tried to prop myself up on my elbow, but Father Rogan gently pressed me back down. He sniffed hard and made a face. "I'd pass out in here, too," he said. "You know, students are not allowed to smoke inside the building."

I nodded.

"Rest for a few more minutes," he said. "Don't rush."

I saw Bastard Bob behind the principal, gesturing to another priest. "No more hard labor for you," he said, peering down at me.

Someone had bumped the overhead light, and the cord swung back and forth lazily. "The nurse is gone for the day," Father Rogan said to me. "But I think you'll be fine in a bit. We'll call your parents."

"No," I said, working myself up to a sitting position. "I'm okay."

"Father Ladd will see you home, then."

"No!" I snapped, propping myself up with my elbow. "Can you walk me to the bus stop, Father?" I said to the principal.

"You've had bad dreams," Ladd said, not moving closer to me. "It's normal. Even though you were only out for a few seconds."

"We don't know that," Father Rogan said. "You said yourself. When you found him."

"He's dazed," Ladd said. "Everything seems confusing. Doesn't it? It's that way when you faint. Like a bad dream."

"I'm all right," I said. "Father Rogan'll walk me out to the bus stop."

"No more smokes," one of the other priests said, with a laugh. Ladd and the others left the room, chattering down the hallway.

I didn't see Ladd again for a couple of weeks. I made sure that I stuck close to other kids when I moved from class to class. One Friday, when we had a short period schedule, he appeared at the end of my lunch table and told me and the other guys to put our trays back on the rack. He acted as if he'd never seen me before.

The weather stayed cool through the rest of September. It seemed like it had always been fall and that it always would be fall. My mother broke out all of our fall clothes and packed away everybody's shorts and swimming trunks. I'd been used to calling Paul every day during the summer, but now I hardly called him at all. I did my homework and listened to my new records. I told my parents that not trying out for the football team or joining the Legion of Mary would help me concentrate on my studies.

On a Saturday afternoon, I marched off to confession with my younger brothers and my little sister. It was the young priest I knew only as the one who said the fastest Masses on Sunday. In the confessional, I felt a familiar relief when I'd enumerated the last sin on my mental list, but somehow it wasn't the same.

"Is there anything else, my son?" he said.

I knew I wasn't there to confess someone else's sins, but the drive to do just that felt as strong and right as the impulse to seek forgiveness for my own. I had found words to confess my sins. Why was I so tongue-tied about the wrong done by someone else? "If I'm leaving something out," I whispered, "I'm not trying to."

"Of course not," he said. I felt my shoulders relax for the first time since I'd entered the confessional. When he gave me my penance and absolution, I walked out into the dim church, found an empty pew in the rear and said the prayers.

The weather heated up again the third week of school. We shed our windbreakers and prayed that a breeze would find its way into the stuffy classrooms. Paul called me right after school that

Friday, and I met him at the playground around four o'clock. We tossed his football around for a while.

"To the woods, Boss," he said.

We left the playground and started walking along the sidewalk.

"How's Central?" I said.

"No religion classes," he said with a smirk. "And no C.C.D. classes, either. I told you." He tossed the ball from one hand to the other.

"Hey," he said. "Meet up with Bastard Bob yet?"

"Seen him around," I said.

"School disciplinarian," he said. "What a joke."

We walked until the sidewalk stopped and then hiked down a winding little hill to the edge of the woods. In the past, we'd trekked down this trail by the creek countless times, disappearing into the jungles of the South Pacific to fight the Japanese or into the darkest corner of Sherwood Forest to help Robin Hood battle the Sheriff of Nottingham.

We worked our way down the trail without having to think about where we were going or how we would get there. Reaching the old stone mill tower that always had been a stop on our tadpole hunting trips, I poked my head in the opening at its base and looked up. Neither of us could fit through the column any longer.

I was throwing stones into the creek when Paul whistled to me. I turned, and he nodded up the trail. "Hot damn," he said in a stage whisper. Two girls, dark haired and about our age, were maybe forty yards up the trail, coming our way. I tried to get a look at them without being too obvious. One was tall and one was short. That much I could see. When I could make out their voices, I started throwing stones into the creek again until the girls passed.

When they were out of earshot, Paul came over to me and put his hand on my shoulder. "They want it," he said. He had a crazed kind of look in his eyes.

"All they did was walk by," I said.

"No, Boss. They want it." Paul tossed me the football and started up the trail. "C'mon," he said.

I followed along.

Paul picked his way up the rocky path then craned his neck for a look around the next bend. He shot his arm out to block me.

One of the girls had been glancing back our way. Now she turned around and whispered something in her friend's ear. They giggled and walked on, occasionally looking over their shoulders.

"Be cool," Paul said. "We track them, but nice and easy."

I twirled Paul's football in my hands as we moved along, slowly gaining on the girls.

The girls turned off the trail at Little Falls and climbed part way down the rocks. When we got to the falls trail, they were down below, watching the water cascade over the rocks into the creek. They both wore jeans and T-shirts. The taller girl sat on a rock that faced the water and fidgeted with her glasses. Her friend stood leaning against a long slab of rock with her thumbs in her pockets. I thought of ads I'd seen for Italian movies. These two didn't wear tight skirts like those actresses, but otherwise they could be right out of one of those foreign movies.

"They want it here," Paul whispered. "Definitely." He lit a Marlboro with his mother's lighter and offered one to me.

I shook my head. I wasn't sure what he was seeing that I wasn't. We watched the girls while they watched the creek. They did not move or look our way. Paul smoked his cigarette down to the end then ground it into the dirt. Finally, the girls started up the rocks.

"I got this nailed," Paul said. He reached for another Marlboro as the girls climbed. He held the pack out for me.

"No," I said.

He lit his cigarette and slipped the lighter into his jeans pocket just before they walked between us to get back on the main trail. Cigarette in his mouth, Paul leaned back against a boulder on the other side of the trail and crossed his arms across his chest. He stared right at the girls. His expression was just short of a sneer. No one said a word. I glanced at the girls at the last second. The shorter one met Paul's gaze and snapped her chewing gum. The tall one with glasses looked from Paul to me then straight ahead. Her blank expression never changed. The girls continued up the main trail toward the neighborhood.

"I thought you were going to do something," I said.

"I did," Paul said. "Now we snag them."

I twirled the football in my hands and followed Paul. The girls were almost at the end of the trail where it terminated at Cresheim Valley Drive. Paul dropped his cigarette and rubbed it out. Traffic zipped by on the busy street, going north toward Chestnut Hill and south toward our houses. Across the intersection, the trail resumed as a macadam road that went up the hill to the train station. As I followed, Paul sped up and then slowed to a saunter when the short girl with gum glanced back. They stopped at the edge of the busy road. I wiped the sweat from my brow.

"I've done everything so far," Paul hissed. "Say something."

Even though I wasn't exactly sure what it was that he had done, I felt caught up in the drama of trailing these girls. We stepped beside them at the edge of the road. I was as close to the one with the glasses as I could be without touching her. Paul tugged at my sleeve. I patted the football. A delivery truck rumbled by. A break was forming in the southbound line of traffic. Finally, I could see an end to the line of cars going north. The girls were about to get their chance to cross the road. I glanced at Paul. He looked like he was going to hit me. I turned to the girl with the glasses. She did not look sexy. Or happy. The explorer guy pulling up next to the iceberg flashed through my mind. And the jellyfish up on the iceberg. I thought about the expression that must have been on my face when I was sitting on that box of paper towels.

"Hi," I said. I smiled when she looked at me.

She glanced at her friend and then turned back to me.

"Didn't mean to surprise you," I said.

Her face relaxed a little.

"Maybe, I'll see you around," I said. I turned and started up Cresheim Valley Drive. I heard the girls' footsteps crossing the road. Half a block later, Paul caught up with me.

"What the *fuck*?" he yelled. "What kind of a move was that?"

"I think it was hard to starboard," I said. Out of the corner of my eye, I could see him tramping along beside me.

"You did nothing," Paul cried. He looked back. "They're gone," he said. "Out of sight."

"You thought they'd stalk us?"

He dropped back out of my view, and I no longer heard his footsteps on the sidewalk. When we got to Paul's street, I turned around and saw him tagging along about twenty yards behind me. His head hung down and his hands were stuffed into his pockets.

"Heads up," I said and tossed him the football. Then I about-faced and continued up Cresheim Valley.

"What are you doing after supper?" Paul said.

I shrugged.

"Yo, Thomas," he called. "You got homework?"

"Same as you," I said without turning around. I kept walking.

"I'll see you," he said. "I'll give you a call."

I said nothing; I just kept walking.

Mt. Pleasant was the shortest way home, but Nippon dead-ended at the avenue right at Scratchy's. The record store closed at five, so I moved quickly. It was still hot, but I was sure it wasn't in the nineties anymore. I felt in my pocket for my money and figured I had enough coins to get a single. I imagined the two girls, relaxed, joking together. I wondered if they'd talk about what had just happened or tell anyone else about it. I never saw those girls again, and I'm sure Paul would have let me know if he had. But then, I didn't see a lot of Paul after that Indian summer. We met other friends and ended up at different colleges.

When I got to the avenue, I actually felt a breeze. It was warm, but it was a breeze nonetheless. Some leaves had dropped down onto the sidewalk from the sycamore trees. Yellow and brown leaves. I kicked through a few of them on the sidewalk and looked up at the swaying limbs, still full of leaves. The leaves rustled as the breeze brushed them together. I told myself it was my own background music. In the quiet between breezes, I started to whistle the tune of the single I was going to buy.

Home

Returning to her third-floor apartment on Tuesday after teaching her first two comp classes of the semester, Sarah Goins discovered the bugs. A week earlier, on moving day, the short woman on the second floor had insisted that Sarah and her brother come into her apartment for iced tea, had told her how lucky she was to be on a safe block, and had showed her the little dolls she knitted to use as covers for spare toilet paper rolls.

When Sarah knocked on her door Tuesday afternoon, the woman opened up only as far as the chain allowed. "There are a lot of them," Sarah told her, "but I'm sure I can get rid of the critters with some spray or something." If fifteen weeks hence she was going to be fit to fill out grade sheets for freshman composition, credit that would transfer to probably any other college in the country, she damn well could take care of some ants and whatever those larger things were.

"Try Kilian's in Chestnut Hill," the little woman mumbled then shut the door.

On her way to the bug spray aisle, Sarah stopped to read the back of a container of grout, suddenly remembering the jagged crack between the edge of the bathtub and the tile wall, and ended up purchasing a putty knife and the grout, along with bug traps and spray.

Before putting on her pajamas that night, she surveyed her work in the bathroom with satisfaction but found herself studying the bleak yellow paint on the walls and wondered why she had not been repulsed by it until then.

Washing up in the sink the next morning, she noticed that new cracks had opened up in the grout between the tub and the wall. Her repair work had been below passing level, she decided. The man at Kilian's had been helpful, but she could not face him having failed something as simple as re-grouting a damn bathtub. Also, the bugs had apparently called for reinforcements, so she used up the rest of her spray can and told herself that things like this take time. She had followed the clerk's advice on the bugs. He would want to know about her progress. In the local telephone directory, under painting and hardware, she found the name of a store that was even closer than Kilian's.

The man at Gable's was sweet. He did not make her feel the way automobile mechanics sometimes did. He spoke of caulking, spackling, and grouting jobs he had done. "You can do this," he told her. She left Gable's with more ant traps and grout, as well as scrapers, sandpaper, brushes, primer, and a pint of Finneran and Haley's finest water-based blue paint.

By the time she went to bed Thursday night, her new grout looked better, if not professionally done, the bugs were nowhere in sight, and she was ahead of schedule with the painting. In fact, she had already painted the finish coat. She had also decided that the peeling paint on the kitchen woodwork was the next target on her hit list.

While eating her toast in the morning, she glanced over her plans for that day of classes. Out of the corner of her eye, she caught a blur streaking across the kitchen floor. It was way too large to be a roach. She dropped her notebook and sat still, waiting for her heart to stop pounding. She waited for more blurs. Nothing. Five minutes passed. It was time to leave for class. She stopped again in the bathroom. Tiny ants ringed the drainpipe below the sink. Her grout work was not as good as it had looked to her six a.m. eyes. A network of little cracks was now quite apparent. She eyed the new paint on the walls with suspicion.

Distributing her handouts before starting class, Sarah was pleased at the banter in the classroom. The students acted like they had known each other for months, and Sarah took this as confirmation that her icebreaker activities on the first day had been a success. She asked them about the assigned reading, but only the guy who had introduced himself as a sports communications major put up his hand. "The poem," he said in a low, resonant voice, "is about the poet's feelings on his first day in college."

The student next to him rolled her eyes.

"Alienation," the sports major purred. "Distrust, with a degree of confidence."

His neighbor popped her gum.

"And what do we know about the poet's background?" Sarah asked the class. Nothing.

"Is Columbia University similar to where he came from?"

Some of them glanced at the guy with the voice. He looked like he was deep in thought but said nothing.

She walked around the room, looking in the eyes of as many of them as would look up at her. "Well?" she said. She wrote the question on the chalkboard, wiped the chalk off her hands, and looked at the class. There had been at least four or five people in each of her other classes who had been willing to play ball. "Anyone?" She walked back to her desk at the front of the room and sat down. "An Ivy League college?" she said, looking from face to face. A student in the back cleared his throat. Her eyes locked on his, with hope. "And the poet's background?" The student looked down at the handout on his desk and thumbed through the pages. From the front row, someone's stomach growled.

Finally, she told the class what she had wanted them to tell her, pouring out everything she could remember about the piece. A few of them took notes; they all looked less ill at ease. She covered what she had planned for the period within thirty minutes and moved on to both sheets of her back-up notes, writing questions on the board before dismissing the class.

In her other comp class, a debate broke out over the meaning of the same poem, and she never got to the end of her plans for the day. She wondered if she might get one or two students from the second class to transfer into the earlier one.

On the way home, she thought about the quality of her grouting and painting work, about the nice man at Gable's, and about the silent blur which had frozen her in her chair that morning. She drove past Gable's, unable to find a parking place. Just past Mount Airy Avenue, she noticed a storefront full of brooms, pipes, stepladders and hats of some sort, all in disarray. She pulled over and parked across the street. Lewis, the sign said. Crossing the street, she made out a smaller and badly hand-painted sign in the window: Hardware—New and Used.

Inside, she stepped around opened, half-emptied cardboard boxes. Except for a small space in the middle, the counter was piled above her height with boxes. She scanned the wall shelving and was drawn to a box containing a jumble of mousetraps. Next to that container was another box full of larger traps she concluded were for rats.

"Pestilence!" snapped a man's voice right behind her ear. She spun around to find a slightly hunched over man, nearly her grandfather's age, stepping toward her. He wore a gray plaid work shirt and dark green pants. His gray hair was uncombed and his grizzled face hadn't been shaved in at least two days.

"Are you Lewis?" she said.

"Irv," he said. He sniffed, wiping his nose with a wrinkled handkerchief. "What do you got?" he said. "Mice, rats? What?"

"Well," she said, "it was small."

"You notice, I used the plural."

"I only saw one," she said. "It must have been a little mouse. It was lightning fast."

He exploded in laughter, shaking his head. He reached into the box behind Sarah and pulled out three small traps. "What else?" he said.

"This is hell!" another man's voice boomed behind her, sounding the same as Irv's.

She turned. These two had to be brothers, maybe even twins. The difference was his plaid shirt was blue, his pants black.

"What do you got?" the second man said to her.

"An answer," Irv barked.

"Right or wrong?" asked the other.

"The proof is in the pudding," Irv grinned, dangling the traps in front of him.

"We'll see about that," the one in the blue shirt said, shrugging. "Tell me your problem, sweetie."

"She saw a mouse," Irv said to him, moving nose to nose with the other man. "Was it in the kitchen?" he said, turning to Sarah.

She nodded. "You're both Lewises?"

"Hal," the other said.

Irv took the traps and walked behind the counter.

"Nine out of ten times," Hal said, "traps are your second best plan."

"Ten out of ten times, you're wrong," Irv said, writing something in a marbled copybook.

"Wait a minute," Sarah said, glancing at the traps. "Those aren't used, are they?"

"No," Irv said. "These are brand, spanking new. But they can be used again and again."

She felt herself redden. "It's just that I saw the sign outside."

"You didn't want the used ones," Irv said. "Did you?"

"No, no, no."

Hal, standing next to her, leaned closer. "They eat the poison," he whispered. "Then they get the hell out of your place."

"Empirical evidence," Irv said. "Where is it with your fancy, schmancy tricks?"

Sarah looked at them. "Both of you remind me of my mother's uncle, Ben. He lived over in Brooklyn."

"Everybody's got a Jewish uncle," Hal said.

"He was lapsed, I think. And my mother wasn't observant at all."

"Lapsed?" Hal grunted. "You don't get any more lapsed than

'Ham and Cheese, Please' Irv Lewis."

"Does the name Maria Grasso ring a bell, Mister Would-You-Marry-Me?" Irv called out in a singsong voice. "Or Mary Ellen O'Hara? Names straight from the shtetl, right?"

"How much?" Sarah asked Irv.

"Give me a buck," he said. "But you're not done."

"Not by a long shot," Hal added.

"I *am* in the middle of some projects," she admitted. "I'm doing some painting."

"Painting," Hal said, brightening.

"Once I get the grout work done around the tub."

"There's grout where you don't want it," Irv said, "and holes where you *want* the damn junk."

Nonplussed, she stared at Irv.

"There is when *he* does it," Hal said.

She stifled a laugh but could not repress a smile. These two were the first people in Philadelphia who had made her laugh.

"I'm better at selling the stuff," Irv said. "I admit it."

"You don't do this home repair bit for a living," Hal said to her. "Do you?"

"I teach English at the community college," she said. "But I am not ready to leave every small job in my life to some specialist."

"And we'll provide you with everything you need," Irv said.

"And depending on who you talk to, you'll get the right information for the job," Hal said, eyeing his brother.

"And always, a second opinion," Irv added. "Did you paint yet?"

"I did the bathroom. And I want to do something with the kitchen."

"She's in an apartment," Irv said. "Am I right, lady?"

"I am," she said. "What's the difference?"

"Where do you live?" Hal said.

"What?"

"Don't worry, nobody's going to stalk you," Irv said. "Even *he* knows that you got to know the place before you make recommendations."

"I don't understand."

"Is it old or new? Is it an apartment house or what?"

"I have the third floor of a Dutch Colonial."

"Oh," the brothers chorused.

"Go ahead, Hal," Irv said, smiling. "You got an easy one."

"Let's talk about the peeling," Hal said.

She stared at him. "In the kitchen. How do you know that?"

"The woodwork. Two, three different shades of white underneath what's on top, right?"

"Is that what always happens?" she said.

They both laughed.

"War paint," Irv said.

"Shut up," Hal said to his brother. "Your place is right here in Mount Airy or Germantown?"

"Mount Airy," she said.

"During the war, they painted those old places with a fish oil based paint. They couldn't get the other stuff 'cause of the war. Anyway, it was cheap, and the crap don't go nowhere." He slapped his hand on the counter. "It'll last longer than the damn houses."

"So, what I painted will all come off?"

Hal gave the same pained expression she remembered old Ben making in every conversation she'd ever had with him.

"Should I have burned it off?" she said.

"Not unless you want to burn the whole place down," Hal said.

"I can't stop myself," Irv cut in. "Don't say she can't burn it."

Hal made that face again. "It's one possible choice," he said. "You can also use something I got here which works in most cases." He asked her what kind of primer she used. When she told him, they both made the same pained face.

She bought the mousetraps and enough of Hal's magic primer and a semi-gloss off-white latex finish to do all of the woodwork in the apartment.

Depositing all of her purchases on the kitchen table, she rushed into the bedroom to find her painting clothes. She had just zipped up her old jeans when she remembered that the welcome reception for new faculty was taking place that evening. She threw her jeans onto the floor, put her work outfit back on, and checked the wall calendar in the kitchen. The get-together would start in five minutes.

Most of the refreshments were gone by the time she arrived. She took a glass of white wine and headed for the only person she recognized, the assistant department chair. He introduced her to the new hire from Foreign Languages, a thirtyish woman with long black hair and a mocha complexion. "Going, going, Goins," he said, laughing. "Sarah Goins."

The Spanish teacher smiled, said, "Excuse me," and walked away. Sarah watched her hustle across the room, insinuating herself into a cluster of teachers having an animated conversation.

The assistant chair took a sip from his Manhattan. "Go. Went. Goins," he said. "I'm forever stuck on conjugations."

She scanned the room but did not see anyone she knew.

"Can't get enough of them," he said. "You know what I mean?

You *knew* what I mean? You *will know* what I mean." He took another sip from his drink, chuckling.

Ten minutes into his narrative of how he had been hired despite the dean's complete lack of a sense of humor, Sarah gulped the last half of her drink. "Time for something else," she said, holding up her empty glass.

The assistant chair insisted on getting her a fresh drink.

"No, no, no," she shook her head. She rushed toward the bar, dropped her glass on a table, and within twenty-five minutes she was changing into her paint clothes.

She returned to Lewis Hardware on Saturday morning with curtain rods on her mind. The collection of painters' hats scattered at the base of the store window seemed to have been augmented. Each one touted some paint company, and she saw that some of them were crumpled and splotched with paint. Hal was at the space in the middle of the counter talking to an elderly Polish-looking woman. Irv was not in sight.

"You don't need a new plunger," Hal said to the woman. "I don't care what he said."

Sarah waited while the woman bought some crystals that Hal guaranteed would fix her drain. "It's the best," he said. "And you deserve it."

"I have a good report on the paint and the bugs," Sarah told him when the woman left. "And I got two mice. I set the traps again." She tried not to look disgusted.

"This weekend, you'll get all of the grout out of there," he said. "Not just most of it."

"I was thinking of working on that tonight."

"Grout?" Hal said, shaking his head. "That can wait till after Saturday night."

"I have a long list to do," she said.

He described what she had done so far as if he had been there and seen it with his own eyes. He walked her through what she needed to do on Sunday. "Are you calling home?" he asked.

"Home?" she said.

"I'm not trying to pry, but I'm figuring you got family you're not used to being away from."

"I'm not a visitor. I live here now."

"Great," Hal nodded.

"The windows need curtain rods. My parents will be coming to visit me one of these weekends, and I want the place to look civilized."

"Civilized is overrated," he said.

She gave him the measurements, and he pointed out the boxes near the rear where she could find the hardware she needed. There was a box of new curtain rods and valances, and another box stuffed with the same things she was sure were secondhand. When she returned to the counter, Hal plunked a handful of screws and nails beside the rods.

"Of course, you've got a screwdriver."

She nodded.

Hal wrote something in his copybook, took her money, reached below the counter and produced the change.

"You don't need a cash register?"

"*He* thinks we do. They stole it. What are you going to do? I'd just as soon write it up. Then I know exactly what we sold."

"Have you been here a long time?" she said.

"Hundreds of years," he said. "It ain't what it used to be, this neighborhood, this city, this whole country. I'm getting the hell out."

"You're moving?"

"Going to Australia, soon as I get out of this dump. They got clean streets there. Beautiful."

"Have you been there before?"

"No, but I researched it. You'd have to be out of your mind to not want to go there. You've seen *National Geographic*, right?"

"Sure," she said.

"They run pictures of Australia every few years or so. That's a good place to see what it looks like. Hey, you must be some heck of a teacher, with all your questions and all."

She blushed.

"Lots of college?" he said.

She nodded.

"Okay, name me two great French painters."

"French? Any particular style or period?"

"Pick a style."

"All right. Monet and Manet."

"Good. It gets tougher. Now, name me two Italian painters," Hal pushed on.

"Michelangelo and uh, Raphael," she said.

"Name me two Irish painters."

"Irish painters?" She shook her head. "I don't know."

"Finneran and Haley," he said and guffawed as loudly as he had the day before.

Sarah got the curtain equipment to the apartment and laid it all out on the kitchen table. She called her parents from the bedroom phone. After covering the usual topics, work and settling into

Philadelphia, Sarah said, "Ben, your uncle from Brooklyn. He died, what, seven years ago?"

"Benny? Yes, you'd just started at N.Y.U."

"He was funny, right?" Sarah said, wandering with the phone to her closet.

"Well, in an odd sort of way."

Sarah ran her hands across the neatly arranged tops, skirts, slacks, and dresses then closed the door, noticing the clink the hinge made. "I liked him," she said. "Didn't I?"

"Why are you asking me about crazy old Benny, Sarah? After all these years . . ."

Sarah opened and shut the closet door again, wondering how she could have failed to hear and feel the hitch in the swing of the door before.

"I guess *some*body's got some free time on her hands," her mother said.

On Monday Sarah found Irv alone in the store.

"My closet," she said. "The door doesn't want to shut when you go to close it. It makes a noise like a thump."

"When it's all the way closed or when it's closing?"

"On the way," she said. "It's the top pin. Yes, it's got a pin. I checked that. I'm not an idiot."

"The pin's too short. Bring the good one in."

She drove to the apartment and, using the hammer her father had given her, knocked the top pin out. She held it beside the hinge it went into. It was not long enough to go all the way through. She returned the pin to its place then checked the bottom one. It was fine.

"They must have replaced the top one some time ago," she said a half hour later, presenting Irv with the good pin.

He shook his head. "He probably sold the owner that piece in the first place."

She would not tell him that she had trapped another mouse the night before. She looked up and down the rows of shelving. There was a flashlight display in one aisle and another one featuring the same flashlights in the next aisle. Nails were laid out beside electrical cords. "Does anybody know where anything is in here, except you guys?"

"People these days don't know diddley," he said. "Besides, that's what I'm here for, and I don't mind working."

She followed him to the middle aisle in the store. Behind a carton of chocolate bars, he found a container of door pins.

"Hungry?" he said.

"No thanks."

The pins came in various thicknesses and lengths. Some had chunks of dried paint on them, others were brass without the shine. He pulled one out and held it up beside hers. "This ought to cost you more," he said. "Can't get these, except out of old houses. Of course, most people don't realize that. They'll buy something brand new that don't fit right. Good for them."

She followed him back to the counter.

"Won't have to deal with people like that when I get to Australia," Irv sighed. "No, sir."

"You want to go to Australia?"

"It's not a new idea. I've had this plan for some time."

"I don't know." Sarah shook her head. "Australia's home to something like seventy-five percent of the poisonous insects and reptiles in the world. I read that somewhere." She watched him ring up the sale on a small cash register she had not seen before.

"Not in the *Geographic,* it wasn't," Irv said. "I don't know where you got that bit of information, but as long as they don't start busing Americans in there, I'll take my chances there any day. No offense, but I can't wait to get out of this dump."

Back in the house, she waved to the bald office worker then clambered up two flights of stairs without becoming winded. She set her little bag on the table next to the stack of essays.

The pin worked perfectly. The ants were gone. She stopped baiting the mousetraps.

She would go back to the Lewis brothers the next day after classes. Between her door and the door to the store, she would come up with something to ask for. One or both of them would be there, like a light on in her window. But first she called and gave her father a report on her classes and on the string of projects she was embroiled in.

"You're full of problems, Sarah."

She smiled, and she knew from the sound of her father's voice that he was smiling, too.

"Like a regular homeowner," he said.

"It never stops," she said.

A Baker

MY ROSALIE, THE twin who lived, calls during lunch break. I don't get calls. I don't want them when I'm standing here by my machine, whirring mostly natural ingredients into Butterscotch Krimpets for Philadelphia and vicinity. On the phone, Rosalie offers a ride home. "Beats taking the bus, Dad," she says. The car's been fixed, inspected. It's the day before the birthday. Last year notwithstanding, for her, birthdays are joyous. She can't get enough of them. That makes them easier for me to get through.

I explain to the white secretary who'd gotten me to the phone that it's not an emergency. I remember when they wouldn't have bothered to pass along a message to a black man on the floor, but this woman's too young to have been here for all that.

"It was my daughter," I say to the woman, "the junior in high school, and shouldn't they know better by that age?"

*

The mixing vat is clean. I clean it myself. Better than the guys on the other shifts. It shines metallic and smooth. It's empty. Ready for the afternoon batch.

I haul the white flour to my workstation and lean the fifty-pound sack against the stainless steel vat. Then the sugar. I walk across the floor to the walk-in refrigerator, lift the steel canister of skim milk onto a hand truck, and wheel it back to my machine.

My Donald, the twin who died, shares a birthday with me as well as Rosalie. Angie called when he didn't wake up from his nap. Back when I was the first black man on this floor and afraid to lose my job. I ran from the mixer to the trolley to the hospital lobby.

"Crib death," the guy said. I'd never heard that before. The words didn't go together.

"What can I do?"

The doctor shook his head.

"Where's my baby?" I yelled.

I screamed until they let me into the room where they had him. I held Donald for an hour, crying.

After eighteen years filling the same vat, clocks don't mean much. One ingredient follows another. Every batch finishes on the nose or a few minutes early. I've never left in the middle of a run, except when Angie called that time. The last item, the small packet of preservatives, goes in. The lid clangs shut on the vat, and I flip the starter switch. I press my palms against the smooth, reverberating machine. It's mixing nicely. Two floors away, other machines are icing and wrapping my morning Krimpets.

I realize I am no longer steamed over Rosalie's call. You always think about other things at the machine, but the work carries you along, evens things out by the end of a batch. I remember going back to work a week after running into that damned hospital, the same place they were born. It was easier going back to work than I'd imagined.

Rosalie drives and I direct. She insists on doing it that way.

"What's your route, Daddy? Don't worry. I'm not going to throw you off your routine. We'll go the way you always go, but for once you can relax."

She looks so pleased with herself, I can't argue. I sink back in the passenger seat and tell her where to go.

"Is this a short-cut?"

"No."

Instead of driving toward the neighborhood, we cross the Schuylkill and head toward center city. We pull into a parking area across the river from Hunting Park Avenue and walk to the water's edge. She sits next to me on the stone bank. Three Canada geese swoop down from the other side of the river and splash to a stop on our right. Rosalie starts talking about the argument she had with her mother last night. I missed it. She doesn't want to ruin the birthday like the year before.

That hadn't been her fault, or Angie's. One screw-up is just that. But you don't want to start something.

I had quit smoking a couple of months before the birthday last year. Or started quitting. More sticks of gum than smokes.

I opened Rosalie's present after we finished the steaks and laughed nervously about the SmokEnders, the book on how to quit, and the packs of Juicy Fruit. Angie went out to the kitchen. I figured she was lighting candles on the cake or something. She yelled for me to go ahead and open her package. I pulled the wrapping off as Rosalie watched. A briar pipe and three packs of tobacco.

"Guess I have to pick my poison," I joked.

I spent the rest of the night refereeing. It couldn't be that bad this year.

Rosalie and I sit watching the lines of cars creeping home on the other side of the Schuylkill. An eight-oared shell strokes downstream toward Boathouse Row. Apparently, she and her mother got into it pretty good. I pull the pipe from my jacket pocket and pack it with Prince Albert. She's sorry about the timing. I light the pipe and toss the match into the river.

"I'm sure Mom's told you about it."

"By the time I dropped the car off and went to Knights of St. Peter Claver, you were both asleep. And you know what mornings are like. What was it all about?"

"Like I told Mom, I'm going to be eighteen, and there are some things I have to be able to decide on for myself."

"So far, so good," I say. She blows out a long slow breath. Four more geese land near us.

"I respect your beliefs, Dad. But I'm not going to Mass anymore, or any of it."

"Go on," I say.

Her friends' parents don't force them to go. She isn't a kid. It doesn't mean anything to her anymore.

I nod and bite down on the pipe. The geese splash each other. I send a puff of smoke out toward the other side of the river.

"It doesn't mean anything to you, so you won't bother with it. Right?"

"In so many words."

"And that settles it."

"Yeah. And Mom can't handle it. All she can do is argue, and then argue some more. Like it's going to make a difference."

I bang the pipe against my shoe. The unsmoked tobacco and ash falls to the water.

To our right, a short, stocky man in his late fifties crunches across the gravel toward the water. The flock of geese has grown to about thirty, and they squawk as the man approaches. He feeds them pieces of bread, donuts, and cookies from two large plastic buckets. They clamor over the food. He gives us a wave.

"Hey, Tom," he calls.

We nod back. With the empty buckets, he trots to a white van and drives off. I stand up.

"Do you understand, Dad?"

"Let's go home."

"Do you come here every day, like this?"

"It's usually a little more peaceful."

I let her drive again. I tell her whatever way she wants to go is fine. She follows the traffic across the Falls bridge and onto Lincoln Drive. I stare out the passenger side window at the wooded hills of the park, the same tree-lined ridges I usually miss seeing for having to steer through the curves on the way home.

*

Angie is in the kitchen. Stirring pots.

Rosalie stops in the foyer to check the mail and allows me to go in first. I kiss Angie and touch the side of her face.

"Is that Rosalie coming in with you?"

"Yeah. How close are we to eating?"

"Five minutes. You got something to do?"

"No. Let's just eat." I point to the largest pot. "Can I peek?"

"Just leftovers. We're clearing out the refrigerator tonight. A little bit of everything."

She turns the burners down to warm and wipes her hands on a towel. "So, how was your day?" she asks.

"Good," I say and wipe my hands on the towel she's using. She squeezes my fingers through the cloth and winks up at me. She looks tired.

"I'm okay, too," she says and turns to open the refrigerator.

"Rosalie," I call. "Let's set the table."

The stew tastes better warmed up than when we had it Monday. We talk about that. And about Mrs. Hillman's heart attack. Nobody has seconds, so we end up with food to put away. We never get to dessert.

Rosalie tries to say something about how red Angie's eyes look and that she doesn't want to cause any more tears in the house. That opens poor Angie like a faucet. The more she cries, the louder Rosalie's voice gets.

"Talk to each other!" I shout, holding each one's hand on the tablecloth. Rosalie keeps on about making her choices, and Angie, who could tell her old boss off any day of the week and who got me through Donald, can't find any more words, and cries like a baby. She's hunched over her dinner plate and looks small to me.

Smaller than I've ever seen her.

"Choice," I say to Rosalie. "You think it's a matter of goddamned choice."

"And I didn't think you were going to argue with me."

"We've done better than argue with you about going to church. We brought you to it. Years of it. Whether you want to believe it or not, it's a part of you. You think you can just walk away from something like that?"

"You must be on the same wavelength with God. Huh, Dad? You two know better than I do, and, of course, you'll always outvote me."

She says she wants more from life than we wanted. She wants to see the Eiffel Tower, feel the ground of Kenya under her feet, write a book. She doesn't want to end up a nervous nag who says the rosary every day, or a factory hand who pretends to be a baker.

"You've been yelling at me all my life, Mom. And you. Hovering over me. Your precious only child. I may be the only one you can sink your worries into, but I'm an adult."

At work in the morning, I shake the last clouds of flour from the sack into the vat. I pour in the preservatives. I remember what it was like loading up the mixer with a hangover. Just bending over hurt. But even with a hangover, after a while, the ingredients almost emptied themselves into the vat.

I remember the exact words Rosalie said the night before and little of what Angie or I said. I can hear her questions and accusations over and over while I lift containers of milk and throw empty sacks into the trash. I hit the starter switch. The machine roars on. I hear my own voice over the din.

"You've never *been* an only child."

The first batch works its way out of my machine. I make sure the equipment is clean and ready for the after lunch load.

I punch out at lunch. Say I'm sick. Drive home and ask Angie to ride with me. We park outside Girls' High, and I stand by the car. She sees us on her way to the bus stop.

"Want a ride?" I ask.

She nods. We all squeeze into the front of the Dodge. We drive down Chew to Penn Street. Turn into the hospital lot. I head for the back to the old part of the complex. I park in a space that faces the old entrance, and we sit there in the quiet, together, for a long time.

The Wig

FROM THE FRONT porch, I can hear my mother-in-law coughing. I have the key in my pocketbook, but I knock. Her footsteps get louder as she clumps her way through the kitchen, the dining room, finally the foyer. Her keys jangle as she fiddles with them on the other side of the deadbolt lock.

"It wouldn't be my Delores, now would it be?" she says. "Not at this time, it wouldn't?"

If she'd stop fooling with the keys, she could see me through the curtains. But of course, she damn well knows it's me.

"I told you I was coming before your treatment today. Remember, Ma?"

"Yes, yes," she says.

Finally, she pulls the door open. I'm holding the screen door, one foot on the porch, the other on the doorstep.

"Takes a construction worker to get this thing open," she says. She steps back, and I enter the foyer, letting the screen door swing closed behind me.

I follow her into the foyer.

"Of course," I say, "the idea is not to leave the key in the lock, Ma, so it's hard for the burglar."

"Yes, yes," she says. "But t'isn't you or the burglar that has to open this thing six, seven times a day, is it then? I leave the key where I can find it. Just like I leave the door where I can find it."

She stands before me like a little soldier at attention. I give her cheek a peck and rub my hand down her arm all the way to her left hand. She catches and squeezes my index finger. "You're too early, girlie," she says.

She wears the same cotton housedress she wore Monday. Her pockets bulge with used tissues, and, I'm sure, cigarettes and lighter. "Gaunt" is the word I've used to describe her to the other girls at the office. Sucked out. Part of her *is* missing: the lung and the part of her stomach they took. But even before that, she tended toward incompleteness; now she just seems that way all the time.

"C'mon, Ma. Let's get dressed."

"You want some tea?" she says. She tromps off toward the kitchen. "I'll just put the kettle on," she calls over her shoulder.

"No, Ma." I follow slowly through the dining room.

She turns to me at the kitchen doorway. "It's a mess, isn't it? A perfect mess."

"Ma," I plead, shaking my head. "Ma," I say louder. "You can't worry about things like that."

"For God's sake, put your hands down," she says. "You look like the statue of the Sacred Heart."

I realize that I've raised my arms in supplication. I drop them to my sides.

"C'mon," she says. "A cup of tea then."

She walks to the stove, lifts the kettle, weighing how much

water is left in it then turns on the burner. I reach into the cupboard for cups and saucers. "It's not a mess," I say, glancing around. "This place looks better than mine, to tell you the truth."

She retrieves the milk carton from the refrigerator and places it on the table. "Well, you've got things to do. You've got a husband. You've got a job. You've got an old mother-in-law to be bothered by."

I lean on the back of my late father-in-law's old kitchen chair and frown at her. Of course, she doesn't say I don't have kids to worry about. But I hear it in her voice. "I can't complain," I say. "Lots of others have it worse than me. But I will complain if you don't get yourself dressed. Come on, it's nearly two."

"Yes, yes." Her voice trails off toward the stairway.

I listen to her footsteps above me. She opens and shuts drawers. Shuffles through her closet. Alone. She must do everything herself. It's a wonder she will let me put tea bags and water in the cups. I run my fingers over the back of Mr. Flannagan's old chair where he patched the cracked plastic with wide strips of duct tape. Sections of his frayed tape have been covered over with new tape. Ma's doing. When he was alive, she would have been shot if he'd caught her tampering with his work. When the kettle begins to whistle, I fill the cups and allow myself to sit in Arthur Flannagan's kitchen chair. When I first dated Brendan, we joked that his dad was the one I was really after. He always looked so fresh in his uniform, even after a long day of driving a trolley all over the city. Sitting tall in his kitchen chair. Quiet.

I hear her coughing her way down the stairs. I remove the tea bags from our cups and pour in some milk. She's only sixty, but she gives off a musty old smell, like something pulled from the basement. Frayed, fading toward uselessness. She breathes out as she enters the room. Taproom breath, my mother called it. Tea and mints on top of whiskey, even a little whiskey, still reeks of whiskey. Mr. Flannagan used to walk down to Gilhooley's on a Friday night, have a draught, and come home with a quart of Ortlieb's that would last him the week. Beer drinkers smell different than hard boozers. They burp and wink, maybe fall asleep. I picture Brendan during the eleven o'clock news. Whiskey drinkers, especially ones who pull it out of the cupboard while everyone else is upstairs or in the parlor, give off that thick sweetness. Too thick. Too sweet. It turns the stomach when you get up close for a kiss.

She draws her hand across the back of my neck before she goes to sit in her chair. The bottle has been moved to her dresser, no doubt.

"You look nice, Ma." She's found that blue flowered top she knows I like. Dark blue slacks.

"How's work, Honey?"

"All right. Slow enough to take an afternoon off."

"I wish I had some scones for you," she says. "Next week I'll bake some. And you can take one home to Brendan. How is my boy?"

"Working. And when he's not at the office, he's working on the Dodge. He sends his love." I sip at my tea. "He thinks it's a great idea, our shopping today." I can lie as good as she can. He would send his love, if he were reminded. He thinks a wig is in order, but he doesn't want to be part of buying one any more than he wants to be part of going to the cancer doctor's office for her weekly treatment.

She looks at the ceiling, self-conscious for the first time today. I've made a point of not saying anything about her hair;

compliments are as bad as insults. The last wispy strands of her once lustrous gray hair have been replaced by salt and pepper stubble of new growth. She usually covers her head with something, anything, a baseball cap, shower hat, one of the boys' old bandanas. "So," she says, "where are we going?"

"I thought we'd try Strawbridge's. You know, out in Willow Grove?" I had hoped it would be far enough away to avoid running into anyone she knew.

She pushes her cup away from her. "Tea's too strong."

I'm only half-finished. "I'll do better next time." I get up and place the cups in the sink.

"Don't do them," she says. "I'll take care of that later. Gives me something to do."

I run water into the cups and leave them in the sink. She pulls a scarf with a pastel print out of her pocket, ties it on her head babushka style and goes ahead of me into the parlor for her pocketbook and her cigarettes. She knows I'll be with her the whole time, but she has to make sure she's got them with her.

She's quiet in the car, content to watch the traffic and ignore me. She opens her pocketbook, fishes around in it, and pulls out some papers. She sits looking at them for a few minutes.

"This came from Michael today." She holds the envelope so I can see.

"Oh. How are they doing?" I say. Brendan's brother rarely writes and never visits.

"Busy," Ma says. "Busy time up there."

"Laurie's about due, isn't she?"

"I'll read it."

She clears her throat and tells me Laurie's expecting any day now. Mike's finished painting the baby's room. Bright yellow. He figures that's a safe choice, better than taking a shot at either pink or blue. I imagine Brendan painting our middle room, the one we'd use if we had a baby. He would buy only blue paint. Mike's got more carpentry work than he can keep up with. Laurie quit her job. Doesn't know when she'll go back to work, but knows it won't be in an office. Her friends had a shower for her last month.

Ma sounds like someone else reading the letter, like somebody at Mass who's drafted to do a reading. I can't tell how she feels about all this. I say, "Gee" or "Isn't that something?" It's the most news I've heard about Mike since he called Brendan two years ago from upstate New York to tell him he'd gotten married. Brendan never calls Mike, and he certainly wouldn't write. So, we only hear about him once in a blue moon through Ma. Ma finishes the letter and returns it to her pocketbook. I still can't figure out how all this strikes her, just like I couldn't really say how Brendan feels about his brother any more. I make a mental note to shop for a baby present.

I can't park close enough to the store for Ma's liking, have to circle the lot twice until I find a suitable space. She studies her face in the vanity mirror and reties her scarf. "If this don't work out," she says, "I'm going to the sporting goods store and buy myself a football helmet."

I walk around the car, but she's already opened the door. "Maybe the Eagles could use me," she says. She's almost laughing. I allow myself to chuckle. She starts walking ahead of me, so I quickly lock her door and dash to catch up. "For God's sake, girl," she says, "we've only got about ten minutes to do this business if we're going to be on time for the cancer doctor, and you're lollygagging like it's the Fourth of July."

It's crunch time; I've agonized over this moment all week. Please, Lord, don't let me say something to set her off.

"Maybe they have something for *you* in this wig shop, Délores. Or is this not your kind of place?"

We enter at the perfume section, the information kiosk ahead of us. "Who doesn't like Strawbridge's?" I ask.

She steams off toward the kiosk. The wig counter is just to the left of me.

"Hey, Ma!" I call.

She reaches the guide and fingers her way down the list of departments. She spins around and points in the appropriate direction. "Some help you are," she says.

The clerk at the counter smiles at both of us. "How may I be of assistance?" the woman says. She is surrounded by hairpieces of various colors and sizes, some on display heads, others in rows under the glass counter.

"Well, I don't see much in the way of hamburgers here," Ma mutters. "So how about something in a wig?"

The saleslady's face reddens. She smiles at me and slides three of the display heads with wigs in front of Ma. "Why don't we start with these?" she says. I wonder how much of this lady's business comes from cancer patients. "Sometimes," she says, "people like to bring in a photo, from before, to help figure out what they would like." Ma unfastens her scarf and slips it off slowly, with surprising grace.

"I think we can narrow it down to gray," Ma says, the sarcasm gone from her voice. She reaches up and pinches a tiny tuft on the top of her head. "Pretty much this color, only a bit longer." It occurs to me that gallows humor may be how she gets through the chemotherapy session every week. I can't say what goes on when she passes through that treatment room door with the smiling black technician. She denies that it's painful, but after three years as her daughter-in-law, I know that truth can become a coloring book in her hands.

The lady brings out half a dozen more wigs. Ma frowns at each of them in turn, but she finally tries one on. The lady shows her how and then explains that it can be combed out, changed around if she doesn't like the style. It's a high quality import. Ma looks this way and that in the mirror. She checks the back with a hand mirror. She shakes her head. The lady pulls several more from a drawer. We've looked at the ones that had been on the bald display heads. Ma tries a few more. I've held my tongue through all of it. The saleslady has done almost all the talking. It's three o'clock. If she doesn't find something here in the next fifteen minutes, we'll have to try somewhere else later. Maybe on the weekend, or next week before the treatment.

"What do you think of this one, girlie?"

"It's nice," I say, drawing out the words. "Better than the last one."

"It's a good color for you," the saleslady says. She adjusts its placement carefully and brushes it out a bit. She nods her approval. It looks nothing like Ma's real hair.

"I might be able to get used to this one," Ma says.

I've turned the price tags over, and I realize that something that looks significantly more real will cost at least two, three times what the ones she's showing us now cost. I can feel Ma talking herself into liking it. She parades around the counter, checks herself in various mirrors. The more she likes it, the more I want her to put it down and walk out of the store. What would Mr. Flannagan make of all this? Brendan doesn't want to even *think* about his shrinking mother with a full head of fake hair, let alone look at the sight. Her Michael's willing to wait until next Christmas to lay eyes on his mother, and by then he'll have a six-month-old kid and a fresh excuse for staying away.

"It's up to you, Ma. You know, we can sleep on it and come back, or shop around some more."

"Don't you like it?"

"It's fine. You look good in it. But don't rush into this just because we got a doctor's appointment." I lean toward her. "There are other stores, Ma."

"I'll take it," she says to the saleslady.

"Very well," the lady says. She stands there face to face with Ma for a moment. She starts to tap her fingers on the counter. "To ring it up," she says, "I'll need the tag."

Ma delicately takes it off and hands it to the lady. She tugs my elbow. "Not like buying a pair of shoes," she says, "where they wrap 'em up or you just wear 'em home."

I rub Ma's shoulder. She looks in the mirror again. I run my hand over her hair, avoiding eye contact with her image in the mirror. We're on a strict schedule for crying. Not a frequent schedule, but we've worked it out so that only one of us cries at a time. Not that we planned anything like that. She would never talk about it. I don't want to set off anything now. Not with her looking in that mirror.

Brendan had ordered me to use my Strawbridge's card, but she insists on paying for the wig. She holds her side through a coughing spell.

"We're late, girlie," she says, then warns me that she won't abide my driving that car too fast. She crosses the lot with measured steps, head erect, pocketbook in one hand, the glossy yellow bag containing the wig in the other. Halfway to the car, I realize that she's not wearing her scarf; it's tucked in her blouse. A warm rush of wind flaps my skirt, stirs through my hair. She slows a little, and I adjust my speed to hers. It's already been a long day for her; I shouldn't have put her through this before a treatment. The afternoon sunlight glints off her head. She'll never take the wig out of that yellow shopping bag. It will sit, still wrapped, in a dresser drawer for however many months she's got left.

I can picture her walking into the doctor's reception area. The familiar pale faces, bony frames, slowly moving through their weekly mime of normalcy, as if this were a hairdressing salon. I see weeks more of these sessions. Injections behind closed doors, slow rides home waiting for and then trying to pretend there is no nausea. I smell hospital hallways and liquid diet spilling through a tube into her stomach, smell these over the fading, but never quite absent odor of tobacco and rye. I sense these things as clearly as if I were remembering them. I hear the priest reading her name in church. I see a baby announcement in the mail. I feel Brendan collapse in a beery heap beside me in bed, drunk in sadness, drunk in anger.

We're three rows of cars away from the Dodge. She stops and hands me the shopping bag. She pulls out her scarf, brushes her nose with it, and returns it to her blouse. She moves away from me through the swirl of wind toward the car.

Shields

Guv saw no point in going to rugby practice Thursday night, not with a cast on his wrist and a weather forecast that made it seem more like February than late March. He tried the television around the time when his fellow backs from the Celtic Rugby Football Club would split off to run plays and do passing drills while the chunkier and slower forwards, a group he considered a subspecies, packed down into opposing scrums, to push each other up and down the frozen field in Germantown for an hour. The club subscribed to the theory that practices should be bloodless games and games should be bloody practices. It was all a little serious for a guy who, already a college graduate and not in medical school, had started playing for Temple Med's team just to meet a player's girlfriend's sister.

On the tube, *The Waltons* was winding down. John-Boy was as wholesome as ever. Guv switched the channel before the temptation to throw something at the bastard with his good hand got the better of him. He thought of Emily Drysdale, as he did whenever faced with the prospect of going alone to a movie or to a nice restaurant, and as usual, the slight twinge passed, followed by the certainty that the breakup had been inevitable and not such a disaster after all. He'd gotten over the guilt of making that nasty phone call; she was a big girl, and after months of demanding that he face what she called his fear of getting serious, she could handle a little name-calling. He went to the bedroom and picked out a fresh white shirt, the navy blue suit he'd picked up at the dry cleaners, and a red tie and hung them on the closet hook. He found underwear and blue socks in the top dresser drawer and placed them on the top of the dresser. In the background, the characters from *Barney Miller* were yakking it up. He pulled the shabbiest pair of black dress shoes out of the closet and gingerly shined them, making sure that the black shoe polish went on the shoes, not his cast. When the pair looked like the others in the closet, he set them at the base of his dresser. *Hawaii Five-0* was a rerun. The ten o'clock shows were a joke. His teammates would be gasping through sprints up the hill now, relief coming only when the city worker pulled the switch on the field lights, instantly plunging the rec center into total darkness.

Stepping outside of his Manayunk apartment, wearing just jeans and a Harris Tweed jacket over the blue Scotland jersey he'd won at the rugby club's Christmas party raffle, he shivered. The guys would be tramping across the dark field toward their cars, steam rising from their muddied and faded jerseys. On Saturdays, their look was clean and green, but at practice motley and torn was the rule. At the bar, with patches and numbers peeling off and with holes and rips abundant, they always looked like a grubby United Nations of rugby teams, disreputably representing an array of colleges, clubs, and national sides.

From the sidewalk outside Burba's, Guv heard a roar that told him that the team was already ensconced at the rear of the bar. The place was in full Thursday night mode when he pulled open the door to the side room. Smoke clung to the ceiling like low cloud cover. The actors from the Allen's Lane theater group had taken over the dart room. Two bald, stumpy thespians, darts in hand, were emoting about a shot that had straddled the line around the bull's eye. At the front of the main bar room, chattering Lutheran seminarians had put three tables together and were scarfing up platters of fried chicken and pitchers of Rolling Rock. Three members of the night crew from the Acme were glued to their bar stools, watching a hockey game on the television, while four of their co-workers played shuffleboard.

He walked past them toward his crowd. Above the jukebox din of Rod Stewart wailing about Maggie Mae, Gene Hart's frenetic TV game call of the Flyers, and animated conversation throughout the bar, the rugby crowd roared again. No one in the bar flinched or turned around. Near the kitchen's swinging doors, most of the shouting or laughing players stood, circled around Tully and veteran Bob Leider. The two sat facing each other on chairs placed back-to-back, hands clasped behind them as they clenched the handles of soupspoons in their mouths. Tully practically vibrated with eagerness. Rookies.

A year ago, when Leon Forest had recruited Guv at a businessman's downtown watering hole during a Friday happy hour, Guv had introduced himself as a former Temple Med player, not mentioning that his playing time had barely spanned a season. He'd thought of his adopted father telling him and his Fitzhugh siblings, "Greenhorns have no cachet." As an experienced recruit, his only initiation had been shooting the boot after he scored his first try for Celtic. He could tolerate being made to stand on a bar table, pull off a muddy rugby boot, fill it with beer and then chug the contents, once. Had they tried to put him through this season-long humiliation, he might have taken up flag football.

Guv took a stool at the end of the bar, reached into the inside pocket of his tweed jacket, and pulled out a Macanudo Lonsdale and his father's whalebone guillotine-style cigar cutter that Dad Fitzhugh had passed on to him when he turned eighteen. He clipped the end of the cigar and lit it, blew a cloud of rich smoke toward the rafters of the old bar, and pocketed the yellowish antique cutter. He watched Tully stretch himself up as high as he could without leaving his seat, rear back, and bring the spoon down harmlessly on the top of Leider's head.

"Thath nothing," Leider barked, his spoon waggling in his mouth as he spoke. He laughed, and the crowd around the two of them jeered.

Ignoring the pile of bills at the end of the bar, Guv dropped a twenty in front of him. Scotty, the bartender, brought him a Bacardi and Coke, scooping up the twenty. "Here you go, Guv'nor," Scotty said.

He nodded to Scotty and turned back to the game. A hand clasped his shoulder. "Guv, my man." Like the rest of them, club president Lester Parullo hadn't called him Vic, Fitz, or Fitzhugh since the road game in Washington halfway through the fall season. His performance in the B game that afternoon hadn't been altogether outstanding, but he had juked his way loose for two long scoring runs. "That guy needs a governor on him!" Yoyo, the charter bus driver, had exclaimed from his sideline lawn chair, while reaching for a Schmidt's from his personal cooler. By the time they returned to Philly, no one was calling him anything but Guv.

Lester took the stool beside him then hollered toward the other end of the bar to get Scotty's attention away from the TV that hung from the ceiling.

"What?" the bartender answered without losing any of his focus on the TV.

"Another ginger ale," Lester said

Scotty ambled down and poured a Canada Dry over ice for Lester. "Power play," he said, scuttling back to his hockey cronies.

Moon Lansing, gold earring glistening, his head covered with a blue bandana and ponytail bobbing behind, sidled over to the bar and plunked down an empty pitcher and mug next to the kitty. He spun around, a maniacal grin on his face, winked at Lester and Guv and disappeared back into the crowd.

"Blackbeard wasn't that fucking scary," Guv said.

Lester laughed. "Blackbeard had more teeth," he said.

The crowd behind them roared, and Guv figured it must have been Leider's turn to take a feeble whack at his opponent. Somebody had to play the victim; it wasn't going to be Guv. He remembered Emily dragging him to a coffeehouse on the Penn campus to hear a grizzled old New York folk singer. During his song about the perils of doing other people's bidding, every verse produced snickers from the herb tea-sipping crowd. "Somebody else," the guy sang in a raspy blues, "not me." Guv had to laugh when Emily poked him, suggesting that the ditty ought to be his theme song. Scotty refilled the pitcher and took a few bills from the kitty. Cigar clenched in his teeth, Guv picked up the pitcher of beer with his left hand and filled Moon's glass.

"You got that left-hand thing down pretty good," Lester said.

"If you can pour, you can tour."

"Tour?"

"Saturday," Lester said. "We're away. We got A and B games at West Point." He sipped his soda. "Going?"

"I planned on it," Guv said, taking a leisurely draw on his cigar. He blew out a long, slow stream of smoke. "Never been there."

"You and your cast can earn your keep. You can type with one finger. We need you to do the newsletter."

"What about Head?"

"His wife's sister's getting married. He can't make the trip."

The crowd behind them erupted into hoots and shouts again.

"That rookie from Jenkintown," Guv said, scanning the crowd. "Where's he?"

"Business trip," Lester said.

The only time you say you can't do something, the old man had said, was when it's something you don't *want* to do. "You think a one handed guy's what you need?"

"You were the English major, right?" Lester said. "You can do this with one finger. Don't worry about being funny."

"Head *thinks* he's funny, Lester."

"Your time has come, Guv."

"Just this once," he said. Behind him, the crowd quieted again. Then he heard another soft knock, followed by a rollicking cheer. Standing behind Tully, Quinn, the fall season's victim, roared loudest.

"Sounds like it's payoff time," Lester said, nodding toward the circle of muddy players.

"Brotherly love," Guv snickered.

Dog had sneaked up behind Tully, brandishing a long, stainless steel serving spoon that Will Dugan had snatched from the kitchen. It was the kind of spoon an army cook would use to stir spaghetti sauce for a whole battalion. Leider's little spoon hovered over Tully's bowed head. Holding the serving spoon just above and to the left of Leider's spoon, Dog made eye contact with Leider. He silently mouthed, "One, two, three," and then slammed the big spoon down on Tully's head just as Leider faked hitting it.

"Gee-thuth!" Tully cried out, surprise and pain battling to claim the expression on his face.

The crowd went wild, several players pounding Leider on the back.

"Good hit!" Dog cried out, tossing the big spoon behind him to Dugan while Tully, still bent over, rubbed the top of his head with both hands.

"Dumb fuck," Guv muttered. This could go on until the last practice of the spring season. Quinn beamed like a proud new father.

Dog grabbed Leider's hand and thrust it toward the ceiling. "Leider wins!" he shouted. "The rookie loses another round to a veteran."

Leider reached over and shook hands with the rookie. Confusion written all over his face, Tully managed a weak smile as he continued to rub the fresh lump on his head.

"Next week," Dog said to Tully, "you go against the great—*Looby*."

Another cheer rocked the barroom.

When Lester adjourned to the corner table with the rest of the selection committee, Mac and Leon joined Guv at the bar. Mac lit a Marlboro, straightened out his six-foot, three-inch frame and blew out two rings of smoke. He was the same height as Guv but had a good twenty pounds on him. His bushy reddish mustache stood out against his pale, weathered skin, but the first thing Guv always noticed about him was the gaunt look in his eyes. Leon was a head shorter than them, trim but muscular.

"At least Guv smokes genuine Cubans," Leon said to Mac. "You could try something interesting from France maybe, or Turkey."

"Gaulois, perhaps?" Guv said.

Mac shrugged.

"Why die for corporate America?" Leon said. He tapped the button he always wore on his faded Public Defenders softball shirt. It pictured the Liberty Bell shot through with an Indian arrow. The inscription read: 'Official BuyCentennial Bullshit Button.'

"Fucking politics," Mac said.

"Everything's political," Leon snapped.

"It's a cruel world," Guv said. "One injustice heaped on top of another; I have to write the fucking newsletter this week."

They guffawed at his misfortune.

"Poor Guv," Leon said. "Some guy in Ireland writes with a pen in his mouth, and you complain."

"In his toes," Guv said.

"In your ass," said Mac.

Leon told them about a guy he'd met in law school who played rugby with only one arm.

At eleven-thirty, Lester reappeared at the end of the bar and read off the selections for the A and B sides. Leon and Mac were both on the A side as usual.

"In England," Leon said, "they just post the selections. They have a big board in the clubhouse, and each side gets listed. And they might have five to ten sides on a club. I played in England

and Wales for a year after the Peace Corps. Scored my first try there."

"On the same field where Richard Burton played once," Guv said, putting his casted hand over his heart.

Mac rolled his eyes.

"It's the truth," Leon protested. He glanced from face to face. "Oh, fuck you," he said.

The rookie and Leider were drinking shots at the other end of the bar. Scotty and a small group of regulars were watching the Flyers game from the West Coast on the TV. Lester, Tuck Willis and Dog took the stools on the other side of Guv. When the others threw dollar bills on top of the shrinking kitty, Guv added a five to the pile.

"The price of beer and everything else is going up," Dog said, "now that the fucking Democrats are back in the White House."

"I'm sure those Republican millionaire friends of yours appreciate the support of a workingman like yourself," Leon said.

"It's only taken your peanut farmer a couple of months," Dog said, "to send the country to hell."

"And Ford left things in great shape?" Leon said. "Presidential pardon, my ass."

Dog drained his beer, gave Leon the finger, and belched.

"Dicks," Leon said to Dog. He turned to Tuck. "Dicks," he said, his voice rising.

"Dicks!" Mac snarled, stabbing his cigarette in the ashtray. "And fuck the both of you," he said, his voice rising. "Can't you find something better to talk about?"

"You're expecting a Mensa meeting to break out at the bar?" Guv said, admiring the un-flicked length of ash on the end of his cigar.

"No," Mac said, glowering at Guv. "I'm expecting the fucking governor to shut up."

Two games ago, Mac had stepped in when some behemoth from Pittsburgh had reared back, ready to cold-cock Guv after a particularly snide comment Guv had made after being tackled. "Put it away," Mac had muttered to the guy, grabbing his forearm with one hand. "Or I'll find you." He saw that same look in Mac's face now. Guv reached for his wallet. "How can I buy you a shot," he said, in mock aggravation, "if I can't open my mouth?" He plunked a ten on the bar and waved to Scotty.

"You'll find a way," Mac said. "And we'll *all* take a shot."

Guv reached for his wallet again.

After they'd downed shots of bourbon, Dog announced that he was going to work for Bob Erving the next day and that got Tuck telling the story about Erving and his father going to a tournament in Florida. Guv figured this tale must have happened several years before he started playing rugby. The ash on his cigar had fallen. He set his cigar in the ashtray in front of him, then topped off everybody's beer and leaned against the bar. Tuck, squat-bodied and perpetually slouched, stood beside his stool, acting out the parts of the story. The Holy Roller hotel manager was finally going to call the cops. Guv knew what came next.

"Erving's old man rips the cord out of the wall," Lester said, "and tells the guy, 'Not on this motherfucker, you ain't.'"

He couldn't help but laugh along with them, even though he hadn't witnessed the original event. The volume of beverages finally got to him. In the men's room, he stood at the old porcelain urinal. Another burst of laughter rose from the rugby guys. Dog's high-pitch howl and Mac's deep roar blended together as if they were a tenor and a baritone in a choir. "Friends can carry you a long way," the old man had told him. "Your father and I would still be friends to this day. Our friendship made all the difference in your life, in all our lives." He knew that he could have far better placed connections than this rag-tag group, but knowing them had opened unexpected doors to him. Guys from the club had introduced him to his current boss, Emily's cousin who introduced him to Emily and, of less duration, the waitress at Tuck's bachelor party. Guv was willing to tolerate their endless capacity for listening to each other's tales; he'd done fine enough for himself since joining the club.

When he returned, they were laughing about the one game wonder, who thought he was helping out by laundering all the jerseys between games at the Sevens' tournament last Thanksgiving. "Numb-nuts must have left them in the dryer for a couple of hours," Guv added, finally contributing to one of their war stories. "After he was done with them, those fucking things wouldn't fit a Pekinese."

Perching himself back on his stool, he worked the cigar in his mouth. Dog brought up the banquet a bunch of them had gone to at the Irish Center, back when Bill Green was running in the Democratic primary for mayor. Tuck Willis had spotted the candidate working his way from table to table, shaking hands. "Tuck started doing the same thing at the other end of the hall," Dog said. "Shaking hands, kissing babies."

"And their mothers," Mac added, sardonically.

Tuck reddened as he laughed, his face registering the same mixture of embarrassment and pride that Guv had seen when other guys had been at the center of one of these stories.

Dog rose from his stool and bent over, mimicking Tuck. "'I'm Bill Green,' Tuck would say, 'and I need *your* vote to be mayor.'"

"I almost lapped him," Tuck said.

"That would have been a first—Tuck catching anybody," Lester said.

"Then," Leon said, "Bill Green hit a table that Tuck had already visited."

"I did the only honorable thing," Tuck said, a grave look suddenly replacing his goofy smile.

Dog raised his beer as if ready to make a toast. "He filled a pitcher and got the fuck out of there."

Guv laughed as loudly as the others, putting down his cigar so he wouldn't choke from laughing with beer in his mouth. The guys were not what the old man would consider the type of friends one should cultivate, but Guv figured this was as close to outlaw status as he was going to get. They were a hoot, as Mom Fitzhugh would say. They might not be paving his way to a summer home on Cape Cod or a seat in the Senate, but they were more fun than any service organization or, God forbid, softball team.

By twelve-thirty, the kitty was gone and every rugby player except Lester and Guv had left the bar.

"Another ginger ale, Scotty," Lester called down to the bartender. "Give Guv a shot and another rum and Coke. He ain't playing on Saturday."

"Just the rum and Coke," Guv said.

Scotty brought their drinks and took a soggy five from the bills in front of Lester. "Barber scored; Flyers are ahead," he reported, before rejoining the other three hockey fans.

"Here's to broken wrists," Lester said, lifting his glass.

At the other end of the room, Scotty scowled at the television. One shuffleboard quoit boinked into another behind them. A burly late-middle-aged man in a dark suit walked in and asked

Scotty for a six-pack to go. He bore an uncanny resemblance to Frank Rizzo, and when Guv turned and caught Lester's eye, they both broke out laughing.

"Hizonnah," Lester snorted.

"Fucking politicians," Guv said, finishing his old drink and sliding his fresh one in front of him. "Who the hell are you supposed to trust?"

Lester shook his head and smirked.

"Sometimes, it's hard to tell who's the biggest asshole," Guv said. "My last semester at Temple, my biology lab partner had dragged me to a couple of anti-war protests," he said, resting his cigar in the dented blue tin ashtray in front of him.

"I thought you went to Bucknell?"

"For a year," Guv said.

"Hey, I nearly flunked out of North Catholic," Lester said. "No shame."

"I lost interest," Guv said. "Anyway, I wasn't exactly Tom Hayden."

Lester nodded.

"One afternoon, this guy takes me to a lecture by some former South Vietnamese government official. We sit in front with a bunch of neatly dressed, short-haired guys."

"ROTC," Lester said.

Guv nodded. "Behind us this sea of long-haired kids," he said, "packed the place to the rafters. As soon as the Vietnamese guy speaks, the freaks howl out a chorus of anti-war slogans. The guy tries to go on, but it's getting ugly. An administrator gets up and says they can ask questions after the speech."

"Right," Lester said, with a laugh.

"'Fucking puppet!' someone screams. The guy I'm with yells,

'Let him say his peace! Then we'll rip him a new asshole!' The guys in the front rows glare at the hippies. When the Vietnamese guy starts again, the longhaired choir in the balcony chants, 'Ho, Ho, Ho Chi Minh! NLF is gonna win!' Everybody behind us gets into it. You can't even hear the little Vietnamese guy.

"Then one of the buzz-cut guys up front screams at the protesters, 'Let-the-gook-*speak*!' He yells it again. Others join him. Now, the six front rows are on their feet, chanting, 'Let the gook speak!' as loud as they can. 'Let the gook speak!'"

Lester smirked, nodding.

"The speaker's mute, staring at the crowd. Administrators confer behind him. It's like a fucking basketball game at the Palestra. All they need are mascots. Red-faced ROTC guys and finger-pointing hippies screaming, back and forth. They look like they're having heart attacks."

Lester shook his head.

"I talked my friend out of trying to get the last word with either group. He was all caught up in it, like there was something you could do." Guv laughed, picked up his cigar, and then puffed on it. "Fucking fools," he said.

"There's all kinds of fools," Lester said. He drank his ginger ale, poured some of the ice into his mouth, and started chewing the ice.

"People think it's all so fucking black and white in this world," Guv said.

Lester raised his eyebrows.

"I mean, it's more nuanced than that," Guv said. "You know, lots of gray."

Lester reached down the bar for a red counterpart to Guv's beat-up blue ashtray and lit a cigarette. He started making circles on the bar with the sweat from his glass. "Three rings," he said. "Ballantine. Remember the jingle?" He hummed the tune from the beer commercial that used to play during Phillies games.

Guv started whistling the tune.

"You know the words?" Lester said.

Guv shook his head. "I forget."

"The shit you don't remember," Lester said, shaking his head. He kept making circles with the bottom of his glass. "These are long days," he said. "I should be home in bed." He took a long drag off his cigarette. "I used to think that when I quit drinking, I'd be able to stay up all hours," he said, his voice dropping to a mumble. "You still run out of gas." With one slow stroke of his glass, he wiped away the circles on the counter. "When I was in Vietnam, they came up with a new design for *bunkers*," he said, a comical look of world-weariness on his face. "The experts."

Guv nodded and smiled, waiting for a punch line.

"Some genius at the Pentagon studied the physics, figured it all out. I mean Mr. Genius spent a lot more than our beer money on this thing, believe me. Machine gun at each corner. *Beaucoup* thick walls. Designed to withstand anything."

Guv checked Lester's image in the mirror behind the bar, watched him grind his cigarette into the ashtray and scowl. He remembered that Moon Lansing and Mac had also been in Vietnam, but he'd never heard them say a word about it.

"This one night," Lester said, "Charlie attacks." Lester jiggled the ice in his drink and then set the glass back down on the bar. "Nothing. The next night, the same deal. We're thinking, maybe those Pentagon experts got something right for a change."

Lester was staring straight ahead at the mirror, but Guv could tell that whatever he was looking at was far away from the bar.

"Night after that," he said, "they send elephants loaded with C-4 explosives right up to the bunker." He lit another cigarette and blew out a long stream of smoke. "Fucking elephants. They were poking at them from behind with sticks, getting them right up on us. We don't shoot. Who'd shoot a fucking elephant, right? And then, ka-boom."

Guv started to laugh, but when he saw that Lester was still not smiling, Guv stopped himself. Lester didn't seem to notice; he took a sip from his drink. Guv glanced around the bar to see if anyone else was listening, but the shuffleboard players were gone and the others were still absorbed in the hockey game.

"The first two times, they just blew up elephant. The third time they blew the fuck out of everything. The ones of us left had to get the fuck out of there fast. Fortunately, Genius Boy had tunnels running out a hundred yards into the jungle. Four directions. I hauled my ass right out of there. Skinny kid from Georgia right on my ass." He took a draw on his cigarette and let out another cloud of smoke. For a few seconds, the image of his face in the mirror disappeared behind the billowy smoke. "Some poor bastard had to stick around. Destroy the guns. Take out the whole bunker. Not me and that southern guy. I got my ass out of that fucking tunnel faster than Bob Hayes and climbed a tree as high as I could. The other guy was in the tree next to me, not three feet away. Stayed there the rest of the night, holding on like a motherfucker."

Guv pictured them, clinging to the trees as quietly as they could. Viet Cong with AK-47s prowling around beneath them. He got the same feeling in his chest that he got when he leaned over the edge of the bridge over the Lehigh River and looked down.

"By morning, the jungle heat had already done a number on

those fucking dead elephants. You don't ever want to smell anything like that."

Guv nodded.

"I don't think about elephants when I think of that smell, though." He flicked the ash from his cigarette into the ashtray. "Fear," he said. "I think of praying for that whoomp whoomp sound of those fucking helicopter blades."

Guv watched him drain his soda then chew the ice loudly. When they made eye contact in the mirror, he could tell that Lester had come at least part of the way back from the dark place he'd gone to.

"That night was not all that fucking special," Lester said. "Moon and Mac got through Khe Sahn."

Guv shuddered, trying to imagine himself where they'd been. "Not my kind of thing," he said.

"It's nobody's kind of thing."

"I was a lucky bastard. Number 321 lucky, to be precise."

"Your number was not your doing."

"You should have been as lucky as me."

Lester looked at him. "I chose," he said.

"Fuck," Guv said. He slid his stool closer to the bar and sipped from his drink "Would you do it again?"

"Nobody does it because they like it," Lester said.

Guv studied Lester's face in the mirror. "Up in that tree," he said. "What did you do? Talk to the guy?"

Lester shook his head and looked off again. "Sometimes, I could see his eyes." He turned and looked at Guv. "I would have killed him if he said a fucking word," Lester said then looked down at his glass on the bar. "I figured he was thinking the same. Didn't open my mouth, but I said every prayer I could think of.

It was a long night. I can tell you that. I said a fucking High Holy Mass up there, Bro."

Guv watched Lester mash what was left of his cigarette against the inside wall of his ashtray until the glow at the end was gone, then push the collection of crumpled butts away from him. Guv brought the cigar to his mouth, but it was out. He set it in his ashtray. He looked at the clock behind the bar. It was after one. Lester was jiggling the little bit of ice in his glass.

He wondered if those memories ever left Lester alone. *Somehow, I'd find a way out,* Guv thought. *Never in a million years, do I get involved in shit that could bring on that kind of grief.* "Jesus," he murmured.

"H. Christ," Lester added, his eyes still fixed on the ashtray.

"Sucks," Guv said.

"Tell me something I don't know," Lester said, with a laugh.

"Like, we have to work tomorrow?" Guv said, gathering up his money.

Lester did the same, leaving Scotty a big tip. "See you Saturday," he said, walking off.

Guv waited until Lester was out of the bar, then plunked down several dollar bills beside his empty glass. Guv called goodnight to Scotty and stepped out into the cold night air.

"Victor!" the pediatrician's office manager called to Guv after he'd packed up his sample case and said goodbye to Dr. Moran. "Do you like the cream-filled or the jelly?" She nodded towards the opened box of donuts on the counter beside her computer.

Perhaps she used the same words and intonation with the nurses, doctors, and other pharmaceutical reps, but Guv was convinced that if he ever made a move, the tall brunette with the sparkling diamond ring would share a lot more than donuts.

He eyed the statuesque, thirty-something holding the top of the box. "You must want to make me fat, Karen," he said. "You wouldn't look like Juno herself if you made a habit of eating that stuff."

"Once is not a habit, Vic," she said.

He had not developed the best client list at Amicus Pharmaceuticals by dallying over sweets with every medical office flirt he ran into.

"Maybe some other time," she said, closing the white cardboard box.

He'd timed his lunch break to miss most of the noon rush. At Jack and Dolly's Diner, a mile from Dr. Clement's office in Montgomeryville, he chose a stool in the middle of the almost empty counter and ordered meat loaf, mashed potatoes, and a green salad. He'd brought only the paperwork he'd need for that afternoon and finished it before the waitress brought his water. In his new Celica's trunk sat all the literature and samples he'd need for his last three visits of the day. The clock above the grill told him that even if Jack dragged his feet in the kitchen, Guv had time to eat, catch his breath, and still arrive at the GP's office on time. Organization, the bane of his college life, was now a main reason for his business success. He closed his file folder and slid it over to make room for his lunch.

"Here, hon," the waitress said, placing salad bowl and dinner plate in front of Guv, everything arriving at the same time, as he had ordered. From below the counter, she produced cruets of oil and vinegar.

He flashed her the big smile, and she smiled back before vanishing into the kitchen.

The end of the meat loaf that was not covered with gravy was moist and hot: not the usual diner fare. Using his fork, he spread the brown gravy over Jack's Lunch Special. It was better than the dry meat loaf Mom Fitzhugh had served the night before the old man's recent birthday party, a weekend reunion in Connecticut that turned into a doomed exercise in nostalgia. At least here, nobody expected anything from him but three bucks and a tip.

"Three years," Mom Fitzhugh had said, when he finally returned her phone calls in January. "All those holidays . . ." Her voice trailed off. He flipped the kitchen calendar to February: nothing. When she said, "It would mean so much to your father," Guv did not believe her, but he hated hearing her cry. Besides, the prospects for this trip were different than those when he'd returned home after flunking out of Bucknell.

He'd been destined for Bucknell because his actual father and the man he called "Dad" had formed a friendship there that grew through college, marriages, and babies. When Guv was a year and a half old, a carload of drunken teenagers had plowed head-first into Geoffrey and Cindy Taylor's new Buick on the Pennsylvania Turnpike. In accordance with their wills, Jack and Marian Fitzhugh took him in, raising him along with their own son and daughter, a year older and younger than Victor. He knew from the start that he was adopted, kept a photo on the bureau of his parents holding him, wrote Christmas cards to the two great aunts on his mother's side of the family, but he grew to be a part of the Fitzhugh family. When he was fourteen, he insisted on taking their last name. "You're a Fitzhugh!" the old man would snap at each of them when the chips were down in school or on the playing field. "You'll come through."

At eighteen, accepted by Bucknell, Guv learned the details of his real parents' will and of the hefty trust fund, set up for the equal benefit of all three children, enough to send him to Bucknell, Derek to Amherst, and Karen to Smith. A free ride. On his real parents' dime. All of a sudden, the family's lifestyle made sense. *His* money. Split three ways. He couldn't blame them. It made sense, he told himself. Quid pro quo. They'd been good to him. Like Looby had said about the spoon scam: the trick is not hitting 'em so hard that they'll get it, just hard enough to keep them thinking they're in the game. All that money. All of a sudden, like a whack that couldn't possibly be delivered by a teaspoon, it seemed so clear that he'd never been as close to them as they were to each other. When they visited, they said he was distant. He went home for Thanksgiving but returned to campus the day after. He floundered through his first semester and flunked out after the second.

"Figures," the old man said. "You never would've gotten in if I hadn't pulled some strings."

A lawyer helped Guv recover what he could from the fund. He ended up at Temple, telling people that he was living on money he'd earned. Having failed at pre-law at Bucknell, he gutted his way through Temple, majoring in English because it bored him less than anything else and because it was sure to piss off the old man.

He washed and waxed his new Celica before leaving for Connecticut, bought Mom Fitzhugh flowers and the old man a box of Cuban cigars, which he'd gotten from an acquaintance who did business in Montreal. He wore a blue blazer, a white shirt with blue and gray striped tie, gray trousers, and dress black shoes.

The family looked like they'd just stepped out of an L.L. Bean catalogue. Hugs all around. He dropped his bags and the gift-wrapped box of Lonsdales in his old room, now painted a Williamsburg green and, except for his old bed, furnished by Ethan Allen. The photo of him and his biological parents had been moved to the array of Fitzhugh family shots on the stairway. A few bites into the meat loaf, it came out that investment banker Derek was working for Houseman and Cower in New York and that Sharon was lined up for a residency in pediatrics at Mass General. Derek's perky girlfriend was a corporate lawyer. "Pharmaceuticals is a great field," she said, beaming at him.

"It's been good to me," Guv said.

"My very first job, as a kid," the old man said, "was as a Fuller Brush Man. Door-to-door, awful. I lasted two months." His smile seared Guv.

Over bread pudding, the girlfriend gushed about how she and Derek were traveling around the region to play cribbage. Mom and Dad were up to their ears in gardening and bridge.

"I'm so boring," Karen lamented. "Work and study. Work and study."

"I'm on a rugby club," Guv offered.

The old man raised his eyebrows.

"Our med school had a team," Karen said.

"I met a lawyer downtown who invited me to join," Guv said. He left out that Leon was a public defender with no plans to move to a more lucrative practice.

The old man was still looking at Karen. "They become doctors," he said. "They can't afford the time for that kind of thing."

"We've got a doctor on our team," Guv said.

"How nice," Mom Fitzhugh said.

"What," the old man snorted, "a horse doctor?"

The rest of the family exploded with laughter. *The real family,* Guv thought.

After dinner, in the den, Guv pulled three Macanudo Lonsdales out of his jacket pocket.

"I quit," the old man said, waving off the offer.

"Never started," Derek said, with a laugh. "But thanks."

Guv pocketed the cigars and sat at the end of their old sofa. Listening to Derek and the old man discuss changing real estate values in the old neighborhood, he fiddled in his trouser pocket until he found his cigar cutter and started rubbing his thumb against it, like a worry stone.

When the women joined them with a tray of brandies, he rose, took his drink and held it up. "A birthday toast to our father," he said.

"Hear, hear," they chorused.

He could feel the warmth in the air; it was practically a Waltons' moment. "And an apology," he said.

"What's that?" Mom Fitzhugh said.

"I realize that the official celebration is tomorrow, but I just found out today that I have to give a presentation on Monday," he lied. "I have to leave in the morning, but I'll be thinking of you all tomorrow night."

His announcement took the wind out of the perky one's sails. He could see that she didn't know whether to be solicitous or to take the old man's lead and freeze him out. For the remainder of the evening, Guv sat on the sidelines as they volleyed back and forth about jobs and vacations.

Turning down his bed, he heard a soft tapping on the door. "Come in, Mom," he said.

She opened the door and stood inside the doorway. "Honey, you know he's not very good at this," she whispered.

He sat on the side of his old twin bed. "Right." He patted the space beside him, knowing that without some sort of invitation, she'd hover at the door.

Smiling now, she padded over to the bed and sat beside him. "Sorry it's your turn to be in the dog house," she said, resting her hand on his. "Derek almost didn't come tonight."

"I'm fine," he said.

"That would be the answer to my prayers," she said, running her hand through his hair.

He leaned away.

"Things don't get better unless you work on 'em," she said.

"For who?"

"For anyone."

A lot of good it had done her, he thought. He kissed her on the forehead, and then she hugged him and rose from the bed. She knew when to leave. He had to give her that.

Rising at five on the day the old man turned sixty, he made the bed, left his gift for him on the pillow, and tiptoed out.

Saturday morning, Guv parked the Celica at the Willow Grove Howard Johnson's between Dog's ten-year-old black Cadillac and Leon's Chevy. He checked the pocket of his Harris Tweed and found the little notebook and pen he'd remembered to stash before leaving the apartment. According to the weather report, the night had brought a killer frost. The forecast was for a high in the forties. He'd put on the Jeff that Emily had brought back for him from Donegal and the woolen knit fisherman's sweater that he liked to tell people he'd stolen from the Clancy Brothers. With jeans, hiking boots, and his jacket, he'd be all right, no matter how cold the winds blew up at West Point.

"We're going in the War Wagon," Leon said, pointing to Dog's Caddy. "Let's do it."

The Caddy was an automatic with power everything, so Guv offered to drive the first shift, figuring he'd be good until New York City.

"The belly of the whale," Mac said, stowing his gear in the trunk. He climbed in beside Guv. Leon, Dog, and Lester piled into the rear.

"No B game," Lester informed Guv on the way out of the lot. "Some bullshit about another team. They're down to just over two sides, so even with guys playing over, they're only good for three games. Guess who gets the shitty end of the stick?"

"Who?" they chorused. "*Who?*" Using the melody to "MacNamara's Band," they bellowed, "Celtic Rugby Football Club, the terrors of the night. Da-da-da-dah. Da-dah-da-dah."

"Us!" Leon yelled. "Us!"

"Fuck *Us!*" they chorused.

"They offered to reschedule," Dog said.

"Fuck that," Mac said.

Most of the Celtic B's were going anyway. They'd have a shitload of frustrated subs and one shanghaied correspondent. The B guys would be pissed, but it wouldn't make a difference to Guv.

Guv rested his right hand on the steering wheel and managed to steer with his left. About an hour up the Jersey turnpike, everybody started clamoring for coffee, and Leon said he was antsy to drive. When Guv pulled into a parking spot at the Joyce Kilmer rest area, he tossed him the keys. "You need a tugboat with this car," he said, as they started towards the restroom. "But I got to tell you, I feel like Elvis, driving this thing."

"You don't *drive* a car like this, boy," Leon said, in his best Elvis impersonation. "You *cruise* in it."

Guv nodded. He looked forward to another driving shift on the way back home in the dark. Cruising. A great black shark, sweeping into the passing lane. Chrome and fins. It was going to be a good day, he decided. The early cloud cover had disappeared. It was warming up.

Carrying their coffees back to the car, they passed an elderly couple trying vainly to coax their little mutt to pee on the little island between rows of parked cars. "Joyce Fucking Kilmer," Lester muttered, then quoted the line from "Trees," prompting a groan from Leon and laughter from Guv.

"Fucking college guys," Dog said, shaking his head. Mac gave Lester and Guv the hairy eyeball, but Guv could tell the big guy was in a better mood than the other night.

When Leon squeezed the car into the northbound traffic between two tractor-trailers, Mac brought up the time that the fullback's dog lapped up the spilled beer around the lip of the keg, rendering him unable to walk—even with four feet. That launched them onto a series of tales that were new to Guv, and which, he was sure, would horrify the family. He wished the conversation were being recorded for the benefit of the old man. When Lester bemoaned the time that he had omitted the names of several players in the newsletter, Guv sneered to himself. He toyed with the idea of doing the newsletter as a villanelle. *Screw the lowbrows,* he thought. No. Just the facts. Simple, elegant prose. Not the memos and letters that made up his writing life now.

At the entrance to West Point, they joined a short line of cars inching toward the checkpoint. "That's Jerry McKay's new van," Dog said, pointing ahead. At the gate, Dog told the guard in the gray uniform that they were here for a rugby game.

"*Match*," Leon corrected.

The guard gave directions to the fields and waved them in.

"You're hopeless, Dog," Leon said.

They drove down winding roadways around ancient buildings that Guv figured must have been around when Ulysses S. Grant was a cadet. They passed a field on which a formation of dress-uniformed, perfectly postured cadets marched. If he'd gone to West Point or Annapolis, he'd be out of the service by now and maybe running for Congress. But Bucknell was all he'd ever wanted, groomed both by genetics and environment, a convergence of influence from his two fathers. He'd ended up like a regular Philly guy, a subway-riding day student at Temple. He watched row after row of trim cadets in gray lines turning smartly on the broad green field.

"Kinda takes the mystery out of what to wear in the morning, I guess," Leon said.

"Yeah," Dog said. "Of course, they don't look nearly as good as you do when you go to work."

"This place is crawling with famous ghosts," Lester said.

"Grant, Lee, Eisenhower," Leon recited.

"Edgar Allan Poe," Guv said.

Mac gave him that look of his.

"Didn't Benedict Arnold sell this place out?" Dog said, watching the cadets disappear in his rear view mirror.

"Looks like we got it back," Lester said.

When Dog parked the Caddy beside a pair of neatly lined

fields with goal posts and corner flags, Leon raved about the quality of the *"pitches,"* prompting a round of groans.

"That's the army for you," Dog said.

"No," Lester said. "That's West Point."

"You fucking well got that right," Mac added.

The wind picked up as Guv walked onto the field. Clouds had returned, and he was glad that he had dressed in layers. A bus with Virginia plates pulled up, and players streamed out of it and onto the field. Dog announced that V.M.I. was going to play the West Point As and Cs. Celtic would get their Bs. The guys in Guv's car pulled on their emerald green jerseys and laced up their boots. Some players stretched by the touchline while others jogged across the field, passing a ball to one another. Lester practiced kicking at goal. Kelly had not shown up yet, so Tully was moved up from the Bs. Guv listed the line-up in his book. Writing Tully's name, he felt resentment for the first time since he'd left the hospital. The injury was no big thing. It would take care of itself. But it would have been nice to be able to tell his grandkids that he'd played at West Point.

Games started almost simultaneously on the two adjacent fields. Guv stood on a bench within the narrow strip between the fields with the B team players. They were all suited up against the possibility that they might go in as an injury substitute. As Dog liked to say, they had a fart's chance in a blizzard. They all wore the club's green windbreaker and paced the sideline or, hands in pockets, rocked back and forth on the grass like vagrants in a park. Sure, one of them could have been pressed into newsletter duty, but he'd already committed himself. They'd get a newsletter they'd remember.

A larger crowd was watching the other game, well turned-out

young women interspersed with uniformed cadets. He watched a back play develop that led to a V.M.I score under the posts. A cheer went up from the Virginians. Minus the uniforms, it would be difficult to tell one side apart from the other. He scanned his own team. The only unifying element among the Celtic players was their green, black, and gold kit, as Leon liked to call it. They ranged in age from late high school to mid-forties and in jobs from roofers and community college students to doctors and accountants.

At half-time Guv drew a line under his notes and made sure he could read his writing. A try by Porter, the conversion by Lester. They were ahead of the West Point Bs by two points. He had lost track of the score of the other game, but the home side was way ahead.

The A side players crouched in a circle near midfield, eating slices of orange and drinking water from plastic jugs. Tuck Willis cleaned up a cut on Mac's forehead and wrapped some tape around his head.

Dog complained about the binding in the line-outs. Leon milled around the rest of the players, muttering something Guv could not hear. More than at any earlier point in the day, Guv felt the urge to play, and he cursed his injury.

The referee whistled the end of the five-minute break.

"Hike up your skirts, ladies," Leon said, now limping exaggeratedly and doing his Walter Brennan. "We're going into hell."

Guv switched sides, leaving the spectator-filled strip between the fields for the empty touchline near the access road. Only he and the West Point touch judge watched from this side, and the touch judge, a baby-faced cadet, prowled the touchline with his flag, following the action and raising his flag at the spot where the ball went across the line. Almost immediately, Looby and Porter mishandled a switch play, turning over the ball to the West Point backs, who promptly scored under the posts. The conversion was good, putting West Point ahead. When Dog dragged one of the West Point backs into touch far down the line, the touch judge shot the flag up smartly, and the two sets of forwards set up for a lineout. A few of the Celtic backs clustered around Lester, looking at his left shoulder. Wincing, Lester worked the shoulder with his right hand. When the ref asked him if he needed two minutes, he nodded and walked around, testing its range of motion and shaking his head. Before the two minutes was up, Lester gingerly walked off the field.

"It's out again," he said, approaching Guv.

Guv glanced across the field at the line of anxious green-jerseyed guys looking back.

Lester raised his arms above his head, slowly rotating them, the concentration of a safecracker on his face. West Point kicked into touch deep down the other side of the field. "We're pissing this game away," Lester said.

"A little more speed on the wing wouldn't hurt," Guv said. "I *know* I would have scored against their wing."

Lester tested his shoulder in the other direction, watching the forwards jump in the lineout down the field. "Maybe," he said. "But how many would you have given up by now?"

Guv felt himself redden. "Hey," he said, "I didn't come up with that guv stuff."

Lester stopped moving his shoulder and looked at Guv. "And Dog's canine qualities are all good?" he said, laughing "You're stuck with the name," he said. He felt the edge of Guv's jacket sleeve. "Who the fuck dresses you?"

"Fuck you," Guv said.

"You *could* tackle like you meant it. Instead of the toreador bit."

There was no venom in Lester's voice; he might have been advising Guv on what grade of motor oil to use for his new Celica. Still, he bristled. It was not the first time he'd seen this side of Lester. After the fall opener against Baltimore, when Guv had asked Lester pointedly if the club routinely gave a Man of the Match award, like Temple Med had, Lester told Guv that even if they did, he wouldn't have gotten it, despite having scored the winning try in his first game for Celtic. "I would have given it to the pack. They were dwarfed by those guys and still won ball all afternoon, pushed them up and down the field. If they don't play like a greased machine, you don't see the ball all day."

Guv couldn't think of a single forward who did anything memorable, and his expression must have said as much.

"Men carry their shields for the sake of the entire line," Lester had said. "Plutarch."

"Plutarch this!" Guv had said, clutching his groin. He'd smiled and Lester laughed.

Across the field, one of the subs was waving. Lester continued slowly gyrating, not looking at the subs. "Give Kelly the finger, will you?" he said.

Guv laughed.

Lester let out a sharp groan that Guv could not identify as pain or relief. "Fuck!" Lester grunted, rotating the injured wing. "There," he said, "it's back."

The ref whistled a knock-on.

"Ref!" Lester called. He held aloft his arms and moved them around for the ref to see. The ref waved him back onto the field.

"Back to Plutarch?" Guv said.

Lester jogged toward where the teams were getting ready to scrum down. "Olé," he said, glancing back at Guv.

When West Point won the scrum, their fly half booted the ball over Guv's head. The West Point touch judge retrieved the ball and tossed it to Jerry McKay, the hooker who served as thrower on lineouts. Guv stood behind Baby Face. The two sets of forwards formed their lines on the touch judge. Guv glanced at Lester, but Lester's eyes were fixed on the middle of the line of forwards. Jerry threw the ball down the middle of the tunnel of opposing players, and Mac towered up and snagged the ball cleanly. The Celtic forwards packed down on him, their human wall shielding Mac and the ball from the Army forwards. In seconds, the ball was out of the mass of forwards and in the hands of the scrum half who spun it out to Moon, who passed the ball to Will Dugan, the inside center. Dugan sidestepped a would-be tackler, twisted away from another defender, and in two strides was up to full speed when, with a crack that made spectators of the other game turn, he knocked heads with a muscle bound red haired cadet. Guv knew from the sound of the collision that the cadet's nose had been broken. Both players fell to the ground, faces covered with blood, and rolled away from the two surging sets of forwards hell-bent on claiming the loose ball. Guv noticed a black shirt on the ground, on the wrong side of the ball. Instead of trying to put himself onside, the cadet reached for the ball. The ref was on the other side of the pile, his view blocked to the intentional infraction. Dog promptly stamped on the player's head, raking him with his boots from the back of his head to the bottom of his jersey. The referee blew his whistle and awarded West Point a penalty.

The redhead was streaming blood but jogged over to where

his teammates were lining up for the penalty kick. His captain ordered him to go off for a sub. Dugan already had an egg-sized lump on his forehead but did not appear to be bleeding. Using his jersey sleeve, he wiped the redhead's blood off his forehead and cheek and convinced Lester that he could play on.

Guv made a note of the time and quickly wrote down as much of the sequence as he could remember, but stopped to make sure he did not miss anything when West Point kicked deep into the Celtic end of the field to restart the game. The sides exchanged kicks until Looby and Porter worked a switch perfectly, sending Tully in for a score in the corner.

By the time the final whistle blew, the West Point As had already won easily over V.M.I., and those players were milling around on the strip between the fields. Celtic had won by the same small margin by which they had led at the half. The teams clapped each other off the field, and the V.M.I. B side players took the field to warm up. Guv put his notebook away and crossed the field. Moon tossed him a can of Rolling Rock then offered one to a guy he'd played against. The cadet turned and surveyed the crowd of spectators. "Hold one for my girl," he said.

With a couple of A-side cadets playing again, the final game began. The West Point guy arrived with his girlfriend, and she took the can of beer from Moon. The boyfriend had a soda can, and she emptied the beer into it. The guy took a drink and passed it to his date.

"You never know who might be watching," Leon said.

"Fucked up," Lester muttered.

"Nobody's perfect," Dog said, popping the top on a Rolling Rock.

"I guess not," Guv said.

Several of the Army players on the touchline had soda cans. When a uniformed cadet with several stripes emblazoned on his sleeve arrived in a jeep and strode up the touchline, the soda cans vanished. When he finally left, the cans reappeared.

By the time the last game ended, Guv was wishing that they had gotten more than just coffee at the rest stop. After following a West Point player's directions, he dropped off his carload of sweaty players at an old gym and sat in Dog's Caddy, watching waves of players go in and come out. It had turned cold again, so he restarted the car and turned on the heater. He went over the scoring from the game, and the numbers he added equaled the scores on the bottom of the page. That was good. But he had lost track of how many lineouts and scrums they had won and lost. No worry, he could make them up, and no one would be the wiser. He had scribbled some notes about the soda can shenanigans and now wrote a headline above the passage: Mere Mortals.

His passengers came out of the gym together, toting kit bags and zipping up jackets. The sun had gone down while they were showering, and the temperature had dropped even lower. Leon was favoring his right leg a little, and they all were walking slower than they had before the game. The tape around Mac's head had been replaced with a small square bandage.

"I got shotgun," Mac grunted, climbing into the passenger side seat. His face was red and his forehead beaded with sweat. He slammed the door shut and rolled down the window. "Let's have some fucking air in here," he said.

"You are definitely part bear," Dog said, squeezing into the back seat beside Leon and Lester.

Guv drove behind a line of cars that wove its way up a series of hills. They circled up and up. Each side of the road was lined with fir trees. It was dark, except for the light of a nearly full moon. The forest on either side of the road looked like it went on forever.

"Are we still in West Point?" he asked.

"I expect to see clouds up here soon," Leon said. "And then some fat lady from a Wagner opera. This place is perfect."

A gust of wind whipped through the car.

"Hey, Mac," Dog said. "I'm freezing back here."

"Roll it up!" Lester said.

Mac rolled the window all the way up, and they continued up the road through the woods.

In the mirror, Guv made out a line of cars behind them, winding their way up the hill. The road crested in a gravel parking area with a fairly steep hill rising up from the far side. He pulled in beside a car with New York plates. The wind had picked up, and it felt ten degrees colder than down outside the gym. Everybody except Mac had pulled on jackets, and they followed a carload of cadets through the parking area and onto a foot trail through some woods to an old Quonset hut in a clearing. The cadets ahead opened the door, and the unmistakable din of a rugby party poured out.

"Hike up your skirts, ladies," Leon said, now as John Wayne.

A cadet standing in front of two kegs handed them plastic cups of draught. On the other side of the building, cadets in gray uniforms served paper plates filled with spaghetti and salad.

Within an hour, the food had been consumed, and two more kegs had been tapped. "Apparently, no drinking restrictions apply at Valhalla," Guv wrote in his notebook. He clipped the end of a Lonsdale and lit it. There was not a rum and Coke in sight, but the beer was cold and he was smoking as good a cigar as anyone at West Point. A group of cadets started singing at the other end of the room. When they called on the V.M.I. players to do a song, they obliged with a dirty one that Guv had never heard before, and then Celtic was called on to sing. Leon and Dog tried to get Mac to sing, but he stayed by the door, cigarette in one hand and cup of beer in the other. Leon and Dog dragged Guv and half a dozen other guys over to the circle of singers.

"Four and twenty virgins came down from Inverness," Dog sang. "And when the ball was over there were four and twenty less." Players from all three clubs roared the refrain. Moon sang another verse, and then a cadet began "If I Were the Marrying Kind." Guv headed toward the keg for a refill. Topping off his beer, Guv felt a hand on his shoulder and turned around.

"Come on, Guv," Jerry McKay said. He took Guv's cigar and waggled his eyebrows like Groucho Marx. "You need to go for a walk," he said.

Guv retrieved his cigar and followed Jerry, his girlfriend, and Porter. They walked down the path, and then stepped off into the woods. Inside the hut, the singers had segued into "I Don't Want to Join the Army." Just enough moonlight filtered through the trees to allow them to see. Guv drew on his cigar, making the end glow. They stopped at a little clearing.

"Marge has a few numbers already rolled," Jerry said. His girlfriend produced a joint and promptly lit it. They heard footsteps, and then Leider and a uniformed cadet approached from behind Jerry. Guv pictured himself behind bars as they stepped forward. The cadet was holding a lit joint.

"Jesus," Guv said.

"Frank, actually," the cadet said, passing him the joint. "Shh," he said. "Be veh-wee, veh-wee kwai-et."

Planting his cigar in his casted hand, Guv took a toke and then handed the joint to Jerry.

"Superb herb," Jerry said.

"Don't worry," the cadet said to Guv. "I'm more the exception than the rule." He took another toke and held it in. Finally, he let it out. "Some guys here don't even drink," he said. He sniffed deeply, closing his eyes. "Of course, what you're smoking there smells as interesting as this stuff."

Guv offered him his cigar, and the cadet took a puff. "Damn," the cadet said. "This couldn't be contraband. Could it?"

The others laughed.

"Gift from a friend who goes to Canada."

"You a professor or something?" the cadet said, looking Guv up and down.

"No, I sell drugs."

They all laughed.

"To doctors," Guv said.

"Does that make it any better?" McKay's girlfriend said, giggling.

"For a pharmaceutical company," Guv said.

"Oh," the cadet said, brightening. "So, you're part of the military industrial complex."

Guv wondered what made the cadet address all of his comments to him. "No, offense," Guv said. "I just didn't expect to see the nation's warriors smoking weed up here."

"Soldiers," the cadet said.

"Pot, weed," Guv said. "Warriors, soldiers."

"Let's call the whole thing off," McKay and his girlfriend sang, off key.

The joint had come around to Guv again, but he passed it.

"It's not the same," the cadet said, reaching for the joint.

"I love this," Leider said. "You guys are having a serious conversation while we get high."

"We're not storybook characters," the cadet said, still looking at Guv. "Just soldiers."

He remembered arguments with the old man, trying to piece together exactly what he'd done so totally wrong. But he'd come a long way since the days when he assumed that he had, in fact, done something wrong every time the old man put him through an interrogation. Here, some crew-cut Boy Scout whose education was being paid for by his taxes was lecturing him. He could hear himself asking the cadet exactly where smoking a Cuban cigar at West Point would place on the list of honor code violations. His lab partner at Temple would have gone down that slippery slope by now, he thought. "Just as long as we don't call you sailors," Leider said.

Everybody laughed. Guv held back the sneer he felt his mouth curling into. Had he really envied these cadets on the ride up here and at the games? Maybe some individuality still lurked inside this kid, he thought, but this place had made him and his cadet buddies bury that deep within their psyches. McKay finished the roach, dropped it, and crushed it with his sneaker.

"Later," the cadet said, shaking Guv's hand.

"Nice game," he said, averting his eyes.

Leider and the cadet left to continue their circumnavigation of the party.

Guv watched McKay and his girlfriend wend their way back to the Quonset hut. Flickers of light dotted the woods, and Guv could just make out little clusters of other smokers in the dark. The sky was filled with stars, as many as he'd seen as a kid in the planetarium at the Franklin Institute when they went to Philadelphia. A shooting star flashed across the sky above the Quonset hut, the first one he'd ever seen.

When he neared the Quonset hut, he heard the voices of the mob belting out the chorus to another rugby song. He went back in and filled a cup half way with beer. Tuck started in on "Swing Low, Sweet Chariot," accompanying the song with obscene hand motions. All of the singers joined in. The redheaded center, sporting a bandage over his swollen nose, belted out the verse. Guv sat on one of the tables they had been using for food and leaned back, closing his eyes.

Somebody shook him awake. "Yo, Guv. Watch it."

He opened his eyes. He had almost fallen over; Lester was standing in front of him, holding him up. Guv sat upright, then stood. He looked at his watch. It was after ten. Lester went back to a group of older guys who weren't singing. The singers had broken into two groups and were in the middle of a song he'd heard once or twice before. "Fuck," Guv muttered, noticing his extinguished cigar on the concrete floor.

A guy wearing a V.M.I. jacket started singing "Red-Haired Mary." While Guv had been asleep, the number of singers had dwindled. Small groups of men were talking and drinking at the other end of the room.

He stretched his legs and walked to the door. Outside, the temperature change woke him completely. He had had more than enough beer for the night. Even more stars were out than before. He was shuffling down the path when he heard what sounded like yelling off in the distance. He started toward the parking lot where the sound had seemed to come from. He heard a shriek and picked up the pace. The screaming became more distinct as he moved toward it, the words almost understandable. He rushed to the end of the path and emerged into the parking area. At the top of the steep hill above the parking area, in the moonlight, he could just make out a figure leaning against a tree. The person pushed away from the tree and then staggered to a halt. It was Mac. "Brilliant *fucks*!" he cried out.

As Guv worked his way through the parked cars toward the bottom of the hill, Leon and Dog rushed past him and stormed their way up the rocky, wooded hill.

"Brilliant fucking geniuses!" Mac thundered.

At the edge of the lot at the bottom of the hill where a small crowd had gathered, Guv stopped. He could see Mac clearly in the moonlight, grasping a cup of beer in his right hand. He raised it above him and stood up straight. "To you," he cried, "from the rest of us!"

When Leon and Dog neared the top, Mac held up his hand, palm out, as if he were about to straight-arm a tackler. They stopped short of him on a rock ledge maybe ten feet below where the big guy stood.

Above the voices of the people milling around behind him, Guv heard the scuff of hurried footsteps on the gravel. He turned just as Lester and Tuck slowed to a stop beside him, panting. They gazed up at the hilltop.

Mac was scanning the sky. "Motherfuckers!" he screamed.

"Let's go," Tuck said, then bolted with Lester toward the hill. Clouds raced across the sky, and now Guv saw Mac hunched over and pawing the air. In the new light, he looked like an enraged bear.

Suddenly, Lester was back, right in front of Guv, glaring. "Let's *go*, Victor," he growled, pulling Guv's sleeve. They quickly caught up to Tuck. In the darkness, the three of them thrashed their way up the hill through the brush and boulders and trees.

When they reached the ledge, Guv looked up and saw that Mac had moved back beside the towering pine tree. He was moaning and shaking but held up his hand warning them to stay away. More voices rose up to them from the parking lot. Just below them, Guv heard muffled voices and the rustle of brush underfoot.

Four cadets approached the ledge and stopped twenty feet from them. Guv recognized one of them but was relieved that Frank wasn't part of the group. Mac cast the contents of his cup over their heads, down the hill. "Great game, gentlemen!" he screamed, leaning against the pine tree. "Great *fucking* game!" He tossed his empty cup at them, but it fluttered away in the wind. He slipped his arm around the tree and slid down until he landed on his rear next to the base of the tree. "It's a game, Leon," he said quietly. "Not a fucking match."

"What the hell's going on?" one of the cadets said.

"Does this guy need help?" a second cadet added.

"Get away," Mac muttered.

The cadets looked at each other, and then one of them signaled and they started forward.

"CHARLIE!" Mac screamed, pointing down the hill, his eyes nearly bugging out of his head.

The cadets froze.

"Hang tight, Mac," Lester shouted. He clambered up the rugged outcropping. He made it to a sapling at the base of the rocky top, grabbed hold, and pulled himself the rest of the way up. Leon, Dog, and Tuck scuttled up after him.

Guv heard the footsteps of the cadets behind him and turned just in time to step into their way. They halted and then the one guy who seemed to be their leader stepped forward. Guv looked at his stern composed face in the moonlight. Guv's teammates had left him to do this. They had gone to their friend and left him to face these cadets, as if this were some kind of tackling drill. He swelled with rage. The wind gusted noisily through the trees, cutting right through his jacket and making him shiver for a moment.

"This is West Point," the cadet said in a steely voice. "We'll handle it."

"He's ours," Guv said, glaring into his eyes. "We'll get him home."

The cadet squinted as he looked up over Guv's shoulder.

Behind him, Guv could hear his teammates moving around at the top of the hill. Then the cadet looked back at him. Slow it down, Guv told himself. He planted his feet and balled his fists. His eyes locked on the cadet's. If he'd stayed in the Quonset hut, he'd still be smoking his cigar and listening to drunks congratulating each other about the games. If only Lester hadn't jerked him along, he'd still be down below in the parking lot. Neither he nor the cadet moved. He could think of no joke that would divert these cadets. Nor could he stand aside and let them pass, unless he wanted to hitchhike all the way back to Philadelphia. He stared into the eyes of the cadet but saw Lester's eyes. No more sounds came from the others behind him. His hands were shaking, and he squeezed his fists tighter. They still shook. Then a loud gust of wind whipped up the side of the hill again and swayed both him and the cadet slightly. Finally, Guv opened his mouth. "I said, he's ours," he said, raising his voice over the sound of the wind.

The cadet held his gaze on him.

Loud talking and laughter drifted up to them from the bottom of the hill. The wind died down. The sound of his breath whistled out of his nose.

"You have ten minutes," the cadet said. He waved his subordinates down the hill, still studying Guv. Then the cadet about-faced and followed the other cadets.

Guv watched the column of men disappear into the brush and darkness. He unballed his fists. They had stopped shaking but felt numb and heavy.

A minute later, the shouting from the lot stopped abruptly. The distant hooting and hollering from the Quonset hut went on and on. Mac was sobbing.

Guv slid into the shadows of the trees. "Fuckers," he muttered. He craned his neck to look above. He could just make them out, but he was sure that they could not see him. Where the rocky top flattened out, Mac sat, facing out over the ledge and the hill below. Lester sat on one side of him and Leon on the other. With Lester and Leon hunched toward the middle, the three of them huddled close, like the front row of a scrum. Dog and Tuck stood close together behind Mac. A sudden gust of wind tilted them forward, and Guv understood why they had set themselves there. Mac had Leon's rugby jacket draped over his shoulders, but even with all of his teammates blocking the wind, he was still shaking a little. In the moonlight, the five of them took on the same gray cast as the rock and dirt beneath and behind them. Soundless and still, except for Mac's keening, they looked like some sculptor's work, like so many statues arranged in a scene. The wind soughed, and he thought for a moment that he had heard Lester calling his name, but then he was sure it was only the wind. "No thanks," he mouthed. Mac's crying had quieted now. His fists lay in his lap. The wind gusted again, bending Dog and Tuck and the pine trees forward.

Lester reached into his back pocket and pulled out a handkerchief or a bandana. He wiped Mac's face then stuck the handkerchief in Mac's clenched hand.

The wind cracked through the trees, and it felt like winter. Still, none of them said a word. Down below, an engine started up, and one car drove out of the lot. A few minutes later, another did the same. A group of people scuffled through the gravel lot, and Guv could even make out part of one couple's conversation. Then, car doors slammed shut, and the voices were gone. After a while, he heard Mac mutter something, and they pulled him to his feet. Dog and Tuck brushed him off; then, they started him down the hill. Guv waited for them to pass before he fell in. The four cadets were waiting, standing near a blue Chevy at the base of the hill. Lester approached the cadets, and in a moment they were talking softly. Guv reached the old Cadillac as his teammates got Mac into the car. Tuck patted Mac on the back and then shuffled off to find his ride. They propped Mac up in the rear seat, packed in between Dog and Leon. Guv climbed into the shotgun seat. Nobody said a word as Lester drove away. Mac passed out before they reached 9W.

Lester stopped for coffee at a rest area on the Palisades Parkway, and they left Mac, still out cold, in the back, covered with a couple of rugby jackets. While Leon and Dog hit the restroom, Lester and Guv got coffee for the four of them. At the service counter, they both popped open their coffee cups. The aroma was bracing and soothing at the same time. Guv poured cream and sugar from packets into the cups for Leon and himself. Lester fixed the other two cups.

"Where'd you disappear to up there?" Lester said, smiling.

Guv shrugged.

"Longest piss in history?" Lester laughed but kept his eyes on Guv's.

"You didn't need me."

"Hardly the point," Lester said. He stirred the coffee in one of his cups, then the coffee in the other.

Guv raised his cup to his mouth, but the coffee seared his lip, and he flinched. He returned the cup to the counter and resealed the lid. *I did the right thing,* he thought, *the bigger thing. I stood up for Mac and the others on the ledge. But it wasn't my choice. I'd wanted to be anywhere but there.*

Guv looked up. Lester still stared right at him. *He knew.* Guv felt himself redden. "Okay, I'm a strange fuck," Guv said. "So what?"

"No," Lester said. "You done good up there."

But Guv knew that he hadn't.

Lester reached over and swept the mess Guv had made into the waste bin between them. Then he stuffed Dog's car keys into Guv's jacket pocket. "Your shift."

Leon and Dog strode around the corner, and they all headed back to the Caddie. Without stirring Mac, they positioned themselves inside the car, Guv behind the wheel. He eased the car out of the well-lit parking lot into the southbound traffic, squinting into the glare of the headlights from the other side of the road.

Dog cleared his voice a few times then started in. "Dave Webster hitchhiked all the way to Windsor, Ontario, for the Borderers' Tournament," he said, his voice just above a whisper. Leon leaned back from the shotgun seat to listen. "Did it every damn time we went there," Dog said.

"I remember," Leon said.

"Last time we went, Webster crashed on Lester's motel floor for the weekend," Dog said. "Lester or Moon would have taken him home." He paused, sipping his coffee. "But the fucker sneaked out of his room and hitched his way home."

"Some fucking people," Leon snorted.

Glancing in the rear view mirror, Guv watched Lester laugh along with the others. He pushed down the turn signal and slid the car into the left lane to pass a tractor-trailer. When the truck's headlights showed up in his rearview mirror, he eased back into the right lane.

"Remember that Irish touring side we hosted last spring?" Leon said. "Who amongst them held the most hot air?"

"Jessie!" Lester hissed. "Their inflatable lamb."

"The lamb!" Dog laughed. "They took Jessie everywhere: the game, the bar."

"Remember the poor bastard they made its guardian?" Leon said. "Some first-tour rookie."

"Richard," Dog said.

"Richard," Leon intoned, "the keeper of the lamb."

"Dick!" Guv blurted out.

They all laughed, even though they were trying to keep it down. Guv checked in the rearview mirror, but they hadn't woken Mac. Dog and Lester had fashioned a pillow for him with their sweats. Lester's handkerchief was still in Mac's hand.

The Interpreter

THE ONES WE get paid for. That's how Janis refers to the calls like the one this morning. Most of the time, calls from people looking into an adoption are no problem at all. In fact, talking with married couples on the verge of taking the big step ranks as one of the nicest parts of this job.

Although Father McCoy is officially in charge, Janis is always here and runs the everyday operation of the office. She and I are pretty much it in this little office. She's never lorded her position over me, though. "Rosalie, I'll treat you like you were my little sister," she said, right when I started here nine months ago, and she has. Every week, she asks how my interpreter training classes are going, makes me teach her the sign for shut-up or good or bad. Ebony and Ivory, that's how she refers to us. "Thanks for giving me top billing," I tell her.

"Here, Miss Mouse," she says, offering me a massive golden apple.

"Thanks," I say, taking it. "Fuji?"

"Right ethnic group," she says, with a laugh. We polish our apples with paper napkins. "Mootsu, I think," she says. "Or Moomoo?"

She's a pistol, as she would say. Lives in the Bella Vista section of South Philly. Her husband, Rocco, is a truck driver whose weekly run out through Lancaster County takes him by an orchard he calls his Dutch Country Apple Detour. This time of year, he's in his glory and is happy to share the fruits of his detour with his wife and her co-worker.

When I bite into the apple, juice splatters all over my lips, and I reach for my napkin. Janis is also wiping the juice from her mouth. Her movement is like the sign for apple, so I show her the sign.

"Maybe that's where they got the idea for the sign," she says.

"Could be," I say. It took her a long time to grasp that interpreting spoken English into American Sign Language is not merely a letter-for-letter or even word-for-word translation.

"I know," she says, "part science and part art." She takes another bite. "I like the signs where your whole face gets into the act, sometimes your whole body," she says, with a mouth full of apple. "Like the way Italians talk."

"Like that sign for sharp-looking or spiffy?" I say.

Face contorted in an expression of either excruciating pain or exquisite pleasure, she purses her lips like Sophia Loren, raises her thumb and index finger to the right side of her mouth, and twists them outward.

"*Va bene,*" I say, surprised I remember any of the Italian that my classmate Nicole taught me in high school.

"I'm Italian by input only," she says, winking. She takes a last bite then drops the core into the wastebasket beside the desk.

"You and your Rocco," I say. "I've always loved that name."

"Of course, Anthony's a good name," she says, coyly. "Nothing funny about a name like that. One of my favorite saints too."

"It's nice enough," I say. I smile.

She winks at me, and I know she won't bother me about my romantic interest of the past six months until after his visit this weekend.

After lunch break, I pull the file for the woman who called in the morning. First time I dealt with an adult adoptee trying to get more information than we can give, Janis listened in. "In class," I told her, "we're always hearing about the ethics of interpreting for deaf people. How you don't intrude, even if you think it would help the deaf client."

"Don't get to put in your two cents?" Janis said.

"It's like a mortal sin."

"They must have seen you coming, Miss Mouse," she said.

"Not that I'd ever want to cross the line," I said.

She laughed. "And be more than a mouthpiece?" she said. "As if you needed telling."

When Grace Harris calls right at three, I try to sound confident. I've read the file and Janis's notes over and over, so, in a way, I feel like I know her. I look at the forms signed a lifetime ago by a woman who was younger at the time than her daughter and I are now.

She tells me all over again about coming back to Philadelphia for her father's funeral and realizing the extent of her mother's Alzheimer's. She repeats the story of a stranger stopping at the house the one day in fifteen years that Grace was out mowing the lawn. The woman was a friend of her parents from the old neighborhood.

"'Your parents were so happy the day they got you,' the woman told me," Grace says. "*Got* me?" she says.

I look at Janis across the way. She is finishing the paperwork for a couple that is a phone call and a letter away from welcoming a newborn into their home. I listen to Grace Harris struggle to stay on top of her tears. I study the names in shadowy typescript that I can know but she cannot. "I can tell you that your birth mother died within ten years of your birth," I say. "I'm so sorry."

The file includes two letters from Father Gerard Pellerin, a friend of the couple. I know that I cannot give her this information either, but I wonder about this couple with a priest for a friend. Gerard Pellerin was a seminarian when he wrote the first letter before Grace was born. I scan the other letter, written by him after he had become a priest, the last entry in her file prior to Janis's research. One sentence catches my eye: "If I may ever be of any service to this child, I will move mountains to help her and her parents." Such commitment. It is love for which he can never be thanked, love that the child is never to know of, let alone feel. I try to imagine being as bold as this priest. How far *would* he have gone to help his friends and their child?

"I intend to look under every rock I can find," Grace says in a grim voice. "It's my right to know, regardless of what you or anyone else says."

"God bless you," I say, knowing that I must sound like a hypocrite to her.

In class, I have no time to dwell on anything but the work at hand. Tonight, I am to be evaluated on the weakest part of my game, as Dad would put it, sign-to-voice interpreting. Watching a videotape of an elderly deaf man signing away in ASL, his fingers flying, I voice everything I can catch. When my performance is over,

I sit, staring at the frozen frame of the old man on the TV monitor and suddenly feel the full weight of the interpreting, the day's work at the agency, and the realization that Anthony is coming to our home for the weekend.

My classmates and instructor know that he is coming tomorrow night. I cannot hide my pride any more than my exhaustion.

"Go, girl," Flo Wright says, as the class breaks up.

We all met Anthony when he visited our third-semester class last fall. Ms. Owens knew him from her time at Gallaudet and arranged for him to come to Philly and talk to us about interpreting for deaf-blind people. When the class took a break, I escorted him to the cafeteria. Seated to his left at the best-lit table in the cafeteria, I finger-spelled and signed in his cupped left hand. We drank coffee and in five minutes were laughing like old friends. His eyesight is not completely gone yet, and I caught him checking me out after I'd given him the two-minute version of my life story. He's built like a linebacker, and I saw strength in his brown eyes, the kind of strength that a deaf farm boy from southern Virginia would need to get through the experience of gradually losing his sight. One good look into his eyes, and I knew this was a man who could handle whatever life threw his way.

When the class ended, he asked if his "new friend" could escort him to the cab that was waiting for him outside. He handed me his card, got me to write my email address on the back of another card, and told me he'd show me around if I visited Gallaudet some weekend. Two weeks later, I took the train down to Washington and stayed at the Sheraton closest to the campus. We walked around the campus and had pizza with two of his friends at The Rathskeller. By Sunday night when the cab came to take me to Union Station, I had told him more about myself than I'd told any boyfriend I ever had, and I felt like I'd known him for years. I felt like I knew who I was for the first time. Standing next to the cab, I kissed him, then pulled his thick left hand to me, slipped my hand inside his, and signed that I'd already made a reservation at the hotel for the following weekend. Now, after more Amtrak trips to D.C. than I can count, it's his turn.

Friday, at work, I'm a mess. Janis gives me space, knowing I'm anxious. At lunchtime, she drops the reddest Mac I've ever seen on my desk. I tuck it into my pocketbook. I eat lunch at my desk, filing as I go, so I can finish a half-hour early to get to the train station by five. When the phone rings, I quickly swallow my bite of sandwich and try not to sound agitated when I answer. It's Grace Harris again. "What can I do for you?" I say, knowing full well the woman wants me to do what I cannot do for her.

"With or without your help," she says, "I'll get to the bottom of this."

I've been on the receiving end of sarcasm and bitterness before but have never heard such anguished determination. I can think of nothing to say.

"It's not your fault," she says. "It's above you. In the Catholic Church, it's always above you, right?" She hangs up.

I throw out the rest of my lunch and clear my desk. I type and file like a terrier. At 4:15, Janis is standing in front of my desk.

"What?" I say.

"You look gorgeous, kiddo," she says. "Too good for this place. She makes that sign, flinging out her thumb and index finger, "*Perfetto*." Then she leans forward and turns off my desk lamp. "Now, get out of here."

*

I've come to associate 30th Street Station with an anxious feeling in the pit of my stomach. But ordinarily, I have something to do—running to the gate, riding down the escalator, looking for a seat on the train. Today, waiting upstairs for his train to arrive, the feeling overwhelms me. Hundreds of people surge to the top of the escalator and pour out across the floor. Finally, I see the top of his head. He's wearing his new jacket, holding a small suitcase in one hand and his long white cane in the other. Decked out and moving with confidence, he looks not much older than I am. I swoop in on him, hug and kiss him at the top of the escalator, and, as always, feel the eyes of dozens of people on us and get the kind of self-awareness that I imagine celebrities must get used to. My insides feel like they might burst with excitement. We stand there, signing to each other about his train ride, the surprisingly hot weather, and my parents. I am dying to bring him home to meet them, but standing here and holding him feels so good that I don't care if I ever move.

At dinner, I don't know who I'm more proud of, my parents or Anthony. We eat with all the dining room lights on. Anthony's the same humble yet amazing man I've seen work his magic with people in various social functions in Washington. Mom and Dad don't gush, but I can tell they're impressed. They ask him questions, and my hands get a workout. But their questions are smart and sensitive, and I hate myself for having worried about my parents embarrassing me. I can tell by Anthony's reactions that he thinks well of them.

When we're done eating, Dad asks Anthony through me if he'd like dessert right away.

Anthony makes the sign for full. I don't need to interpret for my parents.

"Fine," my father says.

"I feel like I'm back on the farm," Anthony signs. He pats his stomach.

"Anthony," my mother says, "I'm glad you liked it."

Flowing through me, the conversation moves more slowly than if he were hearing and sighted, but it feels like a real conversation, not some contrived exercise. Anthony asks my father about his work and his plans for retirement. Anthony's forehead is creased, like it was in the cafeteria when I told him about my brother's crib death. He's looking hard at Dad, moving his head a little bit this way and that, trying to get the best picture of my father that he can in this light. He's taking in as much as he can, waiting for whatever Dad might say next. Waiting and studying. This was the look that got me. His pauses, with that furrowed brow and those searching eyes, are more eloquent to me than some people's poems or prayers.

After lemon sherbet, Mom asks Anthony how he learned he had his eye condition. I've heard the story a dozen times now, so it's an easy sign-to-voice interpreting task. He was a nine-year-old at the residential school for black deaf kids in Virginia. A rare snowstorm sent all the kids and half of the dormitory staff out to a steep hill near the school to sled. His arms float before their eyes. He's breathing through his mouth, making little grunts, popping and whistling air as he acts out the ride down the snowy hill. My parents' eyes are locked onto his face and his flying hands. His hands and fingers become the sleds, the kids, the dorm counselors. His face mirrors the exhilaration of a child on a wild ride. He hoots and squeaks the sounds of the ride, the sounds of his excitement. Mom and Dad are right with him.

He tells of flying down the hill then slowing down and knowing he was near the flatter bottom of the hill. Then he crashed, picked himself up, didn't know what he'd run into. Mrs. Jefferson was wiping snow off him and off herself. She told him he had to be more careful and not to run into her again.

We all laugh.

"At the top of the hill," he signs, "the head of the dorm told me to be more careful. I head down again, pick up speed, crash into the same person."

My mother studies Anthony's face. My father winces.

"The teacher gave me a whack on the head, told me no more sledding today or tomorrow. When I got my sled to the top of the hill, Mr. Martin announced to all the kids that the next ride was the last for the day. I figured, what the heck, took off again. I felt myself going faster and faster. Thought I saw some people. Steered to the right. Then I hit the pine tree. It was small, not much more than a baby tree, but it didn't give an inch. The sled landed next to me, upside down. I felt blood all over my face. Had a lump the size of a baseball. Broke my nose and two fingers. A couple of black eyes. I looked like a raccoon who'd been clubbed. Next day, I saw doctors, had tests. Night blindness, they called it. It got worse over the years."

"Lord in heaven," my mother says.

Anthony laughs. "I got that last ride in, though," he says, clapping his large hands together.

My father nods.

"Progressive deterioration," Anthony fingerspells. "I was able to drive a car during the daytime until two years ago. Now, I'm in a hurry to do everything I can before it gets worse."

We stay at the dinner table, swapping stories. I've never interpreted so much in my life, but I know that I'm in the zone, as

Dad would say. I don't care that I'm doing work that any of my teachers would grade an A. It's a sense of efficacy that is almost intoxicating. A year ago, I knew the rudiments of ASL, but only could imagine doing this.

"Coffee would be great," Anthony says abruptly.

"A man who knows what he wants and ain't afraid to say it," Mom says, approvingly.

When Dad and I take some dishes into the kitchen and put on the coffee, he tells me how amazed he is at my signing.

"And Anthony?"

"Another strong one," he says, fixing his eyes on mine.

"I've never known anyone like Anthony," I say.

"When you do that signing," he says, "and his big hand's right there, all around your hand, going everywhere yours goes. Man, that's something."

I well up.

"Is it hard to tell where his hand leaves off and yours begins?"

"I never thought of it like that," I say, and feel myself flushing.

"You love your work," he says.

"Anthony's not work," I say. I brace myself, expecting the so-far unasked question about Anthony's age, but it doesn't come.

"It's good that you're getting to know each other better," he says, kissing my forehead. I know he's thinking about my fiasco with Ronald. I tell myself that I'm older, wiser.

When we finally decide to go to bed, I walk Anthony up to the second floor, past my room and my parents' room, to the guest room. I go back to signing without using any voice. I apologize for not sleeping together.

"No problem," he signs. "I didn't expect to. Not this visit."

I clamp his hand onto my right hand, press it to my stomach

and sign, "Sorry," larger and larger, trusting that it will impart the depths of my regret.

"I know where I can find you," he signs.

"The door's locked."

He holds the flat opened palm of his right hand up near his mouth and blows out hard as if he were blowing a feather or some insignificant problem right out of his hand.

I punch his arm.

He laughs, reaches around my waist, and pulls me to him. My mother walks by.

I punch him again and then kiss him. "I want to do the right thing," I tell him.

He pats his forehead. He understands.

In my bed, I cannot fall asleep, so I turn on the light. In my bag, I find the massive apple that Janis gave me along with a copy of *The Catholic Standard and Times.* I prop up my pillow and page through the weekly Catholic newspaper for Philadelphia. Per my plan, ten minutes of turning pages has me starting to feel sleepy. Scanning the reports of the comings and goings of clergy in the area, my eyes stop at the name Pellerin under a photo. The blurb mentions several posts in the South that Father Gerard Pellerin, formerly of Philadelphia, has held. In September, he will take over as director of a retreat center in Ohio. He's staying at St. Louise's parish until then. I study the small photo of the thin, slightly graying middle-aged man. Even if Grace Harris somehow picked up a copy of *The Catholic Standard and Times,* his name would mean nothing to her. So much moxie in that woman. All that determination, and she'll still run into that wall when she calls me again. I don't like being that wall. I can't figure this out, can't imagine how anyone could. I set the paper on the nightstand, get up, go to the bathroom, and take a Benadryl. I turn out the light and try to block everything out of my brain.

After the biggest breakfast I've had all year, Anthony and I go into the living room. He sits in Dad's ancient chair, and after positioning the lamp so that it shines on his lap, I sit to his left on one of the massive arms of the chair. I take him through the books of family photos that Mom pulled out for us, looking at my First Communion photos, the block party pictures, my prom pictures with Al Moseley, all of it.

He stops at a picture of my parents out in front of the house. "They don't scare me," he signs. "Not in pictures. Not in person."

"You don't scare them, either," I sign back.

"Can you handle this?"

I sign that I'm okay. I can handle it fine.

"Think you can keep up with me?"

"Yes, you big lug."

I put the albums away and take him down to the basement and into the garage. Dad's reorganizing his tools and hardware. He shows Anthony and me around.

"Just finished tuning up my heart-attack bike," he says. "Doctor says either I exercise and watch my diet or else."

I sign this to Anthony, and he nods, half-smiling.

Dad takes us to the tandem bicycle in the back of the garage. He puts Anthony's right hand on the handlebars, runs it along the top tube of the frame to the seat and then on to the second set of handlebars and seat.

"Oh," Anthony says, raising his eyebrows.

My father and I laugh.

"A bicycle built for two," Dad says, and I interpret. "I got a deal at the junk yard, fixed it up myself. Mom says it'll destroy the marriage. Won't go near it."

"So much for your heart," I say.

Dad laughs and says that she insisted on getting her own bike. He's waiting for the perfect bike to show up at a yard sale.

Anthony's feeling the contours of the bicycle seat. "We should try it," he signs.

Next thing I know, Dad's driving Anthony, me, and the two-wheeled monstrosity down to the Valley Green woods. In the car, I explain that there's an unpaved road along the Wissahickon Creek that horseback riders, joggers, and bicyclists use. "Forbidden Drive," I fingerspell.

He nods gravely but confidently.

"As long as you don't mind sharing the road with bikes and horses?"

He blows on his open hand again: a piece of cake for this guy.

Dad doesn't understand more than "Good Morning" in ASL, but I swear I catch him sneering. He takes us to the bottom of Bells Mill Road where it crosses Forbidden Drive. He gets the bike off the rack, shows us how we have to start and stop together then adjusts the handlebars and the seats for us. The thing weighs a ton.

"One gear fits all," Dad says. "Your mother would give me hell for sending you out without helmets and shoulder pads."

I sign this for Anthony and he laughs. Then he signs to Dad, and I interpret for him: "Our little secret."

"Give 'em Hell," Dad says. He gets back in the car, waves, and then heads up the hill. Anthony is already sitting on the back seat of the bicycle. I climb on, and we start pedaling down Forbidden

Drive toward Valley Green. Right away, we establish a steady rhythm, and in no time we are moving down the broad path along the tree-lined banks of the Wissahickon faster than I'd imagined this beast could go. We pass dog walkers, couples with kids in backpacks, pained-looking joggers. When we get to the waterfall and the covered bridge, I reach around behind me and tap Anthony on the chest. I make the sign for "Stop," giving him a karate chop against his chest. He makes a sound with his voice. It might be "Okay." I'm not sure if he's gotten the idea, and I'm ready to give him another little whack, but he slows his pedaling, and I use the handbrakes to bring us to a stop near the falls. We dismount, and I take Anthony to the fence line above the creek. I point out the falls to our left and the red wooden bridge on our right.

"The last covered bridge in Philadelphia," I sign.

He nods approvingly.

I haven't exercised like this in some time and am sweating profusely, but the breeze along the creek makes the idea of getting back on the bike almost inviting. We cruise by a kid who's chugging along on a mountain bike. He does a double take at us, lifts himself off his seat to get more power, but we pull away. I smile, thinking how I've never moved so fast on a bike. After a mile of flat riding, we reach a bit of an incline, but we push a little harder and climb the slight rise smoothly. The foot traffic gets heavy. I manage to steer clear of a group of horseback riders going the opposite way, but maneuvering becomes tricky because so many people are out for their Saturday exercise. Nearing Valley Green Inn, I steer to the extreme right to avoid the parking area traffic in front of the inn. Anthony slows his pedaling as if he's reading my mind. We pull to a stop at an empty bench in front of the inn.

I point out the ducks and the kids feeding them, the parking lot and the bridge across the creek. When we've caught our breath, we rise to remount. "You don't like the crowds here," he signs.

"Right," I sign.

"What about the regular road?" he signs, nodding toward the bridge.

I tell him that if we go up the hill, we'll have to deal with cars.

He brings the open palm of his right hand near his mouth and blows my concerns right out of his hand with one quick whoosh of air. No problem for him.

We mount the bike again and start pedaling. It's uphill, and the going is tough. There's no traffic ahead, so I weave back and forth across the road to make the grade more manageable. I raise myself out of my seat and strain on the pedals. I hear Anthony behind me grunting and can tell he's also standing to pedal. We slow to a stop.

I stand in place, twist around and sign in Anthony's hand that we're going to walk the bike the rest of the way up the hill. He too is sweating and panting, but I'm sure that he is not happy with this news. He signs something quickly that I don't catch. I'm sure it's nothing nice.

"What?" I ask him.

"Train gone," he signs.

We start walking the huge bike up the hill. At the top of the hill, we stop, and with his hand, he draws my face close to his. "We could have made it," he signs. "I didn't want to stop."

"Crazy!" I sign.

He huffs at me and starts pedaling again. We ride the level street to McCallum, turn right and head back toward Mount Airy.

On the McCallum Street Bridge, I catch a glimpse of the valley along Cresheim Creek below. If anything, it's not much more than a green blur down there for Anthony.

We're going at a faster speed than I'm comfortable with, but I figure the exercise is good for us. When I steal a glance behind, Anthony's got that look I see when he's running a class or when I'm trying to get him to consider ordering something different at a restaurant. We drive along the tree-lined streets in the west side of the neighborhood. Then we're on Wissahickon Avenue, a shoulderless road that runs parallel to Wissahickon Creek high on a ridge above it. When there is a break in the oncoming traffic, cars in our lane roar past us. I pull out of traffic at the top of Kitchen's Lane, and we nearly fall over. I squeeze the hand brakes, and Anthony stops pedaling. I stop the bike at the side of the road. A quizzical look has spread across his face. I explain that Wissahickon Avenue is not a good road for us to be on. He asks where the cross road goes.

"Back down to the creek," I sign. "It's steep."

He squints down the hill. "To Forbidden Drive?"

"Yeah," I sign. "But if we go down, we'll have to ride all the way back up or call my folks from the inn. We can turn back and ride home in ten minutes."

"Thought you were coming out of your shell," he signs.

I sigh. I remember this hill from the summer when I was twelve and rode my bike everywhere. The drop is probably about the same as the one that we climbed in Chestnut Hill, but it occurs in a shorter distance. The road ends at the bottom of the hill. I remember an old stone building and a small parking area right where the hill bottoms out. From there, one rocky trail splits to the left and down a ravine to a small bridge that spans the creek and leads back to Forbidden Drive; another goes off to the right, up another hill a short ways to Monastery Stables. Either way, you'd have to walk a bike like this over that rough terrain. I try to explain this to him.

He makes the sign for chicken.

I want to smack him. "I'm not twelve!" I sign.

He laughs.

I get the same feeling in my chest that I had when we took off our clothes together for the first time, on my second weekend trip to D.C. I hadn't exactly planned it, but there we were. I tell myself that this too will work out okay.

We start down. I wouldn't mind coasting all the way, but Anthony's churning away, so I let my legs fall in with his rhythm. After a hundred yards or so, we fly past the intersection where another road dead-ends into Kitchen's Lane. Now, there's no shoulder on either side of the road, just cobblestone water runoffs with unwelcoming trees and rocks lurking just behind them. It's like that as far down as I can see. I steer to the middle of the road. Anthony makes a little grunting sound with each stroke. I try braking but feel no difference. I squeeze harder on the handbrakes. Anthony's grunts are getting louder and closer to one another. I figure we're halfway down. Gripping the handlebar tightly with my right hand, I reach behind me with my left arm, find his shoulder and tap him twice.

"Whooooooo!" he yells.

It's funny, but it's not. The road curves a bit, and I have to grab the other side of the handlebar to steady the bike. A van rumbles up the hill toward us. I ease the bike to the right, careful not to go too far. When we speed past the van, Anthony lets out another whoop. I blink in the wind; tears build in my eyes. I see the stone building and the split in the road at the bottom of the hill coming to us at awesome speed. Half a dozen cars are parked alongside the rocky unpaved path down to the creek. I grip both hand brakes as hard as I can, but he's not slowing down. I swing my left hand around again and try to find his face. I miss, and the bike swerves to the left. I grab the handlebar just in time to straighten out.

Less than one hundred yards of road remain. I make sure the bike is going as straight as possible and then lash back with my left hand. I catch him in the nose, and he lets out a high-pitched squeal. For a moment, his pedaling eases up, and I squeeze the handbrakes with all my might. But then I realize that he has picked up the pedaling again. I can try a hard right turn onto the uphill path, but a minivan blocks the way. Or I can take the rocky path with the parked cars and the drop to the creek. A Ford pick-up truck is parked dead ahead. Anthony howls. I ball my left hand into a fist and hurl it straight back, catching him under the chin. I drop my feet to the ground and try to drag my heels against the macadam. They bounce up, but I put them down each time they bounce. He laughs again. I brake harder, but we're gaining speed. My eyes are nearly closed by the rush of wind. I scream some wordless sound. We're on the gravel at the end of the road. I move right to avoid a tree, but we crash through a clump of bushes. Steering between the truck and a boulder, I hit a rock. We skid on the gravel and dirt and plow right through another clump of bushes. The bike goes right, and I go left. I break my fall with my left hand then land on my rear. "*Je-sus*!" I cry out.

My index finger is bent at an unnatural angle and feels like someone's broken it off. I feel a bruise on my forehead. Both of my legs are scraped and bleeding. Anthony's sprawled a few feet behind me, still laughing. He looks like he's fallen off the end of a couch. On the ground next to the tree, the bike faces up the hill. The front wheel spins slowly. I look at my tilted-back index finger. When I wiggle the other fingers, they move like they're supposed to move. They don't point backwards inflexibly like the index finger. I start to feel woozy.

"Rosalie!" Anthony calls.

I breathe in through my nose, out through my mouth.

"Rosalie!"

I touch my forehead with my right hand, feel the lump. There's not much bleeding there. My finger hurts more with every passing second. I look at the bicycle again. The wheel has stopped spinning. I take the finger with my good hand, secure it at the base and snap it forward. "Damn!" I scream. I feel like I'm going to faint. I take in a long breath then blow it out slowly.

I feel his hand touch my shoulder. He's next to me on the ground now. He's stopped laughing. I feel his hand move down my right arm to the fingers, then back up to my neck, my chin, nose, cheeks, and eyes. He feels his way across my forehead until he comes to my lump. Gingerly, he touches the edges of the welt. I'm shaking. He inches his way down my left arm, past the elbow, down to my wristwatch, over the back of my hand and stops at the base of my index finger. His hand stays there. I bring my right hand under his and sign, "Broken."

"Damn!" he cries out and signs at the same time. He makes a fist with his other hand and pounds it into his leg.

"Bastard," I mutter.

He settles beside me. I feel him the length of me. He leans his weight against my right side, nudging me an inch to the left.

Then he stops, wraps his left arm around my shoulder and rests his hand there.

I look at my hurt hand. It's cupped, like the letter C, resting on my left knee.

"Okay?" he says and signs. He squints at my face.

My finger throbs with pain, hurts more now than before I tried to move it back into place. Anthony's other hand is in his lap, fidgeting. He closes it, moves it toward my broken finger. He places it under my hand so that mine is resting on his. My hand is warm, throbbing. Below it, I feel the roughness of his knuckles, the ridges of his school ring. I feel the thick vein on the top of his hand. The hand under mine is still and cold. I lean back, away from him, propping myself up with my good hand. The palm of my right hand presses against the cool dirt and gravel. I have no trouble telling where that hand ends and the ground begins or where my hurt hand ends and where his hand begins. The ground beneath me is hard, unyielding. My fingers dig in the dust. The ground feels no more a part of me than the cold, meaty hand beneath mine. I see myself slowly rising, testing my legs, walking away. I close my eyes and breathe as evenly as I can.

"What on earth?" Janis gasps, standing up from her desk as I limp into the office, sporting bandages on my forehead and knee and a splint on my broken finger.

"It was a full weekend," I say, managing a smile. "You've got to be very careful just who you ride a bicycle with." I drop my pocketbook and lunch bag on my desk.

She's standing in front of my desk with her mouth agape, a look of horror on her face. "Is he hurt this bad?" she says.

"I think he'll get over his wounds."

"Do you want to talk about it?" she says.

I shake my head. "Not today," I say, wincing as I sit in my desk chair.

She asks if she can get something for me, and if I'm sure I want to work today.

I arrange my desktop and slide my lunch bag to the side. "I need this job until I graduate," I say. "Not going to let this throw me off any more than it has."

"Well, Miss Attitude," she says, stepping over to her desk. "That mean we're still on for lunch?"

I nod.

"Hey," she says. "How you gonna sign at class tonight with your hand all wrapped up?"

"It's visual language-to-spoken language interpreting tonight," I say. "Somebody else signs, and I say what they're signing."

"Don't lose your voice," she says, "or you'll be down to ESP."

"If I didn't lose it this weekend, I'm not worried," I say. We finally get started with our work for the day. I'm sure that Grace Harris will call sometime this morning, but she doesn't. I pace myself but make good progress with my work. Occasionally, I see myself at the E.R., telling Dad to drive Anthony to the station. There has been an ache in my stomach since the crash, but I have not cried, not even when I explained everything to Mom and Dad, nor when Anthony tried to convince me he should stay the rest of the weekend. I kissed his cheek and thanked him for showing me something about strength. He looked confused.

At lunch, Janis talks about her weekend's worth of gardening and about the movie she, Rocco, and their youngest saw Saturday night.

When she's out at the ladies' room, I get the information I need. A truly brave person would wait for Janis to return, then call Grace Harris and tell her everything she doesn't know. And then a principled person would turn in her resignation. I'm not there yet, but I am feeling a little stronger. At three, I tell Janis that I need to move around to keep my legs from getting too stiff. I find a pay phone around the corner. Call St. Louise's and ask for Father Pellerin. As I hoped, he's not there and I get his answering tape. "Father Pellerin," I say. "Please call Grace Harris." I leave her phone number and hang up. They may stumble around in the dark for a while, but in the end they'll put two and two together. They may even figure out who made the call.

What I've done is not enough to make me feel brave or principled. But at least, they'll know the truth about each other. And that's the least I can do with my newfound strength. "*Perfetto,*" I say, making that sign.

A Private Gig

After dealing with the emergency call to fix a leak in the Castellano's laundry sink, Jimmy Sweeney dropped Kevin off at his baseball game. On his way home he stopped at Todd's Fret Not Shop and bought a new set of strings for his bass. Mary was upstairs, yelling at the teenagers to get their rears in gear. He knew Fats would pick him up at one, so he thought it might be a good idea not only to restring his bass but also to spend a few minutes practicing before the gig. But a Mary Teresa Sweeney, who was on the warpath and who knew he was going back out again in half an hour for the rest of Saturday, could not be ignored.

"These new guitar strings can wait here on the kitchen table," he said, loud enough for his wife to hear from the second floor, "while I strangle those lazy teenage morons who are making life difficult for their sainted mother."

He took the stairs with a heavy foot. She was waiting for him at the second floor landing, her red hair tied up in a green and gold bandana, yellow rubber gloves up to her elbows.

"You can forget that lot," she said, pointing a yellow finger down the hall. "And your strings. And anything else you've a mind to do, except Jennifer's bicycle, *which* you were supposed to have fixed last night."

"Oh, Jesus," he said.

"*He* won't help you," she said. "And I don't see any of your worthless pals lining up to fix the poor child's tire or to do any of a dozen other things that the children's father ought to be doing on a fine June Saturday like this."

He leaned toward her cheek and puckered his lips, but she pulled back and swung into the bathroom. A bucket filled with sudsy water sat on the floor. The curtains had been taken down. The sink was filled with cleanser.

"Ah, don't get your Irish up," he said.

She dropped to her knees. "And don't you be bringing the land of my birth into it," she said. She started scouring the tile floor.

"A na-tion once a-gain!" he bellowed.

She turned and made a face. "Flat," she said. "Like the tire on your daughter's bicycle."

"I'm a bass player, not a singer, but bathrooms make anybody sound better."

"Better than what?" she snorted, going back to her scrubbing. "And with all the time you spend in people's bathrooms, I hope you don't get a notion that you're Mr. Pavarotti. Imagine, a plumber who thinks he can sing."

"Never mind. What's with the teenage mutants?"

"I'm done with them, Jimmy. I've moved on to something else on my list. *As* you can see."

He walked down the hall to Kerry and Tyrone's room. "What's all this?" he yelled from the doorway.

Tyrone, in his underwear, sat on top of a pile of laundry that had been dumped on the floor, while his older brother lolled, half-sitting, in his bed.

"What's all what?" Tyrone mumbled.

"I have no idea what you're doing," Jimmy said. "Sitting there like that. No idea at all."

Tyrone rolled his eyes.

"And you," Jimmy said, turning to Kerry.

"I'm waking up," he said. "I'm just moving slow."

"Slow?" Jimmy said. "People on slabs at the morgue move faster than you."

"Dad."

"Jesus F. Christ. Your mother and I have been up and at it for hours. Even Kevin and Jennifer are out leading productive lives. I only pray to God they don't turn into this shiftless species when they become teenagers."

"Dad," Tyrone said. "Kevin *is* a teenager."

"A technicality," Jimmy said, walking to the side of Kerry's bed. "When I was a lad, my father woke us up every morning with a whack across the head with the newspaper. 'Wake up,' he'd say. 'Life is hard. Move.'"

"Whatever," Kerry said.

"What do you want, Dad?" Tyrone said. "What?"

Jimmy walked to the doorway, closed the door, and turned back to the boys. "Wearing clothes instead of sitting on them would be a good start," he said.

"We'll do the room," Kerry said.

"Before you leave it. Right?"

They nodded.

He returned to Kerry's bedside and picked up a sweat sock

from the floor with the tip of his index finger. "Christ, you won't see the damn floor for hours." He dropped the sock and sat on the side of the bed. "Listen," he said, lowering his voice. "Fix your sister's bicycle now, and I'll give you until tomorrow to finish the room."

"'Til tomorrow night?" Tyrone asked.

"'Til two p.m."

They glanced at each other, then nodded sullenly.

Jimmy told them where to find the flat kit. "And look that bike over like it belongs to Mario Andretti," he said, "and you're the pit crew."

"Michael Andretti," Kerry said.

"Any goddamn Andretti," Jimmy growled. "But do it now. Right now."

Jimmy rushed down to the basement and hauled his amp to the front door. Then he plopped down on the recliner and started restringing his bass. The G-string had been on for a year. It hadn't wanted to stay in tune the last time he played, so it probably wouldn't make it through another gig. Beyond all odds, the E-string had lasted three years. The other two had come from a separate set. He couldn't remember the last time he'd put on a whole set of new strings. He'd treated himself to GHS Boomers.

The boys shuffled down the stairs. "*Before* you eat your Frosted Flakes," he said. Kerry muttered something about being old enough to drink in certain countries, but they went to the basement. Jennifer and her friend Melissa wandered in and sat on the couch across from him. "What are you two up to?" he asked.

"Nothing," Jennifer said.

"We're bored," Melissa said.

"Bored?" he said. They watched him working on the strings.

Please God, he thought, *don't let them decide to go for a bike ride.* "Why don't you have a catch or something?" he said.

"Too hot," Jennifer said. "Mom said to remind you that you're supposed to go to a shower or something at the rectory before that Fats guy comes."

"*Fix* a shower," he said. "Christ. That priest called again."

"She said something about your tithing."

"*Her* tithing," he said. "Might as well be mine. They'll just have to take baths this weekend."

"Why do you call him 'Fats'?" Jennifer said. "Did he lose a lot of weight one time?"

Jimmy dropped the old G-string on the couch and began putting the replacement on. "I don't know, Jennifer." He wound the string, stopping short of over-tightening it. "Maybe he was huge in a past life," he said, reaching for the last new string. It was a beaut, nothing like the cheap crap that it was replacing.

"Your candy salesman is out front, Jimmy," Mary called from upstairs. "He can't find a parking place."

"Jesus," he said. "He's early."

"Candy salesman?" Jennifer said. The girls looked at each other.

"He sells it *wholesale,*" he said. "And he hates children." They ran out front to test their luck anyway.

"Forget about the bicycle, Jimmy," Mary said.

"Nearly done, hon," he said. "The boys'll finish it." Fats tooted the horn three times, and Jimmy packed up the bass.

"You're going to be late," Mary said. "Do you want me to come down and throw together a lunch for you?"

"Thanks," he said. "No." Two more honks. "Damn," he said. "My clothes." He ran upstairs to his closet and pulled out the slacks he used for performing and a decent short sleeve button up shirt.

Mary was waiting in the hallway at the top of the stairs. She wrapped her arms around his neck and hugged him. "Play nice," she said.

He ran his arm around her waist and patted her hip.

"Don't go getting yourself all excited now," she said.

"I'll see *you* when you're better dressed," he said, winking.

"I was better dressed this morning, but yourself was off in dreamland. I couldn't wait all morning for you to wake up."

"Damn," he said.

"I'll see *you* when *you're* better dressed, mister."

The horn blared.

"At least for once, you don't have to drive," she said.

"Don't you murder any family members while I'm gone," he said. He gave her a quick kiss and ran downstairs.

He lugged his amp out to the van that Fats had double-parked. The girls were nowhere in sight. No doubt, they had moved on after finding out there'd be no candy from this candy man.

"Nice van," he said.

"It's a friend's. I got him a bunch of candy and shit for his kid's party. He let me have it for the weekend." Fats took off his sunglasses and placed them on the dashboard. Then he popped open the rear gate and stepped outside the van. "I'll give you the nickel tour," he said.

He pointed out the features of the borrowed van while Jimmy hoisted his amp into the rear next to the speaker columns. "Wire rimmed wheels," Fats said.

"What, are you Vanna White?" Jimmy asked.

"This is the real shit."

Fats looked respectable. White polo shirt, nice jeans, tennis shoes. Other than his receding hairline, he looked like he had the first time Jimmy played music with him at somebody's high school graduation. For all the beer he'd been around, and now all the candy, he didn't have a trace of a beer gut like everybody else their age. Wiry, in a non-athletic way. "How's he get away with it?" Jimmy asked Mary once.

"He can't forever," she said, as confident as if she'd studied the subject in college. "His will be there when he turns fifty, guaranteed. Maybe sooner. A great hideous thing will bloom in all its glory."

"But it all goes through him," Jimmy said.

"No," she said, shaking her head. "All those pints are lined up inside him somewhere, waiting like the troops on D-Day. They'll storm their beachhead."

Fats was checking out his hair in the side mirror, running a comb through it. He turned around and pulled out a cigarette. "Washed and waxed, baby," he said, running his hand on the finish. "Got the kid who loads stuff for me to do it this morning. Gave him a couple boxes of candy I got on an over order."

"Nice," Jimmy said. He fetched the bass from the house and then fit it in between some of Fats's drum cases. Fats had gotten back in the driver's seat that he had down in the lounge position. He was lying back, a pair of sunglasses perched on his nose. "Cruise control, Jimmy," he said. "It'll spoil you."

Jimmy hung his clothes next to Fats's on the hook beside the middle seat.

"Automatic windows," Fats went on. "You don't have them on your van. Do you?"

"Or on Jennifer's goddamn bicycle," Jimmy muttered.

"What?"

"That automatic shit's just something else that'll break down," Jimmy said, jumping in beside Fats.

"You got to think bigger than that, Jimmy." Fats sat up and started the ignition. Then Jimmy's window dropped down halfway.

"Just don't adjust my seat for me," Jimmy said.

On the expressway, Fats told Jimmy that now he couldn't say that he'd never done anything for him. Fats was letting Jimmy ride shotgun, letting him watch the scenery. They listened to the oldies station, and Fats complained about having to deal with people who like candy.

"You hate kids," Jimmy said.

"Not all kids," Fats said. "Just the ones who like candy and the people who sell it directly to them. I try to stay a level away from the kids."

"All kids like candy," Jimmy said. "Besides, they pay your mortgage."

"Fair compensation," Fats said. He hit a button, and both windows shot up. He turned on the air conditioner. "So, how's the Irish lass?" he said.

"The Terrible Beauty. She's great. She was hard charging today, though." Jimmy was surprised that Fats had asked about her. He rarely brought up the topic of wives.

"So what was she so steamed about?" Fats said.

"What else," Jimmy said. "The teenagers."

"What did they do? I know what they didn't do—anything you want them to do."

"At thirteen they turn into another species. Up all hours of the night. Asleep all morning."

"Nocturnal."

"Yeah. They root around in your food, make a mess. They're pretty much raccoons."

Fats pulled onto the expressway part of Route 202. He'd told Jimmy on the telephone that this job was way down in Chester County. Saturday afternoon traffic was heavy.

"Raccoons got those claws or whatever so they can get into trash cans and shit?" Fats said.

"Oppositional thumbs. Great fucking dexterity. They turn on lights and then disappear."

"So, you go through light bulbs like crazy?"

"We get those light bulbs from the blind. They come with a million year guarantee. Not in my house."

"I barter with a guy for all kinds of light bulbs," Fats said. "Cindy wanted to do that blind people deal, but I nixed it."

"Blind people and light bulbs," Jimmy said. "I don't get it."

"They don't make them. They just sell them."

"I still don't get it," Jimmy said. After they covered the blind light bulb stuff, Fats didn't seem to want to talk about anything. This was fine with Jimmy. Usually the guy sprawled on the passenger side of Jimmy's van either sleeping or complaining about the rattle of the wrenches and pipes. Jimmy had known Fats for most of his life, played music with him, gotten drunk with him, but that was it. They'd never been over to each other's house for dinner or anything, never talked about much besides music, other local bands or clubs. Fats was married and had no kids; other than that, Jimmy knew little about him. Jimmy asked about the gig, and Fats repeated what he'd said on the telephone. It was like a wedding, but it wasn't a wedding. Rich people.

Jimmy let him drive and listened to the radio. He recognized some places they passed from having driven the family to Longwood Gardens once. Another of Mary's outings. Each ball game or Stallone movie he dragged Mary to cost him one family trip. He leaned his head against the window and closed his eyes.

A grunting sound startled his eyes open. He had not thought he was tired enough to doze off.

"Enough beauty sleep?" Fats asked.

Jimmy's neck was stiff. He stretched his head one way and then the other. Rolling countryside flew by. They had obviously turned off 202.

"We still in Pennsylvania?" Jimmy asked.

"That's the town we're looking for," Fats said, pointing to a sign ahead. He pulled the van into the right lane.

They were three miles from some place Jimmy had never heard Fats or anybody else mention. "Avondale?" he said. "You said we were going to Hillsomething, wherever that is."

"First, we're going to the Avondale Diner," Fats said.

"You hungry, Fats?"

"A gig this time of day, you eat when you can."

"I thought they were supposed to feed us."

"Yeah, but on a gig day you eat when you can. Right?" Fats launched into one of his sermons. Bottom line, the patrons would give the band something to eat. But Fats said there was no telling when these rich people would get around to it. Jimmy had to agree with Fats about eating when they could.

"Besides," Fats said. "That's where we're meeting the other guys."

Jimmy only got five or six calls a year anymore, and Fats and he never rehearsed. No time. For over twenty-five years they had been a rhythm section, drums and bass. The other musicians they played with came from a stable of about six or eight guys.

Playing with Fats was predictable. They had joked that they were like Steve Carlton and Tim McCarver. They avoided talking about who was the Hall of Fame lefty and who was his journeyman catcher. Once in a while Fats would bring in a new face. Any new guy brought along some surprises. And now, in some country diner, Jimmy was about to meet the band du jour.

"As long as they know what key we're playing in," he said.

"The diner's supposed to be down the road from a garden supply place," Fats said. "And that looks like our garden joint."

"Whatever," Jimmy said. *Great,* he thought. Now he was starting to sound like his teenagers.

Fats pulled into a gravel lot and found a parking spot between a pickup truck and a Honda.

"There's Tink's car," Jimmy said. "So we're Driftwood then? I thought this was more like a wedding."

"Well, it's not a wedding. I don't do weddings. That's the one place I draw the fucking line."

"I know it's not a wedding," Jimmy said. "Maybe it's for somebody's divorce. I don't really give a shit. It's a gig."

Opening the van door, Jimmy felt sick from the heat. He knew the gig was outdoors, but he hoped there would be some shade at least. Tink was leaning against a newspaper box outside the entrance, sweat beaded on his brow. He took a long draw on his cigarette then dropped it and ground it into the gravel. "'Bout fucking time," he said.

Fats looked at his watch. "Sunny spring day like this and you can't enjoy a cigarette?" Fats said. "Two fucking minutes late, and he complains. Jesus."

"How's it going?" Jimmy said to Tink.

"Hey," he said. "How's it going?"

Jimmy hadn't seen Tink since he'd shown up for some stupid karaoke night at Gilhooley's around Christmas time. They hadn't played together in a year. Tink opened the door for Fats and Jimmy. "You buying, Fats?" Tink asked.

"Fat chance," Fats said.

Tink followed Jimmy and Fats into the diner. The air conditioning felt good. They stood by the counter, checking out the dining area. Finally, Fats nodded toward a corner booth. "That's them," he said. "The other guys."

The two guys in the booth were about half their age. One of them looked like the young Peter Frampton. The other one sported a shaved head, three earrings in his left ear, and all black clothing. "Jesus F. Christ," Jimmy muttered.

"Fats," the long-haired blonde guy said, smiling at him. He made a fist in the air like Dennis Hopper in *Easy Rider* and kept nodding his head.

"Keith," Fats said to Frampton, "this is the guy who'll be playing bass today."

Jimmy shook his hand. "Jimmy Sweeney," he said.

"Keyboards," Frampton said.

"Tink here plays lead guitar," Fats said.

"Hey," Tink said, reaching for the guy's hand.

"Albert plays guitar," Fats said.

"Cool," Tink said. They all shook hands again. Tink was nodding like Frampton, his little ponytail bobbing behind his bald top.

Fats went to get the waitress to bring him a chair. Meanwhile, Tink sat next to Keith, and Jimmy climbed in beside Albert. Everybody started sizing up everybody else. Jimmy wondered if the hippies had figured Tink for a middle-aged wanker. They already had some take on Fats. Who knew what these two characters made of him. Maybe they thought he was the fifth Beatle or something.

"I'm a plumber," he said. "Tink's a roofer."

"In my trade we got a saying," Tink said, stretching out his arms expansively. "Only two things you got to know. Water runs downhill and payday's Friday."

Keith looked at Tink like he was speaking Russian. Albert stared with his mouth open. "Cool," he said, finally.

Jimmy pictured these two sitting on a curb with the other freaks down on South Street, panhandling. "You guys do music full-time?" he asked.

They shook their heads.

"You got day jobs?" Tink said.

"Yeah," Frampton said.

"Sometimes," Albert said.

Jimmy studied the two of them. He might not be giving them enough credit. He tried to imagine them doing some sort of job, but all he could picture was them yawning behind the counter at one of those video stores, like the morons at the place up on the avenue who gave you that snotty look if you pronounced some foreign word all wrong.

Fats returned with a waitress and a straight chair. When he pulled in next to Jimmy and Tink, the waitress passed out menus to the three new arrivals.

Jimmy decided on the burger platter. Tink ordered meat loaf. The hippies asked for salads and omelets. Jimmy had figured they wouldn't order anything that breathed or walked around on legs. He would have bet the house on it.

"An omelet like that would be awful good with bacon," he said, looking right at Albert.

The bald kid shrugged.

"Miss?" Jimmy said, waiting for the waitress to look at him. "Do you have bacon?"

"We got bacon, ham, and sausage."

"And sausage," he said. "Bingo. You wouldn't have scrapple, would you?"

"Scrapple?" she said. "We might have some. Sometimes it's a special." She called out to a guy at the kitchen door. He yelled back that they did have it.

"What do you think, boys?" Jimmy said, smiling at the new guys. Frampton gave him a withering look. The face of the kid in black was as red as a steak in the freezer.

"Not on my account," Frampton said to the waitress.

Jimmy turned to Frampton's partner. "How you supposed to decide? They got your four basic breakfast food groups, Al." The bald kid looked down at his menu, even though he'd already finished ordering. Jimmy turned back to Frampton. "What'll it be?"

He flashed Jimmy the same dirty look. "Home fries," he said as if he were saying, "Fuck you." Then he turned to the waitress and said sweetly, "Home fries." Fats ordered a piece of strawberry rhubarb pie and coffee. The waitress walked off with the orders, and Fats announced that he was going to take a leak and then make a phone call. He disappeared around the other end of the dining room.

The waitress brought waters and set-ups. Frampton looked out the window. His buddy with the shaved head closed his eyes. Probably meditating, Jimmy figured. He checked out the rest of the customers, relieved that for once Tink didn't feel obligated to make small talk. The food arrived all at once.

"Ketchup?" Frampton said, looking over at Jimmy and Tink. Jimmy nodded and Frampton slid the ketchup bottle over to him. "So, you guys have been The Groovetones for some time, huh?" Frampton asked.

Jimmy looked at Tink to see if he wanted to answer the question, but Tink was giving Jimmy the same look, so he figured that since he went back the farthest with Fats, he probably should pick up the ball.

"I can't remember exactly when we were The Groovetones. We were The Fulltones for a while. You know, Fats's last name is Fuller. We were The Groovetones before we were the Groovetown Three. That's what we called ourselves after Richie Glover moved to Baltimore and there was only the three of us."

The two young guys looked like they were eager to hear more.

"We were going to be The Brushmen," Tink said. "You know, Fats Fuller and the Brushmen? But Fats thought it sounded too much like The Bushmen, and people might think we were an old R and B group."

"So, what kind of music were you playing?" Albert said.

Tink and Jimmy looked at each other again.

"Well," Jimmy said. "Before Tink started playing with us, when we had Tony Napoli and Ricky Miller, we played hard rock as Bent Elbow Room. We did bars and clubs mostly. I remember playing one bar mitzvah. The same group of us had a few outings as a country and western group, West River Drive, back in the late seventies. Mostly we've been Driftwood."

"Seventies stuff with some Jimmy Buffet thrown in," Tink added. "Fats's philosophy is be ready for anything. Says he keeps up his circus chops just in case he gets a call when Ringling Brothers comes to town. Wedding music's the only thing he'll turn his damn nose up at. That leaves an awful lot of music."

The two guys nodded. Jimmy couldn't figure how all this was hitting them.

"Weren't you and Fats The Driftwoods for a while?" Tink asked him.

"Only two or three times. Fats thought there was a lot of money to be made in bluegrass. He played banjo a little. Terrible. I think he was sick of lugging his drum kit all over East Bumfuck."

Tink laughed, and Jimmy started laughing, too. He thought he saw Albert smile for a moment.

"Drums are a pain in the ass," Frampton said.

They all nodded. Jimmy ate some of his hamburger. It was good, not overcooked like most restaurants did it. He asked Frampton for the ketchup again and put some on the rest of his fries.

"Anybody need salt?" Frampton said.

Tink reached for the salt container.

First the ketchup, now the salt. It wasn't enough to make Jimmy want to invite Frampton over for dinner, but he had to admit the bastard had manners.

"Albert and me used to be in punk bands together," Frampton said.

"Any we'd have heard of?" Tink asked.

"Probably not," Albert said. "Well, maybe The Magic Johnsons."

"Are you kidding me?" Jimmy said, his mouth full of food. He swallowed, so he wouldn't choke while stifling the laughter. "The Magic fucking Johnsons?"

"That's what the man said," Tink said. "Didn't you hear him?"

"Jesus," Jimmy said, the laughter finally getting the best of him. The two kids smiled, like somebody'd just patted them on the back. Tink kept eating.

Frampton said he'd played jazz in high school then was in a

salsa band. Hip hop was cool. They hated alternative, but they'd play it.

Fats reappeared and asked if they'd gotten the check yet.

"No," Tink said.

Fats ate a few bites of his pie. When he finally caught the waitress's eye, he signaled for the check.

Jimmy pulled out a ten, and the others followed suit, each laying their ten in the middle of the table.

"We should get change," Frampton said.

When the check came, Fats took it and snatched up the tens. "I'll leave the tip," he said. "And I'll start a beer kitty with the change."

"So, who are we today?" Tink asked Fats.

"Climate Control Board," Fats said, as if it was the only possible answer to the question. "I got set lists in the van," he said. "And the directions. Just follow me."

The little caravan worked its way down winding roads. Jimmy was sure they must be close to Maryland or Delaware. He asked to see the set lists, but Fats said they were buried in the middle of one of his hardware bags. Jimmy figured it was time to grab the rest of his nap, so he let himself drift off.

The van's bouncing and lurching pulled him out of his sleep. He saw that they were now on a rough dirt road and asked Fats if it was somebody's farm.

"It's a gentleman's farm," Fats said.

"As opposed to a farmer's farm?"

These were not farmers according to Fats. They were all very upper crust and were part of some division of the army or reserves.

"*Our* army?" Jimmy said.

Fats laughed. "First Brigade," he said. "Or First Cavalry, or Troop, or something. They go back to like George Washington or the Civil War. I don't know."

"F-Troop," Jimmy said. They saw some horses grazing in a pasture and then more fields. So far, he'd seen no cows, pigs, or anything else one might expect to find on a farm run by someone who was not a gentleman.

"I think they're part of the National Guard or something," Fats said. "They like an excuse to dress up and ride horses."

"My cousin was in the National Guard," Jimmy said, "but they never let him ride a goddamn horse."

"This outfit don't recruit in neighborhoods like yours, Jimmy. They're horsemen, like knights."

"What's that make us? The court jesters?"

"The guy I've dealt with is fine. A decent guy."

"Do the hippies know they're playing for the Seventh Cavalry?"

Fats grunted.

"That skinhead behind us is probably part Indian," Jimmy said. "He ain't going to like this, playing for the fucking cavalry."

"He'll be cool."

The dirt road brought them to a hilltop from where they could see people and horses down in the valley below. Rolling hills and fenced pastures containing horses flanked both sides of the road. It was like National Geographic pictures of Kentucky that Jimmy had seen in Al's barbershop. "Just like my neighborhood," he said. "Minus the rowhouses and crack dealers."

"You got crack dealers on your block?"

"No, I'm shitting you," Jimmy said. "They're at least a block or two away from us."

"Fucking city," Fats said.

They continued down the road past two large colonial houses and a series of ancient barns and outbuildings. The private road ended at another large house with a wrap-around porch. A barn and a carriage house stood nearby, and inside the huge open doors of the carriage house Jimmy saw a half dozen buggies and sleighs. "They got their very own village here," he said.

"Pretty nice," Fats said.

Cars were parked between the buildings, mostly Mercedes and BMWs. A couple of guys who looked like they ought to be shopping up in Chestnut Hill ambled by. "So, where's the womenfolk?" Jimmy asked. "These guys aren't going to dance with each other. Are they?"

"They'll be here. First, the guys do their little competition. You know, riding and jumping and shit. Then they eat and party. I guess the women are watching their beaus right now. They'll be here for the festivities."

"Maybe they're all out buying gingham down at the general store."

Fats snorted.

"What the fuck is gingham, anyway?"

"Shut up."

They parked behind the main building, and Fats immediately disappeared inside. He returned in a couple of minutes with a sunburned man of about thirty who had a chin that wouldn't quit and a smile to match. His starched white shirt and khaki pants had a military look to them. He gave Jimmy a powerful handshake, a pat on the back, and the smile that he must have ordinarily saved for long lost prep school buddies.

Tink introduced himself when the smiling guy offered his

hand. The freaks, in sunglasses, stood by the side of their car and waved to the guy. They can't be stoned, Jimmy told himself, not this early in the day.

The host told them where they should set up for the gig and showed them the corner of the house that they could use as a green room. He seemed pleased that he had called it that, like he was now a member of whatever secret fraternity he thought musicians belonged to. Then another guy, endowed with the same square chin, popped in and asked if Hank, the hearty guy, could help with something. The new guy's plaid shirt was soaked through with sweat, and he was panting like a plumber's apprentice on his first day of work. The chins left, and the band started the load-in. Following the first chin's instructions, they set up on the big porch on the other side of the house, overlooking a grassy slope. Two white tents set up on either side of the porch and a swimming pool maybe thirty yards straight out formed the boundaries around an abundant space for a large audience.

The plaid shirt guy reappeared and asked if they needed sodas or anything. The hippies asked for diet Pepsi. Jimmy noticed that Fats seemed to warm up a few degrees every time plaid shirt or the first chin appeared. Otherwise, he was his usual miserable self.

The setup had Jimmy in the back line next to Fats, and that was fine with him. They put Tink on the left side of the front line and Frampton and Baldy on the right. They positioned the P.A. columns at either end of the front line on the edges of the porch. Fats's little monitors sat on the floor in front of them. The cavalry were going to present some awards at seven, using the band's P.A. system. Then they'd start eating and drinking, and the band would do the first of three sets. They started a sound check at five-thirty and were done by quarter to six.

The green room was a little library in the back of the house with a bathroom off to one side. Brass fixtures. Beautiful stuff. Probably the original work. A couch and several straight chairs were positioned about the green room. The band brought in their clothes and gear and then settled down for the wait.

Tink broke out a bottle of something and sat on the couch admiring it. Finally, Frampton couldn't stand it any longer and asked what it was.

"Corn liquor," Tink said. He winked. "Moonshine. My birthday present from Fats."

"Store bought," Fats said. "Not quite the genuine article, but it's got a kick. Have a taste, Tink."

Jimmy was surprised to hear him say this. Fats never allowed drinking until at least the second set.

"It'll be good for you," Fats said. "Just don't get any on your clothes."

Fats's generosity also surprised Jimmy. Tink was married to Fats' wife's sister, so Jimmy figured the candy man had dug down somewhere deep inside and found a reason to be nice to the jerk.

Tink unscrewed the cap and took a sip from the bottle of clear liquid. "Hot damn," he wheezed. He kind of snorted and then took another pull on the bottle. "They got an open bar going out there in those tents," he went on, "but you can bet your ass they ain't serving nothing like this shit."

There was a knock at the door. Tink recapped the bottle and slipped it into the bag at his feet. The first chin guy came in and asked if they were all right.

"Just relaxing," Fats said, "so we'll be sharp."

Food, the guy said, would be ready a little after they started the first set, so they'd get fed during the first break. "Do you need anything?" he said. "Anything at all?"

"I noticed a telephone in the kitchen," Fats said. "Could I make a call?"

The chin said he'd be delighted to take Fats to the phone. When they headed down the hallway, Jimmy closed his eyes and rested his head on the sofa cushions.

He heard Fats coming back up the hall and opened his eyes in time to see him put a pitcher of lemonade and five glasses on the table.

"Cool," Albert said. They all reached for glasses and Fats picked up the pitcher.

"Shit," Fats said. "I forgot the ice. Tink, there's a bucket on the table in the kitchen down the hall. Grab some ice for everybody, okay?"

"Gotcha," Tink said. He left and Fats poured lemonade into all of the glasses. Then he picked up Tink's bottle of corn liquor. "Anybody want to get into this stuff yet?" They all shook their heads. Then he topped off Tink's glass with a pour from the liquor bottle. "Hair of the dog," he said to the two hippies. They nodded and sipped at their lemonade.

"What are you doing?" Jimmy said.

"Nothing," Fats shot back. "What do you think I'm doing?"

When Tink reappeared with a bowl of ice cubes, they all grabbed a few and dropped them into their drinks.

"You need to make a little room for the ice," Fats said.

"No problem," Tink said. He took a big gulp. "Whoa," he gasped. "This shit gets better with age." Tink took some ice cubes and splashed them into his drink. "Simply delicious," he said.

"We never saw the set lists," Albert reminded Fats.

"Oh, yeah," Fats said. "My handwriting's terrible," he said, shaking his head. A mournful look came over his face, like he was going to break down. He could have been in a funeral parlor offering some guy his deepest condolences. "I'll just call them out as we go. You'll know the tunes. Nothing really prehistoric. I'll call the key and set the tempo, so you can all just fall in behind me. All right?"

Albert looked somewhat consoled. Frampton just shrugged.

The door rattled with knocking again. "Are you decent in there?" called the first chin. He poked his head inside and winked. He asked if a woman could use the bathroom. The crowd had arrived, and the facilities were all overbooked.

"No problem," Fats said. "We're just doing a little preparation."

Tink mouthed the word, "woman," and winked at Fats and Jimmy. The door swung wide and a smiling blonde in her late twenties wearing a stylish blue top and floral skirt swept by and vanished into the bathroom.

"Oh, Mr. Fats," the chin said. "I almost forgot. You wanted to try the phone again?"

Fats disappeared down the hall with the chin, and the others sat there looking at each other.

"Is he on call?" Albert said. "Like a doctor or something?"

"He's in candy," Jimmy said.

Tink leaned over toward Frampton. "I think she's fucking beautiful," he said, cocking his head toward the bathroom.

"Tink," Jimmy said. He made a cross with his two index fingers like they do in vampire movies.

"All right, all right," Tink said. He slumped back and took another drink.

When the toilet flushed and then flushed again, no one said a word. Tink leaned toward Frampton again. "Courtesy flush," he whispered.

"Tink," Jimmy said, his voice louder than before, but not so loud that the woman would hear. Then the bathroom door opened, and she stepped out again, her smile intact.

"God," Tink said. "It's a beautiful day." He had that same cheery boom in his voice that Jimmy had noticed when the chin first greeted him.

"Yes," the woman said. "We always seem to luck out. You don't even want to *think* about this place in a rainstorm."

"God, no," Tink said. Slowly, a look of desperation spread across his face. Jimmy hoped she'd leave before the moron could do any more damage, but she asked what kind of music the band played. They all looked at each other.

"Fats," Jimmy and at least two of the others blurted out at the same time.

"Is that a style?" she asked. "Like Fats Domino?"

"Exactly," Tink said, leaning forward. "You hit the nail. You really hit the nail. God." He was more excited than he had been when Tug McGraw got the last out in the World Series.

"We play different kinds of music," Jimmy said.

"Not at the same time, I hope?" she said.

Tink rose to his feet and stepped toward her, stopping a few feet short. He looked into the woman's eyes. "Tell me," he said in a suddenly grave tone. "Do you dance?"

"I'm awful," she said. "Two left feet. But, I'm willing to do my bit for the cause."

Tink moved his right foot out a step and extended his left arm as if he were proposing to do the minuet with the woman.

"Thanks for the use of the bathroom," she said. She spun away and dashed out of the room, leaving him reaching for a nonexistent partner.

Tink righted himself, backed up to the couch and collapsed in his seat. "God, I love rich women," he said.

Fats returned, a sour look on his face. "Everything's all right," he said. He sounded like he was telling them he was just about to throw up.

"Well, that's a relief," Tink said. He rose again. "I'm going to see," he announced, "if that lovely young thing left any messages for me in the powder room. Maybe on the mirror in lipstick?"

When he closed the door, Fats topped everybody's lemonade, causing Jimmy's to overflow. Frampton was snoring gently, and Albert was staring out the window. Jimmy wiped off the glass and sipped some of the lemonade. Fats found Tink's bottle and held it in front of Jimmy.

"No, thanks," Jimmy said. He was no puritan when it came to drinking after a gig, but he had enough trouble remembering bass lines when he was sober. He watched Fats pour more of the stuff into Tink's glass.

"What the fuck are you doing?" Jimmy said. "He's already shit-faced."

"The man craves it," Fats said. "Hell, he deserves it. We all deserve it."

"Where's this coming from?" Jimmy asked him.

"Lighten up," Fats said. "It'll be fine."

Jimmy looked at his watch. They had about a half an hour left before they needed to go on. Tink flushed the toilet several times and then returned. He drank half of his lemonade straight down and belched.

"This is fucked up," Albert said.

"Everything is fucked up," Fats said.

Tink kept sipping at his drink and topping it off with the corn. Fifteen minutes before they were due to go on, Jimmy traded his T-shirt and jeans for the dressier clothes. Fats put on a Hawaiian shirt and white pants, and Tink laughed at him, waking Frampton. Tink pointed at Fats's shirt and howled. Jimmy checked Tink's bottle. It was two-thirds finished. Five minutes later Tink was still laughing.

"Shut up," Fats told him.

"Thut up," Tink said, leering back. He laughed again.

"Fuck you, Tink," Fats said.

"Hey, I don't need thith," Tink slurred.

"That's it, Tink. Go home. You're done."

"A gig's a gig's a gig," Tink said. He tried to stand up but instead sank back into the cushions of the couch. "In my trade," he said. "We got a saying."

The two freaks looked at each other. "You are fucked up," Albert said, glaring at Fats. "No set lists, no rehearsal, and then you get the fucking guitarist sloshed and fire his ass when it's time to play. Are you serious, man?"

"You're a better guitarist than Tink," Fats said, "and anyway, we don't need two guitarists for this gig. Let's go. It's time for their presentations."

"Fuck you, you fucking fuck," Tink cursed. He was crawling on his hands and knees toward the bathroom. The rest of the band filed out and took their places on the porch. The hippies still wore the same clothes they'd been in all day. It was still hot, but at least most of the porch was shaded. A crowd had gathered below the porch, dozens of young guys who looked like they might be related to Teddy Roosevelt accompanied by smiling tanned women with great hair, all socializing out there in the sunlight. Poise, Mary would call it. Even in all that heat, they had poise coming out the ass.

On the porch, the two chin guys and a couple other riders stood by a table with plaques and a silver bowl. The first chin welcomed the crowd on the microphone that Tink was supposed to use for his vocals. The riding crowd was louder than the gang at Gilhooley's watching a hockey game, louder than Jimmy had imagined a bunch of Republicans on horseback could be. The first chin had to remind them to quiet down. Then the second chin took over and started announcing the winners of the day's various awards. The first chin walked over to Fats and Jimmy. "Told you this is a real party group," he said to Fats. "You'll see." Fats returned his wink.

"Why don't you give your buddy the rest of Tink's bottle?" Jimmy said to Fats.

"Tell Albert 'Margaritaville,'" Fats said. "He's singing and playing lead."

"Why not?" Jimmy said. He walked over to the two freaks and broke the news.

Albert looked like Jimmy had told him to get an accordion and play a polka. He muttered something to Frampton, and they shook their heads. "I pick the fucking key," he said. "We'll do it in E. The people's key. And tell Mr. Fats to cut the Jimmy Buffet crap. He owes me at least one Dead song."

"What do you want to do?" Jimmy asked him.

"'Box of Rain' is decent."

"I don't think it's a 'Box of Rain' crowd."

"'Casey Jones.'"

Jimmy nodded and headed back to Fats who was still adjusting his cymbals. The chin was bringing victorious riders up to the porch to take bows and pick up their hardware. The older people in the crowd looked pleased as punch to be in the middle of the light brigade and their dates. Jimmy wondered if maybe the older couples had met each other years ago at one of these horsey get-togethers. Maybe the young gentlemen soldiers were their very own horse-riding offspring come today to win a plaque, blow off a little high society steam, and, who knows, maybe even pop the question to some other old trooper's ruddy faced daughter. He was sure that if he scanned some ritzy magazine with photographs of the young and wealthy frolicking on a ski slope in the Alps or out on safari in Africa, he'd see these same tanned faces with the same damn chins smiling at him. If it wasn't someone from this very crowd, it would certainly be cousin Chad and his young Deirdre. Jimmy closed his eyes and pictured the kid from *Deliverance* in a yellow polo shirt and mint green trousers with a white belt strumming a tennis racquet instead of a banjo.

Fats agreed that "Casey Jones" was a good choice. "No funky arrangement," he said. "No slick changes. Do it right off the record." Soon, the chin was thanking everybody, and then he introduced the band. Fats counted off, and Jimmy waited to make sure Albert was really in E before he started playing. Some of the women cheered when they recognized it as a Jimmy Buffet number. A group of troopers getting drinks in one of the tents sang along with the chorus. Albert knew the guitar part, but he left out a verse and sang the last verse twice instead. He was not a happy camper. He started in on the Grateful Dead song even slower than Jimmy remembered the Dead doing it. Dead tunes always dragged on longer than anyone but a Deadhead could stand. He knew what Fats was thinking: here goes half the damn set. A regular fucking "Wreck of the Edmund Fitzgerald." Fats could have gone off, laid some pipe with one of his little squeezes, had a bit of brunch, tossed back a six-pack, and still made it back in time for the last goddamn chorus. Albert's voice seemed better suited for this thing than for the Buffet tune, and the small part of the crowd that was not feeding their faces seemed to be into it. They finished the song in about five minutes, not exactly short but short enough to save Albert's ass for the time being.

"Hotel California," Fats called out.

Albert made a face. "Eagles?" he said. "What the hell?"

"It's not up for discussion," Fats said.

Jimmy stepped closer to the front line, positioning himself between the hippies and Fats. "Do you know it?" he asked Albert. He shrugged and looked at Frampton.

"Do *you* know it?" Jimmy asked Frampton.

"I guess I can get through the words," he said.

Frampton went over to Albert, who looked like he was going to hit somebody. "Do an acoustic guitar thing, man. Play some mariachi shit, some Mexican licks."

"Mariachi?" Albert said, his voice rising at least an octave from the beginning of the word to the end.

Fats hit his bass kick twice, and the freaks turned to him.

"You'll love it," Jimmy said to Albert. "It starts out even slower than 'Casey Jones.' Count it out, Fats."

"One, two, three, four."

Jimmy hit the first bass note and waited, but Albert just stood there looking at the sky. Jimmy played through the rest of the intro. "Any time you're ready," he said. The second time through, Albert joined in, but what he played was almost identical to the licks he'd used for "Casey Jones." Jimmy could hear Fats snorting and fuming behind his kit. Frampton sang the right words, but his voice was flat and it sounded like he was remembering the lyrics just in the nick of time. His voice might work over lots of distorted guitars in some dive on South Street filled with nose rings and marijuana smoke, but here it was a disaster. Jimmy stepped toward Fats. "We're going to get ax murdered," Jimmy shouted.

Fats said nothing, but hit the kick and the snare hard.

"You *have* heard these guys play before?" Jimmy yelled.

Fats snorted again.

Jimmy looked across the lawn. Thank God, most of the people were acting like guests at a wedding reception: talking, eating and drinking. A long line snaked into each of the booze tents. The band muddled through the song, and when they finally got to the end, maybe five people in the crowd bothered to applaud. "This is good," Jimmy said to Fats. "At least we don't have an audience to worry about."

"'Up On The Roof,'" Fats called out.

Frampton and Albert stared at each other.

"The Coasters?" Jimmy said.

Nothing.

"Think James Taylor," Jimmy suggested. "On *Sesame Street*?"

"No," Albert said. "I won't fucking do it."

Jimmy looked back at Fats who was adjusting the clamps on his high-hat and pretending he hadn't heard Albert's refusal.

"I don't know it," Albert said.

"Neither do I," Frampton said.

"'My Girl,'" Fats called out. "Smokey Robinson? Ready?" He turned to Jimmy. "Start it. And one of those bastards better find some sunshine on a cloudy fucking day or I'm going to kick their asses. One, two, three, four."

Jimmy hit the opening notes and was surprised to hear the hippies fall in. When they finished no one clapped, even though it had been their best tune so far.

They played "Brown Eyed Girl" and "Green Eyed Lady." Jimmy was amazed and relieved that Frampton could muddle his way through the keyboard parts. On "Dancing in the Moonlight," Frampton didn't come through with the backing vocals, so Jimmy moved as close to his microphone as his guitar cord would allow and chimed in with his usual monotone.

They closed with The Beatles' "They Say It's Your Birthday" to a smattering of applause. Fats hopped up to Albert's microphone, and while he was announcing that they'd be back after a short break, some people near one of the tents started singing "Happy Birthday" to someone in the crowd.

Fats stood right next to Albert at the mic, glaring at him. Jimmy saw him mouth the words, "Play it."

"No way," Albert said. Jimmy heard the freak's voice boom through the P.A., cutting over the crowd noise. "That's where I draw the fucking line," he snapped. "I ain't playing that shit."

"Yo!" Jimmy yelled. "Cut the mic." The birthday singers cheered for their birthday boy. Fats turned off the mic then started one of the break tapes on the cassette player, checked to hear if it was coming through the P.A., and stomped into the house without saying a word to anybody.

Fats stepped over Tink, who was passed out on the floor of the green room, and disappeared into the bathroom. The two freaks followed Jimmy in from the hallway and they all stood over Tink. He was lying on his side, breathing roughly through his mouth.

"At least he's not hogging the couch," Jimmy said. He slumped into the cushions on the sofa. "Who's got a cigarette?" he asked.

"You smoke?" Frampton said.

"I'm trying to develop the habit," Jimmy said. "I only smoke at gigs." The freaks sat on the floor with their backs against a wall of books. Jimmy spotted the bulge of smokes in Tink's shirt pocket. "Bingo," he said. "James Bond time." He hovered over Tink and slowly inched the pack of Tareytons out of his pocket. Jimmy flopped back on the couch and tapped out one cigarette. "Light, anyone?" he asked.

Frampton pulled a lighter from his pocket and tossed it over. Jimmy lit up and blew out a long, slow stream of smoke. He pocketed the pack and tossed the lighter back to Frampton.

"We didn't do one song that was written in the last fifteen years," Albert said. He pointed to the bathroom. "He's a fucking liar."

A knock on the door drew everyone's attention, and then the plaid shirt opened it and stuck his head inside. He looked serious. "Someone from your band is here," he said. He swung open the door, and a young guy in a Hendrix shirt, his hair in a long ponytail, stepped inside. After the shirt disappeared, the new guy took in the scene then focused on Frampton and Albert. "What are you two doing here?"

"Us?" Frampton said. "What are *you* doing here, Stu?"

"Where's Fats?" Stu said. "I don't care what he's doing, I want to see that fucker now."

Jimmy pointed to the bathroom. "In the can," he said.

"This is too weird," Stu said. The toilet flushed. The freaks stood up and did a little handshake routine with Stu. They all called each other "dude." The bathroom door opened, and out stepped Fats.

"What the fuck is going on?" Stu asked Fats.

"Are you alone?" Fats said.

"Yeah, the other guys bailed. They're back in Philly."

"What other guys?" Frampton said.

"Never mind," Fats said.

"I came all the way down here out of the goodness of my fucking heart to tell you. To help you if you still needed me to play bass."

"Bass?" Jimmy said.

"This fucking sucks," Stu said. "These are the guys you wanted to can?"

"What's going on?" Albert said. "What other guys?"

"You don't want to fucking know, dude," Stu snapped. "I'm outa here." He turned back to Fats. "I came out here thinking I might help you. I don't care about your geezers, but Keith and Albert are my boys, man. This is cold."

"What the fuck?" Frampton said, looking back and forth between Fats and Stu.

"He was going to dump the whole bunch of you fucks," Stu said. "Me and a couple other guys were supposed to do the gig, then we couldn't, and then it looked like we could, so he told us to show up. He said you guys would fuck up before the gig even started and he would fire all of you.

"I said, 'Can't those other guys manage?'"

"'That bunch of assholes?' he said. 'Fat chance.'"

With his left hand, Fats grabbed Stu by the collar and slammed him against the wall. Albert lunged across the room and pinned Fats's right arm behind him. Frampton grabbed Fats around the neck. Fats kept Stu in a choke hold against the wall while the two freaks hung all over his back.

"Yo!" Jimmy screamed. He jumped over Tink and grabbed each of the freaks by the back of their collars. "Everybody let go of everybody else," he yelled. They all froze like parts of some modernistic statue. Then Fats let go of Stu, and everybody else separated. "Now, get the fuck out of here," Jimmy said.

"Jimmy—"

"Shut up, Fats," Jimmy said. "Whoever the fuck you guys are, get your shit and go. That's it."

"We're supposed to get fucking paid," Albert said.

"*All* of us," Stu added.

"Go home now," Jimmy said. "Get out!"

"He's fucking you, *too*, man," Stu said.

"I'll get your goddamn instruments," Jimmy said.

The freaks seemed to have lost their fire. They gathered their stuff from the room.

"Bring your car up to the back door in two minutes," Jimmy said to Frampton. "Fats, why don't you do something useful—like go take another dump."

When the freaks and Stu had shuffled out of the room, Fats started to say something, but Jimmy held up his hand. "Don't say one fucking word," he said. He went out to the porch. The cavalry were eating all over the place. He could smell the beef. He unplugged the guitar and packed it up and Frampton's synth. The hippies were standing by their car when he brought the instruments to the rear of the house. Their buddy Stu was sitting in his car, the motor running. Jimmy brought their amps, and Albert loaded them into the trunk of the car.

Frampton looked at Jimmy with disgust.

"You know what, Frampton?" Jimmy said, "you can't sing worth a shit."

They drove off, trailing dust behind them as they barreled up the hill. Jimmy was relieved that none of the troopers had paid any attention to him when he unplugged a bunch of the setup and sent half of the band packing. Fats could deal with them.

As he neared the green room, Jimmy heard Tink throwing up in the bathroom. Fats was sitting on the couch, a cigarette in one hand and Tink's nearly empty bottle in his other.

"It was nothing personal," Fats said.

"What are you, the Godfather?" Jimmy said. "I can't wait to see what you're going to tell your soldier boys. 'Nothing personal!' You'll be screaming while they rip you a brand new asshole."

Fats took a drink from the bottle.

"Give me some of that shit," Jimmy said. He grabbed the bottle and took a pull. "Yow! Now I'm ready for a cigarette and then maybe the blindfold." He plopped down on the other end of the couch. The bathroom door swung open, and Tink appeared in the doorway, his face wet, his eyes bloodshot and unfocused. He looked like a still from a horror movie. Jimmy passed the bottle back to Fats and took out one of Tink's cigarettes.

"Fats," Jimmy said. "How much are we going to lose? Forget the physical beating we may take. How much money were you in for on this gig?"

"A grand."

Jimmy didn't ask how much of it would have come his way. He figured that even when Fats was planning to pay him, he only would have seen a hundred. He could have done another Saturday call, a backed up toilet or a broken insinkerator, and made a lot more. Or he could have done Father Quinn's shower and held back a couple of those weekly collection envelopes. "So, why did you want to fire my ass, Fats?"

Fats said nothing. Jimmy did not expect him to start acting like he was his friend all of a sudden. Not even Fats could have pulled that one off. Jimmy turned to Tink, still frozen in the doorway. "Sit the hell down," he said. Tink took two steps forward and then fell face first to the rug.

"Am I too damn old?" Jimmy asked Fats. "We're the same age. You weren't firing your own sorry old ass."

"I don't know," Fats said.

Tink was asleep, breathing loudly through his gaping mouth again.

"I guess one geezer seemed okay," Fats said. "I mean, you can't hardly see me behind the drums, anyway. Stu's about as good as you. He did sing some. That was a plus."

"Jesus Fucking Christ."

"I never said you were a bad bass player. You're good."

"Blow me, Fats."

"I thought I needed you; I called you. I didn't plan on all this other bullshit. Look, I don't apologize for anything to anybody."

"And I don't give absolution to nobody."

"Right."

Tink farted in his sleep.

"Great," Jimmy said. Fats passed him the bottle. The corn liquor tasted terrible. "Fuck all those assholes," he said.

"Fuck 'em," Fats said.

"Fucking hippies or whatever they are."

"Dudes," Fats said. "Fuck the dudes."

"And fuck all these rich boy scouts and the horses they rode in on," Jimmy said.

Fats laughed. "Actually, they haven't gotten ugly with us. Yet."

"Right," Jimmy said. "Yet."

"Right," Tink mumbled.

They both looked over at Tink. His eyes were still closed, but he'd started breathing through his nose. "A corpse with bad breath," Fats said.

"His breath's not the only thing that stinks," Jimmy said.

"He looks so peaceful."

"As if he were only sleeping."

There was laughter and some cheering out on the porch. At least a half-hour had gone by since they had stopped playing. "I bet he could play his fucking guitar in his sleep," Jimmy said. "And he'd probably sing better, too."

"No," Fats said. "Oh, no."

"You think that blonde can play?"

A familiar rapping at the door told them that the first chin was back again. "Are you decent in there?"

"Uh, actually no," Fats said.

"I was just kidding, guys."

Fats rolled his eyes. "Oh," he said.

"Seriously, are you guys about ready? The tape ran out, and people are itching to dance."

Jimmy looked at Fats who was staring longingly out the window at the van.

"We'll be out in a minute," Jimmy called.

"For fuck's sake," Fats said. He knelt down next to Tink and spoke to him the way one might speak to a confused child. Tink nodded. He understood what Fats was saying. He would try to make it to the stage. Fats helped him stand up. Jimmy looked around and found his guitar.

"Hey," he said to Tink, "it's only two sets."

Tink belched.

Jimmy brought a desk chair from the room and set it in front of the microphone that Tink was supposed to have used in the first place. He and Fats planted him in the chair and laid the guitar on his lap. Jimmy adjusted the mic stand in front of him. The crowd was milling around between the two bar tents. Empty glasses and discarded plates stained with bits of beef and potato salad were scattered all over the grass. Several horse soldiers were standing by the swimming pool. No one seemed to notice that the band had returned.

"Where's the set list?" Tink asked.

"Play something you know real good," Jimmy said. "Something nice and easy to play."

Tink shrugged. "What kind of music?"

"Something middle groove," Jimmy said. "Not too fast, but don't put them to sleep, either. All right?"

"What happened to those other guys?"

"Who? The Magic Fucking Johnsons? They're off playing with their Magic Johnsons."

Tink leaned toward Jimmy but had to steady himself with his foot.

"Whoa, Bucko," Jimmy said. "Want me to tie you in? Need a seat belt?"

"No," he slurred, righting himself and leaning back in the chair. "Let's do 'Up On Cripple Creek.'"

"Perfect." Jimmy told Fats, who nodded. Fats counted it out, and Tink hit the opening guitar notes right on time. His voice was in some nether world between singing and mumbling. When he got to the chorus, Jimmy realized too late that he was supposed to sing the backing part. On the instrumental break, Tink's playing was pretty clean. Jimmy edged closer to him. "I know you're drunk," he said, "but try not to sing like you're drunk. Growl a little."

Tink screwed up his face. "Grrr," he said.

"No, you moron," Jimmy said. "When you *sing*. Make it growl a little."

Tink sang the next verse a little better. They didn't sound too bad as a trio. It was thin, of course, but they managed. By the last verse a few couples were dancing.

Tink wanted to do "Every Woman I Know Crazy 'Bout An Automobile." Fats gave a what-the-fuck look, and Jimmy nodded to Tink to give it a try. He growled much more on this tune but had a coughing fit when the song ended. Tink asked for water, and the second chin brought a pitcher and three glasses to the stage. Then they launched into Chuck Berry's "You Never Can Tell." Tink's voice started thin and raspy and then got worse. Jimmy watched his mouth. He was trying to sing all the words, but only so many sounds were actually making it out. By the end of the tune, Tink's voice was shot. He turned to Fats and shrugged his shoulders.

"'Time is Tight,'" Jimmy said.

"Booker T. and the MGs?" Fats said. "We've never done that."

"Maybe *he* has," Jimmy said, nodding toward Tink. "At least, he won't have to sing."

"We don't have keyboards," Fats said.

"Whose fault is that, Fuckhead?"

"All right. All right."

Jimmy told Tink and hummed the guitar part and then the keyboard part. Tink nodded and gave him the thumbs up sign.

As soon as they started playing, the crowd began moving to the music. The three of them locked in. It was the tightest they'd sounded all night. Tink's playing had improved immensely since he'd stopped singing. More people joined the dancers. They were shouting and jumping around. Jimmy tried to mimic the Hammond part with his voice. He was sure it sounded ridiculous, but he threw himself into it anyway. He tried to make it sound like they always did the tune this way, like some bizarre kind of scat thing. When they finished, the audience exploded, sounding like it had doubled in size.

"Fucking A," Jimmy murmured. "No more singing." They jumped into "Guitar Boogie Shuffle," "Pipeline," then "Walk Don't Run" and "Memphis." The dancing got more charged up with each song. The horse soldiers were trying to outdo one another at swinging their partners. They had gotten nearly as loud as the band. Halfway through "Memphis," Jimmy realized that he couldn't think of any more instrumentals. When the applause for the song died down, someone in the crowd let loose with a scary laugh and shouted, "Wipe Out!"

"Yeah!" someone else shouted. "The Surfaris."

He'd never been more grateful for a request. Playing "Wipe Out" made him think of "Rumble." Jimmy was ready to end the set after the Link Wray blaster, but Fats yelled, "Rebel Rouser," and off they went, Tink twanging away like a crazed Duane Eddy. When they were finished, the crowd was in a frenzy. Jimmy announced that they would be back after a short break.

"Always leave 'em craving for more," he said, as he and Fats helped Tink stagger back to the green room.

The three of them collapsed on the couch.

"I don't know any more instrumentals," Tink said. Just talking made his voice break up.

"I'm all out," Fats said.

"The sun's down," Jimmy said. "The crowd always kicks it up

a notch after dark. They're going nuts out there."

"What the hell else can we play?" Tink rasped.

"If we'd done that set first we might have gotten away with repeating it," Fats said.

Tink looked at them funny. "First set?" he said.

"Damn," Fats said. "We can't sing for shit. Neither of us."

"It's a party, not a goddamn concert," Tink said. "It's like a fucking wedding." Then he was overwhelmed by another coughing fit.

"We're so close to that money," Jimmy said to Fats. "Between the two of us, we can hit most of the notes."

"I can't sing much more than la, la, la and still keep time," Fats said.

"I'll do the leads," Jimmy said. "You guys just make some noise on choruses. We'll do songs that you don't have to sing good."

"My fucking head hurts," Tink announced. "I gotta lie down."

"No!" Jimmy and Fats yelled at the same time.

It was dark. The troopers had been up and dancing. A short break was best. They didn't want to lose them.

Jimmy and Fats herded Tink back out to his chair, and then they set up microphones for all three of them. The first chin walked over and asked what had happened to the rest of the band. Jimmy couldn't tell if he was angry or just curious. "We only use those guys for the first part of the act," he explained. "We're the heart of the band."

"And the guy in the chair. What's wrong with him?"

Tink winced, reaching for his guitar on its stand.

"He's a vet," Jimmy said. He lowered his voice and said, "It's an old war wound. Poor bastard can only stand for so many hours. It's like having a permanent hangover."

"A war wound?" the chin said, brightening.

Jimmy didn't want him getting within smelling range of Tink. "He's not always comfortable around people. Delayed stress. Know what I mean?"

Tuning up, Tink hit a flat note and grimaced. The chin's eyes were locked on him.

"You're looking at one hell of a brave guy," Jimmy said.

The chin nodded.

"How'd you like the instrumental set?" Jimmy said. "People usually can't get enough of that stuff."

"It was definitely different," the chin said, turning back to him. "I didn't realize your act was so theatrical."

"We try to keep things moving, not do the same thing all night. We get a little offbeat in the third act."

The chin stared at him. "More offbeat?"

"Don't worry," Jimmy said. "You'll love it."

"Okay," the chin said. "You need anything? More water?"

"You know, some beer would be nice. We haven't had a taste of beer all day."

The chin left and Jimmy took a deep breath. He looked at Tink and Fats. "Think festive," he said. "'Mexican Hat Dance.'"

They both stared at him like they hoped he was kidding.

"A bridge," he said. "Between the instrumental stuff and the rest of the night. It'll set a tone."

"No shit," Fats said.

They played through the tune five times, and the swells were swinging their partners around like they were trying out for *Oklahoma*. The place was decorated with little lights that twinkled along the porch and along the flaps of the booze tents. Guys in tuxedos and uniforms and women in formal dresses were lined up in front of the bartenders and scattered across the lawn and around the pool. Jimmy was sure that if he wandered through the parking area, he would find more than one Jaguar. He remembered Kerry talking about his book report on *The Great Gatsby*. This place was crawling with Jay Gatsbys and Daisy Buchanans.

The crowd applauded loudly when they finished the tune. No one in the band had said a word to the audience all night. Things were going much better than Jimmy had expected. It was time to take a chance.

"Good evening, Ladies and Gentlemen," he announced. "We hope you're having as much fun as we are." The crowd over at the pool let out a cheer. The dancers in front of the porch seemed content to catch their breath after their hat dancing. Over on the far side of the pool, three guys in uniform and two women stood, swaying on the tile, arm in arm. They waved to the stage and kept singing the song by themselves. They kick danced like a chorus line, shouting "Olé" at the end of each line. They danced forward, somehow holding on to each other and their drinks, and then with a great lunge the five of them kick-stepped right into the swimming pool. The huge splash soaked the couples sitting at the tables near the edge of the pool. A great cheer went up from the rest of the crowd.

"Well, we hope you can manage to loosen up a little," Jimmy said. That line was met with hooting and laughter. "A little birdie told me," he went on, "that a certain couple here are not far removed from their blessed union. From their glorious, nuptial celebration. Am I right?"

"What the hell are you doing?" Fats whispered.

Jimmy waved him off with his left hand. "Am I right?" he said louder. He hoped one couple and only one couple might respond to this. The crowd buzzed and laughed. He could drop it and look like a fool or push it and end up looking like a total idiot. "Didn't one of your own, one trooper, recently march down the aisle with a lovely lady?" he pleaded. The crowd converged around a couple in the middle of the lawn. The bathroom blonde stepped in and hugged the woman. There was more hooting. Jimmy thanked God for May and June weddings. "Can we bring the happy couple up to the stage for a moment?" He knew exactly what Fats's face looked like about now, so he didn't even bother to look back. Besides, he wasn't worried anymore. The crowd paraded the couple up to the porch. He recognized the guy as one of the winning riders. "I'm sure the senior officer here will be more than glad to come to the stage and present the couple to this assembly." He gestured for the couple to come to the microphone. A uniformed man about Jimmy's age trailed them. With all the medals, patches, and gold braid he had plastered on his jacket, Jimmy figured he must be a general or something.

When Jimmy did plumbing work for rich people, he usually dealt with the woman of the house. He could remember standing in the bathroom of some big house up in Chestnut Hill telling some biddy she would not be able to flush her toilet or run her shower the same way anymore, basically laying down the law about the wonderful world of waste fluids. Now this guy, who could buy the whole block of rowhouses where the Sweeneys lived, was looking to him for direction.

"If the principals can all find a drink," Jimmy said to him, "then I think you, sir, can present them with a toast?"

The general nodded and beamed as if he'd just gone into a strip joint and gotten lucky. The first chin appeared with glasses of champagne for the couple and the general. When the general lifted his glass, he had to wait as the crowd roared.

"Jack Sinclair doesn't deserve to be honored twice today," he said. The crowd laughed. "But, Lynne here certainly does."

Oohs and ahs emanated from the crowd. Jimmy felt goose bumps form on his skin.

"You were the horseman of the day, Jack," the general said. "But as proud as I'm sure you are about that, I bet you're prouder yet to be standing next to this special lady."

Jimmy sneaked a look back at Fats and wiped at his eye. Fats sneered and gave a rim shot.

"Lynne," the general went on, "I can't say that I hope Jack has retired the cup today, but I do hope that you've retired Jack." The crowd cheered. "Ladies, troopers, I give you one damn lucky trooper and his beautiful bride. Troopers. Hip, hip."

"Hooray!"

"Hip, hip."

"Hooray!"

"Hip, hip."

"Hooray!"

Everyone lifted their glasses and drank to the couple's health. The pair hugged each other and the general and then Jimmy.

The general patted him on the back. "Great stuff," he said. "Bloody great stuff." Jimmy turned around. Fats looked like he'd shoot him if he had a gun. Jimmy winked at him.

The chin brought three glasses and a pitcher of beer and left them on the porch floor.

"What's next, Maestro?" Fats said.

"A cold one," Jimmy said, pouring two beers. He tossed the third glass onto the grass and handed a glass to Fats. Jimmy looked back at the audience. "Because you can never get enough of a good thing," he said into the microphone, "we're going to dedicate the rest of the evening to Jack and Lynne." More cheers. "Now you'll all have to help. Are you ready?"

A modest cheer went up. He took a long drink from his glass then put it on the floor.

"I said, are you *ready*?"

They roared back.

"You put your *left* foot in," he sang, "you put your *left* foot out."

Tink and Fats started playing and the crowd sang along with "The Hokey Pokey." After that, they played "The Electric Slide" and "New York, New York." They played "Golden Slippers," and all these people who'd probably never even been to a Mummers' Parade did the Mummers' strut. Jimmy led the band through "The Bride Cuts The Cake." Fats looked paler and paler with each song. They slowed things down with "Daddy's Little Girl" and "When Irish Eyes Are Smiling." They swirled through "Hava Nagila," and they sprouted wings for "The Chicken Song." The chin brigade was slumming it, and the band was there to serve the schlock up for them. It was the cheap wedding reception that every one of these people would be horrified to book. When the band had run out of songs, the crowd screamed for more. Jimmy toasted the troopers, the happy couple, the United States of America, Kate Smith, the Philadelphia Flyers, and then got everyone to stand and sing "God Bless America." Jimmy listened to Fats and Tink. It was the tightest they had ever played. *We're whores,* he thought, *all three of us. But at least we're thousand dollar whores.* He belted out the last line of the chorus, and the crowd, arm in arm, roared the line along with him. They were whores, all right. And the upper crust loved them.

Jimmy played a dance tape through the P.A. while the three of them started to break down their gear. They drained the last of the beer that the chin had brought them. The bathroom woman came up, planted herself next to Jimmy and handed him a bottle of some import.

"Thanks," he said. "Great timing."

"I'd hoped so," she said. "You guys were great."

He thanked her again, told her he was glad she'd had a good time. She clinked her bottle against his. He took a long pull on the beer. "Good stuff," he said.

She asked him about his instrument, told him how she thought the bass was underrated. He nodded. She asked if he gave lessons, and he laughed. Then he apologized for laughing. He knelt down and placed his guitar in the case. She wanted to know when their next gig was.

"Our drummer does our bookings," he said. "I really don't know when or where we'll do this again." He wiped down the strings on his bass, tucked the cloth in its little compartment and closed the case.

"Do you play with other bands?"

"Yes and no." He rose and picked up the case. "I've really got to get moving here," he said. "It's a long way back to the city. I'm glad you enjoyed the music."

"You were wonderful," she said. She smiled. "Thanks."

He shook her hand, turned, and walked toward the parking area. A couple holding hands stopped him along the way and told him how much they enjoyed the evening. After he untangled himself from them, he put his bass in the back of the van and returned to the stage.

The crowd had thinned a bit, but there was still a critical mass of revelers. A few of them danced until it was time to unplug the cassette player and carry off the speakers. Fats and Jimmy carried the first speaker back and lifted it into its position in the van.

"That blonde broad gave me her card to give you," Fats said. "Helen." He held out the card. "She's a lawyer."

Jimmy didn't respond, so Fats wiggled the card a few inches in front of his face.

"She likes the band," Jimmy said. "I told her you do our booking."

"She wants you, you fucking dope. That babe was coming on to you like a bitch in heat, and you didn't even fucking know it."

"So, I'm stupid," Jimmy said. "I can do stupid real good."

"You fucking pussy," he said.

"Why don't *you* go sniff her out."

"I would," Fats said, heading back toward the porch. "But it's *your* ass she wants, pal," he called over his shoulder.

Jimmy watched Fats disappear behind the building then looked up at the stars. He thought of the day he'd met Mary Teresa at the hardware store, her red hair flowing down her back, her face aglow. *Ah,* he thought, *smiling to himself, the Terrible Beauty.* Then he headed back to the porch. Everything was broken down, and all they had to do was load up. Tink and Jimmy carried the other speaker column out to the van. A few more trips and they had the stage cleared.

"Hey, guys," a trooper called. "There's sodas in the pantry. Have as many as you want."

They thanked him and started filling up the van with their gear. "I'm going to be right next to you when you get paid," Jimmy told Fats. The first chin showed up and helped them lift the last amp into the back.

"You guys are without a doubt the most eclectic band we've ever hired," he said.

"That's us," Tink said.

The chin followed them into the green room and handed Fats a two hundred dollar cash tip and a check for five hundred. The man was now drunker than Tink. He clapped them on the back, winked, said he had unfinished business and then left.

"I've seen more than my share of winking today," Jimmy said.

Fats put the money in his wallet and slipped it into his trouser pocket.

"You lied about the thousand, didn't you?" Tink said to Fats.

"Well, they got their fucking money's worth," Jimmy said.

"You got an advance. Didn't you?" Tink said. "They gave you a check before the gig. Right?"

"I see your headache's gone," Fats said.

"What did they give you all together?" Jimmy asked him.

"A thousand. Along with this two hundred."

"Hot damn," Tink said. "That's four hundred each. Two hundred a set."

"For you, maybe," Fats said.

"Tink and me are splitting the two hundred in cash, right up front," Jimmy said. He stuck out his hand and waited until Fats retrieved his wallet and handed over the bills. "How were you figuring on paying people today?"

"Checks."

"Write us each a check for three hundred." He handed Tink a hundred in cash. "And we know where you live, Fats, so these checks will do no bouncing. No bouncing whatsoever."

Fats wrote the checks, and then they all left the green room. Fats and Jimmy stuffed their clothes and the rest of their gear into the back of the van. They stopped by Tink's car. He'd just finished loading, and he had five cases of soda stashed in his trunk.

"Nice, Tink," Fats said.

"They *said*," Tink said. He slammed the trunk shut and got into the driver's seat. A six-pack of Bud was nestled on the passenger seat.

"Sure you can make it home?" Jimmy asked Tink.

"Follow the North Star," he said. "Right?"

Tink stayed right behind Fats's van as they wound their way past the parked cars, barns, and paddocks filled with horses. Jimmy pressed the button on his armrest and watched his window come down. The air was bracing but felt good. Then they reached the county road and left the dust behind. Fats and Jimmy sat in silence until they'd driven many miles.

"Jimmy," Fats said. "These people really dug all that shit. I mean, if they called me up next year or the year after and wanted us to come out here again."

"Fat fucking chance," Jimmy said. "They can call me if they want a fucking booking. That guy with the chin asked me for my number, and I gave him my business card." He figured he could lie as good as Fats. He saw the diner up ahead. "Your rich friends never fed us," he said. "If that diner's open, I say we hit it."

"Back to the scene of the crime, huh?" Fats said.

"Something like that," Jimmy said.

"All right. I can eat."

"You can pick up the check, too," Jimmy said. "And Tink and me are going to be bottomless pits."

Fats mumbled something Jimmy couldn't catch, then pushed down the turn signal lever, and eased across the yellow line onto the crunchy gravel of the parking lot.

Jimmy heard a toot from behind. Someone yelled. He turned around just in time to see Albert dart to the edge of the road and heave a plastic cupful of beer at Tink's car.

"Fuck you!" someone yelled.

Tink accelerated and drove right past them and around to the back of the diner.

"You fuckers!" Albert yelled. "You cheap goddamn fuckers!"

A hail of gravel hit the rear window. The three hippies were running up to the rear of the van. Stu reached Jimmy's side as Fats jammed it into gear.

"Get the fuck out of here," Jimmy said, holding the button in place until the window was all the way up.

He saw Stu grabbing for his door handle, so he hit the button that locked the door. Stu slapped his hand against the window as the van lurched forward. Another round of gravel sprayed against the back of the van. As they raced around the rear corner of the diner, Jimmy caught a glimpse in the side mirror of three guys running the other way.

"They're doubling around to meet us," he said.

Fats slammed on the brakes and skidded to a stop behind the diner. Tink's car wasn't there.

"What the fuck?" Jimmy said.

Fats made a U-turn and accelerated back the way they'd come in. A car cruised by on the road, so Fats screeched to a stop. Jimmy spotted the three guys milling around the entrance to the diner. Albert had the newspaper box in his hands, but when he saw that Fats and Jimmy were well out of range, he dropped it, and the three of them dashed toward the van.

"Tink must have blown right by them," Fats said, waiting while another car drove past the diner.

Stu threw something, but whatever it was fell way short. Fats floored it, and they sprayed gravel behind them as they pulled out onto the road. Something smacked against Fats's side of the van. "Fuck you!" Albert yelled.

They screeched away, both of them screaming then laughing. Jimmy looked back. Frampton was standing in the middle of the road, giving them the finger with both hands.

"Shit," Fats said. He took it up to sixty-five and held it there.

"They're done," Jimmy said. "They're not coming after us."

"Well, fuck them if they do."

"They weren't waiting for us. They probably just came out of the diner and saw us. "

"Assholes," Fats said.

"Your friends," Jimmy replied.

Up ahead, they saw the back of Tink's car. Fats creeped up close and then flashed his highbeams. Tink's car shot ahead.

"You scared the living shit out of him," Jimmy said.

"Stupid fuck," Fats muttered. He flicked his lights again. Tink swerved a bit before blinking his own lights and slowing down to sixty.

They passed another diner, but neither of them felt like tempting fate, so they kept making time toward home.

When they turned onto the Schuylkill Expressway, Jimmy checked behind them but saw no familiar looking cars. "They don't know where you live. Do they?" he said.

"No," Fats said. "And I ain't in the phone book."

"That, I can understand."

They stayed behind Tink until they got back to the neighborhood. When they turned off the avenue to get to Jimmy's house, Tink hit his horn and kept going.

They arrived at Jimmy's place after midnight. The lights were on in the teenagers' room and downstairs in the living room. A parking spot was open right in front of Jimmy's van, and Fats pulled in. He turned off the engine and popped the rear gate. When Jimmy got out, Fats did too, and they met at the rear of the van.

"Another surprise," Jimmy said.

Fats helped him carry the amp up to the porch. Jimmy opened the door, and they brought the amp inside. The TV was on, and Tyrone was sprawled out on the fully lowered recliner, watching *Saturday Night Live*. "Hey," he said.

"Hey," Jimmy answered.

Tyrone waved to Fats. "The candy man," he said. "Hey." The TV audience laughed. Tyrone's expression never changed, but his eyes stayed locked on the screen.

Mary bustled in from the kitchen. "Alive!" she whooped, heading straight for Jimmy.

"You're a sight for sore eyes," he said. They met in the middle of the room and hugged. He remembered that the van was open. "Just a sec," he said, patting her hip. He went out to get his bass and his other stuff. Fats followed him. Jimmy figured Fats was going to take off.

He pulled his gear out of the van, and Fats closed and locked the rear gate. "Tyrone," Fats said.

"Don't mind him."

"No," Fats said. "The name. That couldn't have been your idea?"

"Not my doing. We'd named the first one for Mary's father's county in Ireland. When the second one came around, there wasn't much choice. Mary and her mother's side of the family are from Dungannon in County Tyrone. Dungannon might have been a better choice, now that I think about it."

"Tyrone," he said. He shook his head. "Irish."

Jimmy looked up and down the empty street then leaned toward him. "He may not be the only Tyrone who goes to Holy Cross, but I'll bet he's the only Irish one."

Fats laughed. "Hey, we ought to get something to eat," he said.

"Oh, that's perfect," Jimmy said. "Mary's not fixing anything for you. You fucking weasel."

"No, Mother Teresa can join us."

"Mary Teresa," Jimmy corrected Fats.

He brought his bass and other clothes to the living room, sat his instrument on the floor, and put the clothes on top of the amp. Fats stayed behind him at the door.

"Were they nice to you?" Mary said. She took his hand and gave it a little squeeze.

"Let's just say it's been a full day," Jimmy said.

"Oh, that sounds as bad as can be," she said. "Take a load off." She sat in the rocking chair and gestured toward the couch. Fats sat in the middle of the couch, and Jimmy sat at the end by Mary. Tyrone stared at the TV. "I thought these private gigs were supposed to be a step above club dates or weddings," Mary said.

"Weddings," Fats muttered.

"Well," Jimmy said, "at least we didn't have to worry about having enough people turn out or getting somebody to do the door."

"Mary," Fats said. "How about a late night pizza?"

Jimmy gave Fats the once over. He sounded like a kid who'd been grounded, trying to cute his way back into his parents' good graces.

"I'll call for one," Fats said. "I mean, if you're going to stay up. Hey, I'll treat the whole clan."

"I had pizza for supper," Tyrone said in a low monotone, still gazing at the TV.

"I don't know," Mary said. "It's been a full day here, too." She patted Jimmy's right hand. "And I'm betting this one here's ready for dreamland."

"Mary," Jimmy said. "They never fed us. You and Fats and I could pop out, get a hoagie or a burger. I mean, it wouldn't quite be a night out."

"Not quite," she said.

"Gilhooley's?" Jimmy said. "A cold beer? A sandwich someone else makes? No mess to clean up?"

"A cold one," she said.

She was teetering on the fence. "Of course," Jimmy said, "I don't know if you're really dressed for the occasion."

Mary hauled off and punched his arm. "*You,*" she said, her face instantly red. She gave his arm another shot.

"You can go to Gilhooley's looking any old way," Fats said.

"I know," Jimmy grunted, rubbing his arm.

"Kerry's not due back any time soon," Mary said. "Tyrone, the young ones are sleeping. Would you guard the castle for us?"

He nodded.

Jimmy clapped his hands together, startling Tyrone. "Great," he said.

"We're *going out!*" Mary said, slapping the sore spot on Jimmy's arm.

"Jesus," he said, wincing.

She was out the door before he could get up off the couch.

Jimmy told Fats they'd take both vans, so they all could go

directly home afterwards. The parking spots on the avenue were all taken, so Jimmy pulled his van into the municipal lot next to the bar. Fats parked three spaces away. When Jimmy turned off the ignition, he heard the rhythm section of a band playing Chicago blues. He'd forgotten that the bar was featuring music that night. The band finished a song just as the three of them reached the front step, and Jimmy swung open the door to a round of applause. A guy at the door told him the band had already started their last set, so he didn't have to pay the cover, but Jimmy stuck fifteen dollars in his hand anyway.

The tables and chairs at the far end of the room had been removed to make space for dancing. The floor was filled with gyrating couples. One table in the front near the short end of the L-shaped bar was vacant. The stools were all filled. They headed straight for the open table.

"All the things that I like about a bar," Mary said. "Noise, smoke, and a crowd."

"Let's make sure the kitchen's still open," Jimmy said.

"What'll you have?" Fats asked.

"Anything," Jimmy said.

"Pitcher?" he said.

Mary and Jimmy nodded in unison.

Jimmy watched Fats waiting at the bar. When Fats turned to get a better look at the band, Jimmy noticed a snugness in the fit of the candy man's shirt. It was the unmistakable beginning of a belly. When Fats walked toward them with a full pitcher and three glasses, the drummer's modest paunch jiggled slightly with each step.

"The kitchen's about to close," Fats barked over the noise as he landed his load on the table. "But they'll make sandwiches for us."

Fats filled their glasses while they decided on cheesesteaks, then made his way back to the bar to place their order. Jimmy recognized some guys from the trades sprinkled amongst the mob. Half of the crowd was on its feet.

When the song ended, the crowd whistled and cheered. Mary leaned close to Jimmy's ear and shouted, "That was a good one!"

"'Stormy Monday,'" he shouted back.

She nodded. "Do you see the Gilligans from church?"

"Yeah."

Fats returned with napkins and ketchup. One of the band members was introducing the next tune. "Don't you know the guitarist?" Fats said.

Jimmy nodded.

Fats topped off their glasses. When the band started playing, they raised their glasses, clinked them against each other, and tasted the beer.

"You won't believe who's at the other end of the bar," Fats said.

Jimmy stood up, but the people at this end of the bar blocked the view. He moved a few feet over and stood on his tiptoes. Tink was holding court at the bar near the bandstand.

"He's buying rounds for everybody in sight," Fats said.

"Jesus," Jimmy said.

Between songs, Jimmy tried to explain Tink to Mary. The band started a slow tune he wasn't familiar with. Gil brought them their cheesesteaks and a plate of hot peppers. After Fats whipped out a couple of twenties and paid him, Jimmy thanked Fats. When Mary started to thank him too, Jimmy was afraid she'd go overboard, but she didn't.

"I played with the keyboard guy," Fats said.

"He's better than Frampton," Jimmy said.

The beer was cold and went down fast. Gil brought over another pitcher as the band segued into "Sweet Home Chicago." They finished their cheesesteaks and enjoyed the music. Dancers filled the floor and made it hard to see the band.

"Want to get out there and move around?" Jimmy asked Mary.

"Nah," she said. "I'll move around a little here. That's enough for now."

"All right," Jimmy said.

"Tell the truth," she said. "You're relieved. Aren't you? You don't want to dance."

"It's up to you," he said. "I'd find the energy. I can dance or not dance."

"Pish."

"There's no satisfying the Terrible Beauty," he declared.

She smacked him in the arm.

"Jesus," he wailed. "How do you always find that spot?"

She beamed.

He filled her glass as the band started what he thought might be a B.B. King song. When the song ended, the guitarist announced they had time for another couple of tunes. He said he recognized some other musicians in the crowd and that maybe they'd help out on the last few songs. Jimmy looked at Fats. They both shrugged.

"Don't worry, Mary," Jimmy said.

He heard the guy call out his name and Fats's and Tink's. The crowd let out a roar of approval.

"We got to do something," Fats said.

"I'm not doing anything but drinking this beer."

The audience clapped rhythmically.

"Tink's not moving," Fats said. "And you're out of gas. I'll go up."

"Knock yourself out," Jimmy said. He watched Fats wade through the crowd to a smattering of applause. "Want some more beer?" he asked Mary.

"My beer's full, Jimmy," she said. "You can go up. I don't mind. Really."

"I mind."

Fats adjusted the drummer's seat while the band's drummer grabbed a pair of maracas. The bandleader said one guest was better than none, but the guitarist and bass player would welcome a break if Jimmy and Tink changed their minds. Jimmy waved and smiled. Tink had his back to the guy. He was gesturing wildly. Then he laughed at the guy next to him and clapped him on the back.

"Suit yourself," Mary said.

The band launched into "Tore Down."

Jimmy saw Gil heading in his direction. The guy couldn't be expecting him to go up and play. Gil was out of breath when he got to their table. He nodded to Mary then leaned in close to Jimmy.

"Jimmy. I've been out back for fifteen minutes."

"You got the wrong guy. Grab Tink. If he's still conscious."

Gil pressed his hand on Jimmy's shoulder, and Jimmy's shirt instantly felt soggy and cold.

"Your hands are all wet, Gil."

"You've got to help me," he said. "I can't stop the toilet in the ladies room. It's all over the floor. Christ, it's all over me."

"Ever heard of a shut-off valve?" Jimmy said.

"Broken."

"There'd be one in the basement for the whole building," Mary said.

"I can't get it to budge," Gil said. "I don't have the right tools. I need a professional. Please, Jimmy."

"Jesus," Jimmy said, glancing at Mary.

"Sure, there's two other plumbers dancing on the floor as we speak," Mary said.

"With all due respect, Mary," Gil said. "Would *you* hire one of those clowns? Even sober, I mean."

She frowned at him.

"Jimmy," he said. "It's all over everything. Think of the women. What are they going to do?"

"Oh, for Christ's sake," Mary said. Jimmy thought she might hit the poor bastard. "He can't," she said.

"What do you mean?"

She looked up at the band. "It's Saturday night, Gil," she said. "The man's got another call." She leaned toward Jimmy and put her mouth next to his ear. "And I'll see *you* when you're better dressed," she said. She touched the spot on his arm tenderly with her finger.

Jimmy rose and started making his way toward the band.

Acknowledgments

I THANK SENA NASLUND, my teacher and mentor, for her guidance and encouragement, without which this book would not exist.

The following people also have provided timely and valuable assistance to my writing: James P. Brady, Vince Castronuovo, Susan Dodd, Elaine Terranova, Gladys Swan, Dianne Benedict, Sharon Sheehe Stark, Art Roehrig, Phil Ruggiero, Michael Napoletano, Marian Lorenz, Bill Kulik, Paul McGarvey, Tony Wychunis, and the late Max Eirich. In large and obvious ways and also in ways of which they may not even be aware, they have helped me write the stories in this collection. I am deeply grateful to them for sharing their wisdom, talent, and inspiration.

My children, Stephan and Anna, have blessed my life from the day each of them was born; Kathleen, my wife and best friend, has made everything in my life better. I thank them for being *mes raisons d'être.*

About the Author

NED BACHUS RECEIVED a BA from Temple University, an MA from Gallaudet University, and an MFA from Vermont College of Fine Arts. A Community College of Philadelphia faculty member as a counselor from 1974 to 1989 and as associate professor of English from 1989 to 2012, he received various awards for service to students, including the Alana Collos Award for Teaching Excellence and the Christian and Mary Lindback Award for Distinguished Teaching.

His stories have appeared in various publications, including *The Louisville Review, Calliope, Antietam Review, Meridian Bound, Carve,* and *The Evansville Review.* He has won fellowships from the Pennsylvania Council on the Arts and was awarded an artist residency at Cill Rialaig Project in Ireland.

As a songwriter and solo artist and as a member of the Philadelphia-based band, Sacred CowBoys, he has recorded several CDs and performed in music venues throughout eastern United States; his songs have been performed and recorded by various artists in the U.S.

He and his wife, Kathleen, now live in Maine.

Fleur-de-Lis Press is named to celebrate the life of Flora Lee Sims Jeter (1901–1990)